THE EASY WAY

THE WAY HOME
BOOK 1

MAY ARCHER

ACKNOWLEDGMENTS

A huge and heartfelt thank you to the village that made this book possible: Leslie Copeland (magical, rock-star professional beta reader), Ann Attwood (proofreader extraordinaire), Shanoff Designs (cover design genius), Jane Henry (mentor-bestie), Kara Kelley (moral support), my awesome family, and the amazingly supportive M/M readers and writers who have taken the time to read, review, and/or advise me.

I am a lucky person to have each of you.

CHAPTER ONE

"Oh, I feel good about this one, Cort! I feel like a man who can't lose!"

Kendrick Cortland, better known as 'Cort,' smirked at his partner. "Uh huh. Then take the shot, Derrick."

Derrick Green squeezed his wadded-up ball of paper and eyed the recycle bin behind Cort once again before giving him a mistrustful glare. "You can't cheat, dude. No moving from your seat, no-"

"No wheeling the chair," Cort said, impatient but amused. "I know the rules of office basketball, Derrick. *Take your shot.*"

Derrick pursed his lips. "You forget I've been your partner for four years. Only reason you bothered to learn the rules was so you'd know how to bend them."

Cort laughed. The man wasn't wrong.

"I'm telling you right now, I'm not staying here a second after five just because you liked to hear yourself whining," Cort warned. "I've got plans."

"Yep. *That's* the level of dedication I've come to expect

from my partner," Derrick teased, aiming his paper ball once again.

Derrick wasn't wrong about that either. Cort liked his job, and some days he'd even loved it – the thrill of out-thinking criminals, the occasional feeling he'd helped some-one. More and more often, though, closing a case felt like lopping the head off a hydra - the next day, two more would spring up to take its place. And when it came down to it, the most important investigation he'd conducted in the last year wasn't on the FBI's books at all.

"Hey, wait!" Derrick let the paper fall to the desk and pointed an accusing finger at Cort. "That means you're not coming to Garvey's with us tonight?"

"Nope." Cort shook his head apologetically. "Not tonight."

"Breaking tradition! We close a case, we go to Garvey's!" Derrick's brown eyes were as mournful as a basset hound's. "But, fine. *Whatever.* Your *plans* are more important than hanging with your coworkers."

If Derrick only knew. *Understatement of the millennium.*

Cort had plans that would help him locate his brother and hopefully take down a powerful, entitled criminal busi-nessman in the process. So, yeah, just *slightly* more impor-tant than downing flat beer at Garvey's Pub. Not that he would share any of those plans with Derrick.

From the other side of the cubicle dividing Cort and Derrick's shared space from the rest of the office, Natalie Marquez's deep voice shouted. "For God's sake, Derrick, take the shot. Our boy's got a date, and it's about time he got lucky."

Cort rolled his eyes, but didn't correct her. It hadn't been more than a month or - fine, maybe *two*, since he'd brought someone home, but not because he *couldn't*. If you had a good build and a decent-looking face, finding a hookup was child's play, and there was no more *luck* involved in the process of 'getting lucky' than there was in ordering a hamburger at the drive-thru. The problem was, those hookups were about as stale and unsatisfying as the dollar-menu burger.

"So, who's the lucky gal?" Natalie, their computer specialist, peeked her platinum-blonde head above the divider. "Or is it a guy? It's a guy, isn't it?"

Cort shook his head. His bisexuality wasn't something he'd ever hidden - nor was his personal life something he liked to discuss. "No comment."

He cracked his knuckles as a spurt of nervous energy wormed its way through his gut. Part of him was excited that after months of planning, watching, and waiting, it was finally time to take action – the first step on a long path to getting his foster brother Damon back, and taking down the people who'd framed him - but he wasn't particularly thrilled that tonight would involve what essentially amounted to unauthorized spying. Sinking to the level of the people he wanted to take down was sometimes necessary, but never fun.

Nothing more than a simple conversation, he reminded himself.

Cort's desk phone rang, and Derrick groaned.

"Game over, buddy. Shoulda taken your shot while you had the chance," Cort said, shaking his head with mock sympathy as he reached for the receiver. But the voice on the other end chased the smile from his face.

"Cortland, I need to see you in my office immediately."

Agent Sean Cook, was one of the good guys - the kind of idealistic boss who didn't have grand career ambitions and genuinely cared about his staff. His tone now was stiffer and harsher than Cort had ever heard him use before.

Cort's stomached plummeted and his fingers clenched tightly around the phone.

In a career distinguished mostly by his ability to skirt the law and bend the rules, Cort was used to being in trouble. The question usually wasn't *whether* he'd done something wrong, but *which* of those things he'd been found out on, and he wouldn't have lasted long at this job if he let himself get riled every time he was called on the carpet.

Today, though, he was pretty sure he knew exactly why he was in trouble, and he was afraid there'd be no bouncing back from this one.

Using agency resources to track his brother had been a calculated risk. Time to pay the piper.

"Coming, sir," he said, putting the receiver back in its cradle.

Without a second to lose, Cort removed a tiny thumb drive of pictures from his top side drawer and put it in his pocket with a grim smile. Then he unlocked the top middle drawer of his desk and took out the thin sheaf of papers he'd printed that morning. Holding them under the desk, out of Derrick's view, he folded the stack in half and quickly slipped them between his sock and his shoe. Not comfortable, but effective.

The beauty of low-tech, baby. Nobody thinks to look anymore.

He stood.

Derrick glanced up in concern, their game forgotten. "Cooksy wants us?" Derrick was on his feet and reaching for the jacket hung over the back of his chair without waiting for Cort to reply, but Cort stopped him with an outstretched palm.

"Not us, man. *Me.*"

Derrick's eyes narrowed. "You? Just you?" There was a thread of hurt in his voice as he added, "What's going on, Cort?"

Cort cleared his throat against the niggle of guilt that tried to lodge there. He and Derrick Green had been partners for years, and the man had earned Cort's trust. Derrick wasn't an idiot - he knew Cort didn't share any details about his personal life, but he probably thought Cort had enough team loyalty to share information that would impact their work, their partnership.

Cort hadn't.

And yeah, it was partly because making personal connections was sticky as hell – telling people your shit compelled them to get involved in your life and vice versa. But he also reasoned that if he'd told Derrick about Damon's disappearance, about the lies and the cover-ups, Derrick's neck would be on the chopping block too.

Cort forced a smile to his face. "I feel like I may be getting some unexpected time off. You behave yourself, Derrick."

Derrick shook his head, stunned and suspicious. "What's this about?"

But Cort was already on the move, grabbing his gun from the lock box in his desk and sliding it into his holster - temporarily, at least - before snagging his own jacket and his FBI cell phone on his way out of the cubicle.

"Cort?" Natalie called, but Cort didn't pause. He turned to flash her and Derrick a quick smile and salute as he pulled his jacket on. He wondered what the office rumors would have to say about his departure once it became known. Probably something like *Cortland went vigilante and got his ass reamed again.* If he were suspended or even fired, they'd likely think nothing of it. Derrick would get a new partner, Nat would find someone else's love-life to live vicariously through, and that would be that. There was an upside to not putting down roots.

He pulled in a steadying breath. The familiar smell of

stale coffee and donuts made his chest inexplicably tight, and he had to mentally roll his eyes at himself. *Jesus, Cortland.* If they could distill that odor into a candle fragrance, no sane person would buy it, but here he was all wistful because he knew he probably wouldn't smell it again.

When he turned around a bank of cubicles and got a direct line of sight into Sean Cook's glass-fronted office, he saw the man was not alone. Mark Porter, Special Agent in Charge and general boil on the ass of humanity, sat in a chair in front of Cook's desk. Neither man looked happy, but Sean's face was flushed and his pale eyes flashed with temper.

Stick to the plan. Deny, deny, deny, and buy yourself some time.

As Cort approached the office, Cook glanced up from his desk and the look of disappointment and anger he leveled at Cort could have singed the hair off his head. Cort lifted a hand and ran it through his messy blondish mop. *Still there. Barely.*

Porter caught the direction of Cook's glare and turned his head, too, leveling a look of disgust at Cort. He stood as Cort entered the office. "Agent Kendrick Cortland?"

Cort nodded and responded in kind. "Agent Porter."

Cort put his hand in the pocket of his suit jacket, and smoothed his thumb over the surface of the lucky quarter Damon had given him a few years back. *I knew this was going to happen,* he reminded himself. *I owe Damon more than I can ever repay.*

"Have a seat, Agent Cortland," Sean said stiffly, gesturing next to Agent Porter.

Cort sat stiffly. *Think about Damon. Think about Sebastian Seaver. You're about more than your badge.*

"You know why you're here, I presume," Porter said.

It was the kind of bullshit interrogation tactic they were

taught on day one in the Academy. Did he think Cort was an idiot? That he'd start babbling?

"I'm afraid I don't, sir," Cort replied, spreading his palms out flat in front of him and attempting a smile.

"Cort, enough with the bullshit," Sean said. "You started working with me right after you left Quantico. You don't have any tricks I don't know about."

But growing up in a house where the very act of breathing was often grounds for punishment meant Cort knew better than to volunteer information. "Why don't you tell me what you think I've done," he said.

Porter leaned forward and grabbed a tablet from the desk.

"How about unauthorized use of Bureau assets, for starters? This image turned up on a facial recognition scan at the airport in Barbados, but the face isn't linked to any ongoing investigation in our database. Running a trace using facial recognition software without authorization is a serious offense."

He turned the display towards Cort, who kept his expression blank when he saw the picture on the screen. There, in grainy color, was a man with shaggy, prematurely-gray hair and a beard, his baggy clothing barely concealing his tall, lean frame. It was the very same image Cort had printed out that morning, the one now growing damp inside his shoe, and it finally proved a suspicion that had only grown stronger for the past six months.

Cort's foster brother, Damon Fitzpatrick, who everyone on earth believed to be dead, was actually very much alive.

Cort put his hand back in his pocket and fitted the quarter between his fingers. *Flick and roll, flick and roll.* "Wow, yeah. I would imagine it's serious. And you think *I* had something to do with running the face through the system?"

"Don't play dumb, Agent Cortland," Porter warned. "It's not a good look on you. Now, how about if you tell us who this man is and why you were searching for him."

Cort made a non-committal noise. "I wish I could, Agent Porter," he said, a slight bitterness in his voice. He wished Damon *could* have a fair shot at coming forward and clearing his name without having to deal with Sebastian Seaver, the heir-apparent to the global Seaver Tech conglomerate, and Cam Seaver, the younger brother who always covered for him.

Agent Porter puffed out his chest and stared at Cort. "Agent Gigi Weston recalls you initiating a *flirtation* with her a few months ago," he continued.

"Gigi?" Cort asked, rolling the name around his mouth as though trying to place it. "Oh, the redhead on the seventh floor?"

"Yes," Porter huffed.

Cort nodded and smiled. "Right, I remember. She's a lovely woman. I do remember chatting with her a few months back."

"She said she offered to show you the facial recognition system," Porter prompted. "And you seemed extremely enthusiastic. She assumed you had a romantic interest in her, and asking her to show you the system was just a way to break the ice. But it wasn't. Was it?"

"I don't understand what you're getting at," Cort lied. "I do remember her chatting to me about the computer, but… Well, you know me and computers." He shot Sean a self-deprecating smile. "I was sort of flirting with her at the time, but then circumstances changed."

"You mean you got her to show you how to program a long-term search and then ditched her?"

Cort blinked. *Right on the money.* "No. I mean, I remembered there's a no-fraternization policy in the office."

This time it was Sean who snorted. "You honestly mean to say you were flirting with Gigi? Just last week at Garvey's, you took off with some guy named Tom."

"Your point?" Cort retorted, allowing his very real impatience with this topic to show. Yeah, he'd been flirting with Gigi to learn her programming system, but he *could* have flirted with her for other reasons. *Jesus.* They needed to cover bisexuality in the next sensitivity training.

"And what about *this*?" Porter tapped his tablet again and showed Cort a split-screen of two very official-looking letters.

Now this *was* a surprise. He hadn't expected anyone to catch him on this rule-bending so soon.

Although Cort didn't need to read further than the company header at the top of the one on the right - Seaver Tech - to know what he was looking at, he carefully read the entire thing, then shifted his attention to the letter on the left and read through that one too, as though his own signature wasn't affixed to the bottom, buying himself a minute to compose himself.

"This looks like a pretty standard letter from the FBI giving notice of a potential investigation. And the other one looks like the typical, rich-corporation boilerplate reply, saying they're far too powerful and entitled to take our investigation seriously. Nothing out of the ordinary."

Cort glanced up and met Porter's eyes. They glittered with anger, and somehow it calmed Cort. He could deal with anger.

"It *wouldn't* be out of the ordinary," Porter agreed. "If this were in our jurisdiction to investigate! This isn't Cyber Crimes, Agent Cortland, and no one in the hierarchy has ever authorized an investigation into Seaver Technologies!"

Cort clenched his jaw, gripping the quarter in his hand so tightly he knew it would leave a mark on his palm. "Perhaps you're not aware, but we received a tip regarding a very clear data breach–"

"An anonymous tip about a data breach which, I will repeat, you have no authority to investigate! Without a warrant, you're only going on an unauthorized fishing expedition. You don't take up a position against a company as powerful as Seaver Tech without dotting your I's and crossing every damn T." Porter's eyes were hard as stone. "If they chose to take further action against us for harassment, it would leave *us* open to litigation, and after the year the Seavers have had, we never would have won."

Rage blossomed in Cort's chest. The *Seavers* had a tough year? They didn't know the half of it. And now they were getting off scot-free, without any repercussions, as they always seemed to.

Porter shook his head in disgust. "You're lucky they seem to have dropped it after this letter."

Those words were like tiny pins that pricked the dam of Cort's composure, unleashing a deluge. "I'm *lucky*? I was *doing my job* and investigating illegal activity! Jesus!" Cort locked his teeth together, trying to rein in his temper.

Porter opened his mouth to reply, but Sean cut him off. "Cortland, this isn't your first rodeo, so don't start talking to me about how conducting an investigation within the boundaries of the law is compromising your morals. There are rules and procedures we need to follow, and *you know it*. You know exactly how far to push the line without crossing it, and you also know better than to pull a cowboy, vigilante stunt like this." He motioned towards the letter on the tablet.

Sean was right. Cort did know better. He'd sent the letter weeks ago, in a spurt of impatient frustration, wondering if he'd ever see Damon again, if he'd ever have enough information to make Sebastian Seaver pay. It had been stupid and he'd known nothing would come of it, but he'd hoped it would make the bastards at Seaver Tech sweat, if only for a minute.

Now, knowing he had nothing more to lose today, he crossed his arms over his chest and stood firm. "What I *know* is when assholes like Sebastian Seaver say *jump,* we say *'How high, sir?'* He can get away with anything."

"Ah, and that offends you because only *you* should be able to bend the rules? You're Kendrick Cortland, the Robin Hood of the FBI!" Porter scoffed and it took all Cort's self-control not to wipe the smirk off Porter's face with his fist.

"I think we've heard enough," Porter told Sean, then he stood and looked down at Cort. "You're hereby suspended without pay, Agent Cortland, until the Office of Professional Responsibility can investigate your involvement in this matter. Sean, take his gun and badge. I'll get Vasquez, and we'll escort him out of the building." Porter turned and left the office, almost gleeful.

Cort found his ass stuck in his chair and a lump stuck in his throat. The words had hit him like a sucker punch, even though he'd been expecting them.

"Sean, *if* I were to break the rules, it would be to help someone who didn't have the power to help himself," Cort said quietly. If this was the last moment Sean would be his boss, it was somehow important that Sean not think of him as an asshole.

So stupid.

Sean shook his head in disgust. "You think I don't know that? Christ, Cort. That's not the issue. Not for *me,* anyway. You see this piece of crap?" he demanded, pointing at the framed inspirational poster that had been hanging on his wall for as long as Cort could remember, the word Teamwork emblazoned over a sunset skyline. "You think I keep this here because the freaking scenery inspires me? I've been preaching this to you idiots for years, but you just won't get it. There's no 'U' in teamwork. You don't close cases on your own, you don't go into a sketchy situation without backup, and you don't go off half-cocked just because, *for reasons I can't fathom*, you hate rich people in general and Sebastian Seaver in particular." Sean shook his head sadly. "Until you learn to trust someone, Cort, until you can really believe other people have your back, you're gonna be shark bait for guys like Porter...*and* guys like Seaver."

Cort ground his teeth together to keep silent. Sean Cook didn't know a single thing about his life beyond the black-and-white statistics of his personnel file - the number of foster homes he'd been in and out of, the number of schools he'd attended, the number of jobs he'd worked to get himself through college. Nobody knew what went on in those homes behind closed doors, or what it was like to grow up in the poorest, sketchiest neighborhood of an affluent town. They didn't understand the loyalty a man earned when he stood in front of a closed fist to protect his brother.

Men like Porter existed only to serve fat cats like Sebastian Seaver, and Cort would be damned if he'd play that game, even if it meant surrendering his badge.

He took his FBI cell phone out of his pocket, but before he could set it on the desk, Sean shook his head. "Keep it. We'll need to contact you."

Cort nodded robotically, his stomach churning. The worst had happened, professionally-speaking, but he reminded himself that now he could focus more fully on finding Damon. *Another thing to blame Cam and Sebastian Seaver for.*

A knock at the door signaled Porter's return. He'd

found another agent and was ready to escort Cort out of the building. Cort stood and mechanically removed his gun from its holster, placing it on Sean's desk. It was *weird* setting his badge next to the gun. He felt a flash of panic, followed by an unsettling weightlessness, like the gravity holding him in place had somehow reversed itself. Who was he without his badge?

It was time to find out.

He nodded once at Sean. "Thank you," he said, and he knew Sean would understood those thanks had nothing to do with the bullshit he'd just spewed, but with the years he'd spent teaching Cort how to be a good agent.

Sean nodded.

Cort turned and shouldered his way through the doorway, pushing himself between Porter and the other agent. Porter put a hand on his shoulder to stop him.

"Just a second, Cortland."

"What?" Cort sputtered as the agent gestured for Cort to put his hands in the air. "You can't do that."

"Oh, you'll find we can," Porter said pleasantly, patting him down.

Porter removed Cort's phone, keys, and wallet, then came upon the thumb drive Cort had stuck in his pocket.

Porter smiled. "Well, now. Look at that. You weren't taking information out of the building, were you?"

"Hey!" Cort protested. "That's personal!"

"This is an FBI-issued thumb drive," Porter corrected him. "I'm afraid whatever's on here is going to have to remain in evidence. You can be sure I'm going to go over it with a fine-toothed comb, myself."

Cort let his anger rise to the surface. "Good luck with that!" he spat.

He grabbed his belongings from Porter's hand, then

strode down the hall toward the elevator with the two escorts hot on his heels.

Cort powered through the revolving door and out onto the rain-swept Boston street before he allowed himself to take a deep breath. If he wanted to help his brother, he needed to play by a different set of rules than Sean Cook did - rules that involved using Cam Seaver to find Damon.

CHAPTER TWO

Cam watched a plane flying past the window, red tail-lights flashing in the darkening sky as it circled a spot above the airport. Perhaps the biggest perk of being in the sixty-fourth-floor ballroom of the opulent Cabot Hotel on a night like tonight was the uninterrupted view of Boston in all its hazy August twilight glory. From up here, his perspective was skewed just enough to make the brightly lit freighters in the Harbor look like wind-up toys. Even the plane in the distance seemed like something he could grab out of the sky, superhero-style, and set safely on the ground where it belonged.

Sadly, Cam's reflection in the glass mocked the very idea of him achieving superhero status. With dark brown hair that constantly flopped on his forehead and freckles all over his cheeks, he looked more like Clark Kent's thinner, geekier twelve-year-old brother, playing dress-up in a thousand-dollar suit. Besides which, logging a thousand hours a year playing League of Legends online didn't exactly qualify him to join the Avengers. He wondered how long he'd have to make polite conversation before he could make his getaway.

He wished, not for the first time, there were even *one* person at this party who was here for *him*.

Cam stared at the reflection of the party in the window, the bright lights and the languid, unhurried movements of Boston's ultra-rich, interspersed with the quicker and more deliberate steps of the servers who roamed the party serving champagne and canapes. There were hundreds of men here tonight. No doubt dozens of them would be thrilled to leave here on his arm. The trick was finding a guy who wasn't interested in Camden Seaver, President of Seaver Tech, but in plain, nerdy Cam. If such a unicorn existed, Cam hadn't found him on Grindr.

The plane was edging lower, beginning its descent. Superhero or not, Cam's eyes fixed firmly on those flashing red lights, and he guarded it with the force of his stare until it dipped behind another building and out of sight.

"Cam?"

With a guilty start, he turned away from the window to find several pairs of eyes watching him intently. He stifled a sigh. "Sorry. Yes?"

The biggest *downside* to spending this evening in this sixty-fourth-floor ballroom was being here as the host of the annual SafeWater gala - the party of the season for Boston's elite, all to benefit the clean-water charity Cam's mother had started decades before. Cam had somehow been coerced into giving a speech and glad-handing all the donors, probably because it hadn't even occurred to him to fight this stuff anymore. Just a typical Friday night when you'd inherited the top position at one of Boston's biggest corporations.

The small group clustered in a semicircle around him, all high-ranking members of Seaver Tech, watched him expectantly, waiting in vain for brilliance to fall from his lips. His chest felt tight, and he resisted the urge to tug at his collar.

Though not everyone had such high expectations.

"Daydreaming again?" Drew McMann snorted.

Cam ignored him, pushing down the instinctive flare of temper in his gut. To acknowledge Drew's months-long post-breakup temper tantrum would only encourage him to be an even bigger and more controlling asshole. If the idiot weren't so freakishly good at his job as the head of Seaver Tech's legal department, Cam would have fired him a long time ago. Still, he was pleased when Drew rolled his eyes a moment later and walked away to share his sunshiny personality with some other lucky guests.

Mrs. Yates, the head of Seaver's charitable foundation, sighed and gave Cam an encouraging pat on the arm along with a watery smile, like she assumed grief, rather than annoyance, was distracting him. The woman constantly surprised him with her ability to read tragedy into every situation. *He* wasn't the Seaver brother who was stuck wallowing in grief after their parents' deaths in a plane crash thirteen months ago. Cam had been done with *his* grieving for nearly a year.

He gave her a bright smile and grabbed a flute of champagne from a passing waiter, needing the quick buzz. "Your team outdid themselves tonight, Mrs. Yates. I'm sure we'll be raising plenty of money for SafeWater."

"So thoughtful of you to say," she began, but Cam didn't hear anything else. A stranger walked through the door, and Cam's thoughts stuttered to a halt.

Holy, holy shit.

Who the hell was that?

The guy standing in the doorway was huge - easily over six feet tall, with improbably wide shoulders tapering to a trim waist like an animated Disney hero. His golden-brown hair was messy - not in the accidental way of Cam's cowlicks, but like he'd *earned* that messiness from frantic hands running through it in some dark closet or shadowy hallway. The very idea sent a bolt of electricity to Cam's groin. He'd never felt an instant attraction like this before *in his life.*

The man strode into the ballroom the way a Viking might have walked through a sleepy village he intended to pillage, lips turned up in a confident smirk, and all Cam could think was, *"Yes. Finally, yes." This* was a man who wouldn't be careful. He would take what he wanted, and Cam would yield, and all the thoughts that buzzed in his head like angry bees would be silenced. It would all be as easy as breathing. He squinted just a little bit to see what color the man's eyes were.

Then the stranger paused a few paces inside the room and threw a flirtatious smile at Misty Sturmacher, his eyes straying to her barely-contained breasts, and Cam felt his face go hot.

Typical, Seaver. Lusting after the hot, straight guy.

He snapped back to reality, where Mrs. Yates was still speaking in mournful tones. Cam slugged down his champagne like medicine, an inoculation against contagious misery.

"… just wonderful, and your speech tonight was the cherry on top! But I can understand how distracted you must be, on a night like tonight. I only wish your brother were here to see it."

Cam shut his mouth so quickly his teeth clacked together. Trust Mrs. Yates to bring up the one thing everyone else in the room was wondering about but not daring to mention.

"I'm sure Bas is every bit as proud as I am," he deflected

smoothly, even though most days Cam wasn't sure Bas remembered his own name, let alone the existence of the SafeWater fundraiser.

"And where *is* Sebastian?"

Cam turned to face the man on his right. If Mrs. Yates could be trusted to stumble onto minefields where angels feared to tread, Emmett Shaw, the junior U.S. Senator from Tennessee and Cam's honorary uncle, could be trusted to follow right behind her, leading a big brass band.

Cam gave him what he hoped was a patient smile. "Working." *Obsessing, drinking, grieving. Always grieving.* "You know how he is when he's working on a project."

Uncle Shaw shook his sandy-blond head. "Utterly consumed, no doubt. Just like your father. But we'll be seeing you in St. Brigitte! Next week, isn't it?"

He exchanged a glance with the tall, dark-haired body-guard-slash-assistant who followed him everywhere, and the assistant nodded. "Next weekend, sir. We arrive a week from today."

"Good man, Jack," Shaw said with a smile, patting the man on the shoulder. "Don't know what I'd do without this guy, I really don't."

Jack looked at Cam intently, almost unnervingly so. The man was attractive, with blue eyes, tanned skin, and a distinctive mole beneath his eye that gave him a rakish look, but he wasn't Cam's type at all.

Jack winked and gave him a small smile. "I enjoy making myself indispensable."

Ugh. Definitely not his type.

Cam blinked and turned back to Shaw, so distracted by Jack's weird look – was it *flirtation*? –he almost missed what Shaw had said. "St. Brigitte?" he repeated.

"Mm. The Tyndalls' private island, for their annual charity do. I know for a fact you and Bas were invited.

Good publicity for the company *and* for public servants like myself." He winked at Cam.

"No," Cam said flatly. "I won't be going. And I sincerely doubt Bas will either." He didn't think Bas had ventured out of his apartment in weeks.

Shaw sighed. "If I've told Sebastian once, I've told him a million times - you need to lean on the people around you in times of crisis! I really think I could be a help to you, Cam, if you let me handle some projects for you. I helped your dad found Seaver Tech, and I haven't been out of the game very long, either." He gave Cam the you-can-trust-me smile he'd used to win his Senate seat two years ago, just around the time he'd left his position at Seaver.

"And I'll tell you the same thing Bas told you, Uncle Shaw," Cam said coolly. "I appreciate the offer, but we've got things under control."

He knew Shaw meant well, but his constant offers of help over the past year had become grating - more like a condemnation of Cam's ability than a sincere desire to help. Though maybe that was Cam's own insecurities talking.

"You two are so stubborn." Shaw shook his head with fond exasperation, and not a strand of his hair changed position. "I'm going to keep asking. And just wait until your Aunt Lucy hears you've refused our help again."

Lovely. He couldn't wait.

Shaw turned to congratulate David Pearce on landing a new contract and Cam flagged down a waiter who scurried over to replenish his drink.

"Yeah, I was pretty thrilled it came through," David was saying. "Especially given the possible FBI investigation. But Drew said it's been handled."

Cam's attention was caught. "*Investigation?*"

David's eyes widened and he glanced quickly from Cam to Shaw to Drew, who stood nearby talking to socialite

Lydia Tyndall. "We received a notice from the FBI a couple weeks back about an investigation into a security breach originating at Seaver Tech. They were asking to talk directly to Sebastian, since he's the CEO and head of development, so any security breach would be in his purview."

"And mine."

"Well, right, but…" David swallowed hard. "I tried to get in touch with Bas first. When he didn't return my calls or emails, I worried the investigator would start calling my team, so I got Drew involved."

Cam watched Drew shake Mrs. Tyndall's hand and walk towards the main bar at the front of the room. "Did you." It wasn't a question.

"He sent them a letter, or whatever, but I don't know whether they're going to drop it." He paused to lick his lips. "He sent out a company-wide memo saying nobody should allow FBI agents on the premises or answer any questions without consulting Legal first." David glanced at Shaw again, then back to Cam. "I would have thought he'd have told you?"

Cam nodded, his eyes still on Drew. "So would I."

"Likely he thought he was helping you out, my boy," Shaw said jovially. "You've got too much on your plate. More than you can handle. It's what friends do."

No. Taking control without giving someone a choice was *not* what friends did.

Cam plastered a brittle smile on his face and excused himself from David and Shaw. Drew had gone too far, and it was past time they had a reckoning.

God, what I wouldn't give to have my parents here.

The thought surprised him. It had been a long time since anything like that had popped into Cam's head. After his parents died and Sebastian checked out, Cam had done a bunch of bargaining with the Universe. *How do I do this job?*

Tell me what to do, and I'll do it. The Universe had sent him nothing but the echo of his dad's voice: *Seavers never back down, Camden.*

It hadn't been easy, but Cam had learned how to fake competence like a champ. He was not a self-made billionaire like his father, a tree-hugging philanthropist like his mother, or a tech genius like his brother, but he was *the only goddamn Seaver in the room.*

Now, he carried the Seaver name before him like a shield, drew himself up to his full five-feet-ten, and locked eyes on his target at the bar.

CHAPTER THREE

Cam crossed the floor to the bar, his eyes trained with dagger-like intensity on Drew McMann's familiar taut shoulders, struggling to remember why he'd ever liked the guy.

Drew was someone's idea of the perfect specimen, no doubt - dark hair and eyes, shock-and-awe brilliance with all things legal, intense focus. He was an amazing litigator and generous, careful bed partner. Outside of the bedroom, though, he'd been an absolutely shiteous boyfriend, accusing Cam of inventing drama every time he took exception to Drew's high-handedness. And *still* Cam had wanted them to be able to work together, for the sake of their history - their parents' friendship, Drew's decades-long friendship with Bas. But if Drew's bullshit was going to undermine Cam's position at Seaver Tech, Cam wouldn't tolerate it.

"Drew, I need to talk to you."

Drew took a sip of his drink - bourbon, no doubt - but didn't turn. "That's novel. I thought you preferred ignoring my existence."

"I attempt to ignore your *attitude*," Cam corrected. "What is this FBI investigation, Drew? And why the hell did I have to hear about it from David Pearce?"

"It's not a big deal." Drew waved a careless hand in the air. "I took care of it."

"The big deal is you didn't *tell* me, Drew." Cam darted a glance around to verify that they were alone, and caught sight of the broad-shouldered blond from earlier, standing near the exit. He was alone, a drink in his hand, and if it weren't so utterly impossible, Cam would swear the guy was looking right at him.

Focus Seaver. On Drew, not the Viking.

He turned back to Drew and lowered his voice as he continued. "You didn't give me a chance to figure out how I wanted to deal with it."

Drew finally turned to look at him. "Why is it you can never trust me to handle things for you? Why do you have to be such a control freak?"

The irony of the statement seemed to sail over Drew's head.

Cam rolled his eyes and Drew's nostrils flared. "Fine, you want to know? Yeah, the FBI sent us a notification that they're investigating a data breach that came from Seaver. It appears some classified information may have been accessed."

"But we have security clearances," Cam said in confusion.

"Come on, Cammy. You know information isn't all classified to the same degree." The look Drew shot him was the dictionary definition of condescending. Coupled with the stupid fucking nickname, it sent Cam's blood pressure soaring. "They're saying we didn't have authorization to access the server that was accessed, and it wasn't accessed in an approved manner, using government-supplied credentials."

"Jesus. They think we hacked them?" Cam demanded in a harsh whisper. "What do we need to do?" His fingers clenched tightly on the glass in his hand.

"We don't need to do anything! I told you, it's bullshit and it's already been taken care of." Drew took another sip of his bourbon.

"So, there was no breach?"

Drew looked at him like he was an idiot, then gave him a smug smile. "Of course there was a breach. We did our own internal investigation of the equipment and the credentials used."

"And?" Cam demanded.

Drew shrugged, and Cam lost control of his temper.

"God, Drew! This is what I fucking mean! You can't give me even half an answer. Tell me!"

"Tell you?" Drew slid back from the bar and leaned toward Cam, all cold anger and intimidation. "Tell you the electronic signatures indicate Bas was the one who hacked them? Tell you your brother probably didn't answer the FBI's questions because he knew he could incriminate himself? Tell you the best way to handle this was to throw our weight around so nobody looked too closely? Tell you Sebastian could go to jail for a very long time if he actually got caught? How much do you *really* want to know, Cam?"

Cam felt gravity tilt slightly, so his feet no longer felt firmly planted on the ground. "Bas?" He could only manage to utter the single syllable.

Drew's anger seemed to drain out of him as he took in Cam's shocked expression. He blew out a breath. "Cammy—"

Cam shook his head. "How is that... It's just not... *No.* Not possible."

Bas had graduated college at seventeen. He'd designed artificial intelligence technology in high school still being used by the military today. If he wanted to hack a system to obtain information, he'd take every piece of information right down to the size of your dick and you'd never even know he'd been there. Cam knew jack shit about hacking and electronic signatures, but he knew that much.

Drew sighed. "I don't know how it's possible, but Bas is messed up right now. You know it. I stopped by his house the other day, and he was sitting in the dark watching home movies from when we were kids. You and him, me and Amy, our parents, the Shaws. He's still grieving, still obsessing about the crash." He took a deep breath. "And the agency he hacked was the NTSB."

Cam reached out a hand to steady himself against the bar and motioned to the bartender to get him another of what Drew was drinking. The floating feeling he'd experienced a moment ago got worse as he processed Drew's words. The National Transportation Safety Board had investigated the plane crash that had killed Cam's parents and Drew's sister Amy… but none of this made any sense.

"There's nothing to hack there, Drew," Cam said, shaking his head. "The investigation was concluded two months after the crash. We all got the report. The pilot was seen drinking heavily before the flight and failed to check the engine. It was pilot error."

Drew nodded. "I know. But you know Sebastian never accepted it. He wanted accountability. He wanted somebody punished."

Cam rubbed his fingers against his forehead again. It had been impossible to punish anyone, of course, when nobody had walked away from the crash. He remembered Bas's reaction vividly, since it had involved piles of shattered glass in the living room of their parents' home, and had preceded Bas falling off the face of the earth for a solid week. It had been the first disappearance of many.

"What the hell was he looking for when he hacked them?"

"You think I'd know?" Drew snorted. "Two years ago, I could have told you every single thought in your brother's head. We shared *everything*. But I lost him after the crash the same way I lost Amy."

His words were so bleak, the sentiment so close to what Cam himself had felt, that Cam felt his anger subside.

"I think it was probably even earlier," he said quietly. "You thought he was crazy when he asked Amy to marry him."

Drew chuckled. "True. I never understood what they had in common. Amy was… Well, you know. Flighty. And Bas was *mine*. My friend, I mean."

Cam nodded. Bas and Drew had been inseparable. He wondered for the first time if missing Bas had prompted Drew to start dating Cam in the first place. Trying to substitute one brother for the other. It had never really been about *Cam* at all.

He glanced back at the spot where his Viking had been standing, but the man had moved, maybe even left for good. He scanned across the far side of the room, but there was no one there.

Figured.

"I don't like thinking about this shit," Drew said, drinking deeply. "And I know *you* don't like thinking about it either - God, you never even visit your parents' graves. I didn't want the investigation to bring it all back, so I made sure it went away."

"I don't need to visit their graves, Drew. There's nothing there but names and dates." This was familiar territory, too - an argument they'd had a hundred times. Cam wouldn't be baited. This wasn't about *him*, this was about Drew keeping things from him.

Drew pierced him with a glance. "And you don't need to cry. And you were fine boxing up all your parents' shit and selling the house two months after they died. And you don't need to hang out with your friends or volunteer anymore."

Cam sighed. "Can we please not…"

"You run away from everything emotional," Drew concluded.

Cam shook his head firmly. "And here we were getting along for a whole five minutes." Why was everything with Drew so fucking complicated? He hardened his voice. "From now on, full communication. Understood?"

Drew lifted his drink in a mocking salute. "Sure thing, boss."

Cam slammed back the rest of his own drink and straightened. It was still early, but surely he'd endured enough torture for one night. Time to go. Maybe he'd see if the sexy Viking from earlier was out in the lobby, and…

Ha. Cam couldn't even complete the fantasy.

A guy who looked like that would want nothing to do with a man like Cam. Cam would just head home and play video games.

"Well, if it isn't the gentlemen of the hour!"

Cam turned to see Lydia Tyndall beaming at them, and Cam found himself returning her smile with practiced ease. "Thanks so much for coming."

Lydia's smile grew even warmer. "Camden, dear, I wouldn't miss it. SafeWater was like your mother's third child, after all. She'd be proud to see how well you've done with it."

Cam's coughed to cover the sudden tightness in his throat. "Thank you." *God.* This was why he preferred spending his evenings gaming. Emotions were exhausting.

She turned to Drew and put a hand on his shoulder,

then beamed at them both. "And now the two of you will return the favor when you come to St. Brigitte next week!"

The Tyndalls' fundraiser, the one Uncle Shaw had mentioned. "No, I'm afraid I can't make it."

Mrs. Tyndall looked crestfallen. "Oh, but Camden!"

Drew looked annoyed.

"I told Lydia earlier we'd be attending," he said in a harsh whisper, the kind of whisper that said *Don't be childish, Cam. Don't argue in public. We'll discuss this later.*

Once again, Drew had made a selfish decision without consulting or considering him at all. Immediately, his anger was back.

He set his jaw and lifted a hand to motion for the bartender. *One more drink, to keep me from committing murder.* But his hand dropped just as quickly.

The Viking was sitting at the other end of the bar, his eyes unmistakably fixed on Cam. He raised a single eyebrow and nodded to the seat next to him, a challenge and an invitation all rolled into one.

Cam was transfixed by the way the light played over the man's hair, bringing out flecks of gold, glints of copper. Then the guy smiled - a teasing, lopsided grin - and Cam's stomach inverted. Did he know who Cam was? Had he focused on Cam because of his name, or the tragic legend of his family? In that moment, Cam couldn't find it in him to care. The man's eyes - Cam still couldn't see the color, dammit - were curious, hot, and fixed on Cam. For that look, Cam would be anyone the Viking wanted - Superman, Clark Kent, or anyone in between.

The man smiled again, wide and predatory, and every instinct in Cam's body jumped to life, but he had no interest in running away. He couldn't wait to get closer.

He turned to Lydia again. "I'm sorry, it's impossible."

Nothing they could say would get him to fly to St. Brigitte, and Drew knew it. He *knew* it, damn him.

Drew was glaring daggers at him, but Cam wouldn't, *couldn't*, back down. Instead, he held Drew's angry glare for a minute, letting his own eyes go flat and cold. He would not be manipulated or pushed around, and Drew needed to understand that.

A second later, Drew ground his teeth together and looked away. *If that PBS nature special on wolves was right, I'm pretty sure Drew's now my bitch.*

He gave Lydia an apologetic glance. "I'm really very sorry."

Lydia nodded, seeming resigned. "Alright. Well, I'll leave you both on the guest list, just in case." She glanced back and forth between him and Drew, confused.

Whatever. Let Drew figure his way out of this one.

"If you'll excuse me, I see someone I need to speak to," Cam said, before kissing Lydia on the cheek.

He stalked toward the far end of the bar, his gaze locked on the man who was - *holy shit* - waiting for him. His heart lurched into a disjointed quick-step, and lines of poetry, actual *poetry*, leaped into his head. *Jesus, he was a handsome man.*

And that was before the man smiled at him like they'd known one another for years and slid out the stool next to his.

"Well, Camden Seaver," the man said, sending an honest-to-God shiver down Cam's spine. "Looked like you handed that guy his ass." He nodded in Drew's direction without breaking eye contact. "Remind me not to piss you off."

Cam laughed out loud before he'd even fully processed the man's words, and then stopped, stunned. When was the last time he'd laughed like that? He honestly couldn't remember. The vise he'd felt clamped around his chest all night loosened and dropped away.

"Let me get you a drink," the man said.

His eyes were green. Bright, bright green.

And just like before, all Cam could think was *Yes. Finally. Yes.*

CHAPTER FOUR

"Okay, I've got one!" Cam said, swaying forward to put his hand on Cort's forearm.

Cort, who sat on the stool next to his at the little bar, while the fundraiser was in full swing behind them.

Cort, who was actually *Kendrick Cortland*, even though nobody had used his first name since elementary school, and who'd gotten pissed off in a really cute way when Cam had tried.

Cort, who liked drinking Jameson, which showed excellent taste, and pineapple on his pizza, which was totally disgusting.

Cort, who agreed *Firefly* should never have been canceled, but who had never in his life seen *Stranger Things*, which was a travesty.

Cort, who was sexy as fuck and looked at Cam with a combination of amusement and lust which scrambled Cam's wits faster than the whiskey they'd been drinking in copious amounts.

Cort, who was now his best friend.

"You ready? Never have I ever had sex with two people at once."

He and Cort stared at each other, smiling, then Cort grabbed his drink and sipped.

"Ha! I knew it!" Cam laughed. "Deviant."

Cort grinned. *"Prude.* It's not even that unusual. First time was with these identical twins, Claire and Beth Knight, senior year of high school after we won our homecoming game. I was so fucked up, I hardly remember most of it, but I became a school legend."

Cam laughed out loud. "So, what you're really saying is there might have been only one girl, and you had double vision?"

Cort pushed his arm so hard, Cam would have fallen off his barstool if Cort hadn't also grabbed him around his bicep and pulled him back onto the seat as though he weighed nothing whatsoever.

"No, seriously!" Cam laughed as Cort wrapped an arm around the back of his neck to hold him steady. "I knew a guy on one of the humanitarian trips I took who had double vision all the time, not just from drinking. The trick is to cover one side." He demonstrated, clapping his palm over his right eye. "Now your brain can't get confused by any mixed signals."

"You know the weirdest stuff. You learned that on a humanitarian trip?" Cort's thumb brushed the side of Cam's neck in a casual way, which nevertheless made Cam's pulse pick up.

Cam shrugged and lowered his hand from his eye. His face was inches away from Cort's now, and he felt heat climb his cheeks at the proximity. *When was the last time he'd been this turned on?*

"Yep. They don't always have the access to surgeries or other interventions, so they go old-school and low-tech. But it works." He moved back slightly and took a sip of his drink, trying valiantly to cover his arousal. "Also handy when you're playing video games after a couple of beers and need to shoot a target."

Cort threw back his head and laughed out loud, his hands dropping to his sides. "You are... not like I thought you'd be."

For just a second, Cam tilted his head, trying to figure out whether there was a thread of disappointment in Cort's voice, whether he was just another person who preferred the image of Cam Seaver they saw in the newspaper, but the grin on Cort's face said he was pretty pleased by whatever he'd discovered.

Cam laughed again. The champagne he'd guzzled earlier was fizzing and popping, inflating an invisible balloon inside him, filling all his empty places and lifting him away from the tethers of gravity. A voice in his head which sounded like Drew's suggested he should be suspicious of the feeling, but he couldn't quite bring himself to care.

"Fuck you. *My* turn," Cort said, his evil, teasing glare making Cam's pulse thrum wildly. "Never have I ever dated anyone on the Hundred Richest People in America list, or whatever they call it."

Cam rolled his eyes and obligingly took a drink.

"Yeah, somehow I figured," Cort smirked. "Bet that's how you picked your dates in high school."

"Not *me!*" Cam elbowed Cort. "Other people. Or their *parents* anyway. My parents grew up normal, middle-class all the way. Seaver Tech didn't take off until after Bas was born, so they were really chill. But other people's parents, not so much." He winced. "One time in college, before I decided I wanted to work with non-profits, I was interning with one of my dad's best friends. He tells me I'm doing such an amazing job, showing so much potential, all that good stuff. He wants to take me out to lunch, right? And I'm down with that because I think it's gonna buy me a serious *in* with my dad, you know? Like he's gonna be genuinely happy with me for once because I pleased this guy."

Cam laughed softly as Cort's forehead creased in thought.

"So anyway, I get to the restaurant, and he's got his whole family there - wife, son, and his *beautiful snowflake* of a daughter, Arcadia."

"Arcadia?" Cort repeated. "For real? Only a millionaire could name their kid that."

"Oh, shut up. People all up and down the socioeconomic spectrum name their kids unfortunate things, *Kendrick*. We haven't cornered the market on this shit."

Cort rolled his eyes, making Cam laugh.

"So, Mr. Shaw, my dad's friend, sits me on one side of the table between Cady and Cain, his son, and the whole time, he's telling me how amazing Cady is - she's in this fucking *sorority*, and she's won this debate thingy. He was, like, ready to negotiate a bride price right then and there. Like, how many goats will you give me for my daughter?" Cam snorted. "And you wanna know what was really funny? I had dated *Cain* for a while in high school! I guess his dad just never knew. I mean, *I* certainly never told."

Cort snorted. "You shoulda told him to offer you a *groom* price instead."

But Cam shook his head and winced. "Oh, believe me, not from this guy. Nope. *No.* I kinda feel bad for Cain, because he's, you know, gotta be seeing Narnia from that deep in the closet. But he was also kind of a pretentious prick back then, and totally emo for the longest time, so I was not gonna involve myself in that hot mess."

Cam shook off thoughts of Cain Shaw and gave Cort a

winning smile. "Okay, forget that shit. Moving on. Never have I ever had sex in a public place."

Cam sized Cort up, watching him reach for his glass, waiting to see if he would drink, but he didn't lift his hand off the bar. They both burst out laughing.

"You're lying! I've only known you for a couple of hours and I can already tell you've got to be lying," Cam said, shaking his head sadly at the glint in Cort's eyes.

"No!" he said, nodding his head.

"Oh my God!" Cam said, pointing at him. "You just did the thing where you nodded and said no! Total indicator you're lying!"

"What?" Cort's expression was startled and maybe a little embarrassed. "I did not!"

"Did too," Cam teased. *God*, he liked this guy way too much already. He cast around for a safer topic to return to. "So, uh, public sex?"

"I haven't, really! I mean, unless... Wait, how are we defining *sex?*" Cort demanded. His green eyes danced and his mouth twisted up in a lopsided smile, which made Cam's cock twitch. "And for that matter, how are we defining *public?*"

Cam raised a brow. "Public, like if someone could catch you. Sex, as in anything beyond petting."

"*Petting*," Cort echoed, giggling. "Who the fuck says petting?"

"Me, clearly," Cam defended himself. "And I mean, isn't that what you do with girls? You, like, pet them?"

Cort dissolved into laughter and slumped on the bar, clutching his stomach. "Oh, holy shit. Oh, God."

Cam felt his face flame. "Dude, like I'd have the first clue what to do with a girl...*woman*... whatever."

Cort laughed softly. "Not even the first clue, huh?"

"Well, I took AP Biology, but ah, no. No practical

knowledge," Cam confirmed. He put his hand over his mouth. "I cannot believe I just said that."

Not that Cam had a problem outing himself - he'd never really been *in* the closet, not from the first time his nanny had shown him an ancient episode of The Brady Bunch and he'd realized Peter did it for him way more than Marsha. Still, he wondered about the man in front of him, and the alcohol made him bolder than he otherwise would have been.

He licked his lips. "You do, though, right?" he asked Cort, who was still chuckling. Cam felt his face flush red. "I mean, beyond Cindy and Becky?"

Cort frowned, apparently trying to follow this inarticulate question, then he smiled again, and Cam forgot to be uncomfortable because the way Cort's mouth hitched up at one corner made Cam's stomach swoop.

"Beth. Claire and Beth. You have the cutest freckles," Cort said softly, then he blinked as if he hadn't meant to say that. He cleared his throat. "But yeah. I mean, yeah, I like women."

Cam nodded and looked down at his whiskey. *Well, of course.* Hadn't Cam seen Cort's fascination with Misty Sturmacher earlier in the evening, when he'd first walked into the ballroom? It was alright. It was fine. They were just two new friends having a drink at a party, and it was absolutely *not* disappointment making it hard for him to breathe.

Cort put his hand over Cam's where it rested against the bar, and leaned toward him slightly. "I am also attracted to men."

Cam's head shot up and he sucked in a breath, but Cort's eyes were focused behind Cam's head. "Speaking of which, the man you were talking to earlier is watching us right now."

Cam shifted in his seat, but Cort's hand trapped his.

"Don't turn to look," he said softly, his breath hot on Cam's ear. "Unless you *want* him to come over here. He's staring at you like he wants to know what color your boxer briefs are."

A bolt of acute lust shot straight to Cam's groin - a one-two punch of Cort's warm hand on his, and the words he spoke. He loved the way Cort touched him, and had seemed to find excuses to touch him all night. "How do you know I wear boxer briefs?" Cam whispered.

Cam wondered if he imagined the hitch in Cort's breathing.

But before Cort could speak - and Cam was *dying* to know what he would have said at that juncture - a hand fell on Cam's shoulder.

"Cammy."

Drew's voice held long-suffering disapproval, like Cam was a dog who simply refused to heel. Cort's eyes met Cam's, and he raised an eyebrow which spoke volumes. It reminded him of the wordless communication his parents had sometimes shared. *Who is this guy? Why is he claiming you? What are we going to do about it?* But he didn't pull back from Cam's space. He looked ready to fight.

Cam very nearly laughed, and shifted himself closer to Cort.

"My name is Cam. Or Camden. Now go away, Drew," he said without turning around.

Drew sucked in a pissed off breath. "We need to talk."

"Again? We talked earlier, and I heard enough. If and when I want to talk to you again, I'll call you."

Cort smelled *delicious* - like a weird combination of pine and oranges. Trees and citrus had never made Cam hard before, but somehow right now, they were everything. He leaned into Cort and inhaled deeply, and watched in fascination as Cort bit his lip and shifted in his seat.

Oh, fuck yes. This was happening.

"Cam!" Drew pulled at Cam's shoulder and tried to spin him around on his stool, but at the same moment, Cort splayed his hand on Cam's waist beneath his open jacket, keeping him locked in place. Cort's entire body tensed, and his head went back just slightly so he could meet Cam's eyes again. *Am I beating this asshole up? How do you want me to play this?* The questions were as clear as if they'd been spoken out loud.

Though he'd never aspired to be the prize in a tug of war, Cam loved the feeling of Cort's broad palm against his flank, the heat of him seeping through Cam's thin shirt. Though *Cam* knew Drew was nothing more than an annoyance, he liked that Cort seemed ready to step up if Cam wanted him to. But what he fucking *loved* was that the guy hadn't moved his ass from his seat without checking whether Cam *did* want him to. Almost like he expected Cam could handle himself. Almost like he trusted Cam's judgment.

Imagine that.

Cam smiled wide, euphoric in a way that had fuck-all to do with his whiskey.

Cort looked confused - and no wonder, because Drew's hand was still on Cam's shoulder, pulling like a freaking tractor beam - but his lips tipped up too, like he couldn't help it.

Cam shook his head and, still smiling, turned to face Drew. "What. Do. You. Want?"

Drew's nostrils flared and he darted a glance at Cort before looking back at Cam. He looked tired and pissed because Cam wasn't falling in line with his plans. The fragile peace they'd achieved an hour ago was definitely over. "I want to discuss that stunt you pulled with Lydia."

Cam calmly sipped his Jameson. His eyes were on

Drew, but he was one hundred percent aware of the warm body at his back, supporting him. "There is nothing to discuss. You completely overstepped by accepting Lydia's invitation when you knew I wouldn't fly to St. Brigitte. I corrected your error."

He tried to turn away, but Drew stopped him and rolled his eyes. "I'm sorry I made plans for us without consulting you, Cammy," he drawled, making it sound like their argument had been a lover's spat. "But get over it and talk about it like a grown-up! It's not about you and me, it's about what's best for Seaver Tech, and you're the president."

Cam jerked his shoulder out of Drew's grip and glared. "Don't fucking tell me how to do my job or how to be a Seaver. I'm not a child, and I have a perfectly valid reason for not wanting to go."

Behind him, Cort tensed, likely bracing himself for a fight, and from the corner of his eye, he saw Cort's knuckles whiten on his glass.

Drew frowned, and then as he looked at Cam, the light seemed to dawn. He closed his eyes tightly for half a second in realization. "What, still?"

"Yes, *still*," Cam said, hating Drew for always making him feel so fucking *weak*.

"But what about, you know, your doctor? Doesn't she help?" He gave Cort a cautious glance, like he didn't want to give too much away.

Cam snorted. Because *now* Drew cared about embarrassing him? Yeah, right. "You mean my *therapist*. And what about her? She says not to allow *anyone* to push me past my comfort level, or to take risks unless I can completely trust myself and the people around me."

Drew ground his teeth together then glanced away. His eyes landed on Cort again. "And who are you?" he demanded.

Cam could still sense Cort's tension from behind him. Cort's chest was pressed against his back, and he could feel Cort's indrawn breath down to his toes.

Cort didn't say a word, allowing Cam to decide if and how to answer. But Cam had nothing to hide. "This is my friend Cort."

"Cort," he drawled. "And how do you know Cam, *Cort*?"

Cam felt Cort shrug, then his hands fitted to the sides of Cam's torso. "We have lots of interests in common."

"Like what?" Drew demanded.

Like we both like Jameson and we both like to fuck men. It was on the tip of Cam's tongue, but he refrained from commenting. He deserved a medal.

"Like none of your business, and Cam asked you to please move along," Cort said.

Drew hesitated, glaring back and forth between them, but Cam had endured enough.

"Move along, Drew. For God's sake, for *my* sake, for the sake of our friendship... hell, for the sake of karma and peace on earth and *whatever the fuck you want*, please, just go."

Drew ground his teeth together. "We will be discussing this *tomorrow*."

Cam rolled his eyes and made a mental note to shut his ringer off. Tomorrow was Saturday, anyway. They watched as Drew stalked off towards the exit, and then Cam turned to face Cort.

Cort's gaze was still on Drew, and Cam was once again reminded of a predator. But unlike the way he looked at Cam, Cort's eyes now were cold and calculating. A predator *on the hunt* with no trace of playfulness in his gaze. Cort glanced down at Cam and smiled. "Do you know CPR?"

"Pardon?"

"CPR. Mouth-to-mouth resuscitation. Could you save my life if I suddenly dropped dead?"

Cam shook his head. "Uh. Sort of? I was a lifeguard back in college. Is that, uh, likely to happen?"

Cort grinned and looked over towards the elevators again. "Only if looks can kill."

Cam groaned at the joke, but the happy bubble which seemed to surround him, surround *them,* was safely back in place.

"Wanna tell me who that jerk was?" Cort asked easily, relaxing deeper into his stool as the elevator dinged. "The introduction only went one-way."

Cam got the idea that if he said *no,* if he said he didn't want to talk about it at all, maybe Cort wouldn't press him for answers. But he also didn't want to start anything with Cort tonight - *oh, please God, let them be starting something tonight!* - without explaining exactly who Drew was and was *not.*

"Sorry. That was Drew McMann. Ex-boyfriend. And current head of the legal department at Seaver Tech. He's also my older brother's best friend, and was mine too, for a while. His dad is my godfather. My mom was his sister's godmother."

Cort winced. "Ouch."

The guy didn't know the half of it. Hardly anybody knew *anything* beyond the stupid tabloid stories, because Cam sure as hell didn't talk about it, not to the media and not even to his friends. But for the first time maybe *ever,* Cam kinda *did* want to talk about it. Maybe it was the whole strangers-on-a-bus thing, the freedom that comes from not knowing anything about a person, not even their last name. Or maybe it was the way Cort looked at him, like Cam's name didn't impress him at all. He wanted Cort - hell, he'd been half-hard for the guy since the moment he'd spied him across the room earlier. But he found he wanted Cort to know about him, too. He liked that Cort listened.

Cam drank the last few drops in his glass and met Cort's eyes. "Another?"

Cort blinked for a second and hesitated. "Think it's a good idea?"

Cam shrugged. "Define good." Cort raised an eyebrow, but Cam propped his elbow on the bar, and set his chin in his palm, returning his skeptical look with a smile. "Seriously! I mean, if you mean good as in wise, then maybe it's not a good idea. But if you mean good as in what would be most fun, then it definitely *is* a good idea. And if you mean what's the easiest and *rightest* thing..."

"The rightest thing?" Cort snickered, leaning into Cam's space.

"It's a word, *Kendrick*," Cam said primly. "The *rightest* thing, like what your instincts tell you is the right thing to do. And that would definitely be to have another drink. With me. Now. Don't you think?"

Cam held his breath, watching Cort's reaction. Then Cort nodded slowly, and that funny euphoria hit Cam again.

He gestured to the woman behind the bar, who hurried over to refill their glasses.

Cam took a slow sip of the liquid, figuring out where to begin. Sharing had never come easily to him, partly because of who his family was and partly because of his own nature. It didn't help that he could still hear Drew's voice shouting warnings in his head. *What if he's a tabloid reporter looking to sell your story? What if he's a business competitor looking to steal company information? Don't share too much, or you'll look weak.*

He looked at Cort, at the way the man's broad shoulders were aligned perpendicular to his own, so fucking warm and solid; at the tiny white scar on the upper corner of his lip; at the scruff on his jaw; at the intensely curious look in his eyes, like Cam was a puzzle he was piecing together and he wanted to get it right. What had started as simple physical attraction to this man had morphed into something more. He felt strong and totally in charge, even though Cort was so much bigger and more assertive than him. He loved the way Cort laughed at his jokes, like his laugh was rusty and he was surprised to hear the sound coming from his own chest. It all combined to make his attraction ratchet higher and higher.

So, without formulating an agenda or carefully determining how much he wanted to say, Cam started to speak.

"You probably know my parents were killed in a plane crash a year or so ago."

Cort nodded once. He didn't interrupt to offer platitudes, which made Cam like him all the more, but his green eyes took on a vulnerable cast for a second which made Cam wonder whether he'd lost someone he loved, too.

Cam cleared his throat. "Drew's sister Amy, who was also my brother's fiancée, was killed too." Cort's head went back in surprise and Cam nodded. "Yeah, most people didn't know they were engaged. It was a new thing. Happened only a couple of days before the, ah, crash. All of us - me, my parents, and Sebastian, plus Amy, Drew, and *their* parents, the McManns - were supposed to go and celebrate with Emmett Shaw's family."

"Wait, wait. The Mr. Shaw you were talking about before, the one who was best friends with your dad, is *Emmett Shaw*? The senator?" Cort interrupted.

Cam nodded. "Yep. Yeah, he was in business with my dad a while back. They founded Seaver Tech together, along with Jonathan McMann, Drew's dad. Dad had bought Uncle Shaw out of the business a while before the crash - I'm guessing maybe so he could use the money to move out of state and fund his whole political thing? But they stayed really close friends."

Cort nodded, but there was an appraising look on his face which Cam understood without explanation.

"Yeah. I know what you're gonna say. He's not *quite* as violently conservative in real life as he is on the campaign trail," Cam said quietly, his finger tracing the rim of his glass. "

"Huh," Cort said, tilting the liquid back and forth in his own glass. "I don't know whether it makes it better or worse that Senator Shaw says all that shit on TV when he doesn't really believe it."

Cam nodded. He wondered whether his parents would have kept ties with the Shaws if they'd lived. He very much doubted it. Emmett Shaw was a different man these days, and even though Cam still called him "Uncle," he found it hard to talk to the man for more than a few minutes at a time.

"Anyway, he has this cabin in the mountains of Tennessee. I mean, it's a cabin like Versailles was a summer house, you know?" He rolled his eyes and Cort snorted. "Huge contemporary monstrosity with lots of steel and glass, but it's got a kick-ass hot tub."

Cam liked the way Cort looked at him sideways and smiled at that, as if maybe Cort was picturing him in the hot tub. He felt himself flush and wondered for a second if he should be embarrassed, but he wasn't.

"And then?" Cort prompted.

Cam took a deep breath and got to the part of the story that had his arousal fleeing. "We were all supposed to fly out together in the evening on my parents' plane, but at the last minute, Emmett got tickets for some benefit show that night. Libraries for under-served communities in Tennessee." He chuckled without humor. "Everybody knew

Charlotte Seaver was all about benefits for every-damn-thing, so you know *obviously* she had to be there." He swallowed.

Cort leaned into him, and Cam sucked in a breath. It was a matter of a couple of inches, but seemed to speak volumes. *Control yourself, Seaver.*

"It's alright to cry, you know," Cort said offhandedly.

Cam stared at him. "I don't cry."

Cort's eyebrows shot up.

"Anyway," Cam continued. "Emmett made arrangements for them to fly down earlier. Amy tagged along to do some shopping, and the rest of us were flying later. They crashed into the mountain. There were no survivors. Everyone already knows that part. *An American Tragedy* they called it on the news." Cam cleared his throat, but it didn't get rid of the lump there. "I should have been on that plane."

"If you'd gone, you'd have died too."

Cort's words hit him like a slap and he looked up. The man's eyes were hard, burning.

"Whatever happened that day, you couldn't have prevented it. Maybe *nobody* could have prevented it. But if you were on that plane, you would have died too."

Cam nodded. He knew it. Mostly. Maybe he'd have been the one to notice the pilot had been drinking. Maybe he would have been the only one who wasn't too consumed with the excitement of the engagement and the party to recognize something was wrong.

"I mean it, Cam. Grief fucks us all up. Makes us think crazy things we know aren't logical. Don't play those games. Nobody on that plane would have wanted it for you."

Cam cast his eyes to the ceiling and nodded. That much

he knew for certain. His parents would have been glad he wasn't there, that he and Bas had lived.

"And that's why you took over the company?" Cort asked gently.

Cam glanced at him. "The company was supposed to be Sebastian's baby. He's the computer genius, you know? My dad had been grooming him to take over for years. But losing Amy on top of our parents put Bas in a really bad place." He licked his lips and confided, "He's holed up inside his house. He tried to *hack the NTSB*, for God only knows what reason, and it's like he doesn't care if he gets thrown in jail by the FBI. I'm scared for him."

Cort winced and sat back in his seat, looking uncomfortable. "Damn. And you always step in to take care of him?"

Cam shrugged. "He's my brother. Of *course* I do. I always *will*. But as far as the company goes, it was time for me to take on more responsibility, anyway."

"From what you've told me, that sounds like something that would have come out of your ex's mouth," Cort said with a wink. He motioned the bartender to refill their glasses.

Cam snorted at how quickly Cort had figured Drew out. It probably *was* something Drew had said, if not in those exact words.

"But now you're all grown up, and you're the president of Seaver Tech. That's gotta be stressful." The words were a tease, but the look in Cort's eyes and the way he laid a hand on Cam's thigh, turning him on the stool so they were facing each other fully, made heat surge through Cam's gut. "How do you blow off steam?"

Cam raised an eyebrow at the deliberate flirtation. Was he trying to distract Cam now that things had become too heavy?

Did Cam care?

His dick certainly didn't.

"I run," Cam said blandly, resting his elbow on the bar. "Half marathons. I log probably thirty miles a week."

Cort's answering smile was genuine. "No shit?"

"Nope. And I play video games."

The way Cort's smile widened was more arousing than the hand currently caressing Cam's leg. "Yeah, you mentioned that. Sometimes with one eye closed." He laughed. "Which games?"

"Uh, League of Legends, a couple of first person shooters. And I'm developing a game with our software team based on a series of YA fantasy novels, which… Well." Cam shrugged and braced himself for ridicule, for more of the "Grow up, Cam," he'd always gotten from Drew.

Cort grinned in the lopsided way Cam was already starting to find familiar - way too familiar for an acquaintance that could only be measured in hours. "So, what you're telling me is, you shoot people for fun? That's kinda badass."

Cam burst into laughter. Badass? He'd been called that exactly never, but he *kinda liked* it - and liked it even more because everything about Cort said his flirtatious teasing hid genuine interest. He couldn't remember the last time he'd felt this good, or done something for *himself* like this. Cort didn't want to talk about Seaver, didn't seem to care about his job or his bank account, didn't want Cam to put on some kind of fake persona. He couldn't believe someone like Cort could be into him in this way.

"Yep. That's me. Totally badass and dangerous. I like to shoot stuff online for fun, and I can run far, far away very quickly."

Cort nodded with mock-seriousness. "Duly warned."

"What about you?" Cam asked, leaning his elbow against the bar.

"What *about* me?" Cort returned. His eyes turned a shade more guarded, and despite the way the alcohol and the man were making his brain buzz, Cam read that as a flashing sign saying, "Proceed with Caution." Cort didn't want to talk about himself, didn't feel the desire to share the way Cam did.

So fine. Okay. Strangers at a bar don't have expectations. Keep it casual.

Cam leaned in closer to Cort's heat, loving the way Cort's body responded, the sharp exhalation of breath that warmed Cam's cheek.

"What do you do to blow off steam?" he asked. Seduction and flirtation were not his forte, but tonight he felt bold.

"Sometimes I like to just *scream*."

Cam snickered. "What?" He'd expected to hear… well, something more violent maybe? Something more befitting the man's heavy muscles and the way he'd tensed at a perceived threat. Cort's entire demeanor blared "man of action." But his face held the same sincerity as before, and maybe just a trace of vulnerability.

"True story. I just go someplace alone and let out all the anger, all the frustration, all the shit I've dealt with all day. You should try it sometime. You know, if the shooting thing doesn't work."

Cam shook his head, amused and charmed. He gave a pointed glance around the room. "Pretty sure it wouldn't go over too well around here."

Cort grinned. "True. It's harder to find places in the city. Especially in exclusive hotels." His grin turned cagey. "But not impossible, if you know where to look."

Cam's eyes widened. "You want us," he gestured

between them, his hand brushing the hard wall of Cort's chest in a way that made his own thoughts blank momentarily. "To scream? Inside this hotel? Is the ensuing arrest all part of the fun?"

Cort laughed.

The sound was so potent and rich that if it could be distilled into liquor, Cam would happily have drowned himself in it.

When his laughter subsided, he looked at Cam with affection no less potent than the laughter. If he wanted Cam to scream right here, right now, he'd do it and damn the consequences. But instead, he stood up and held out his hand. "Come with me?"

It was not a demand or an expectation, but an offering. Cam was vividly aware he knew nothing about Cort - the Jameson hadn't dulled his thoughts to the point where he could forget it. Everyone wanted a piece of him - his money, his influence, his name on a fucking computer program, and maybe Cort was no exception.

But for years, everything in Cam's world had required cold logic, scrupulous planning, and straight paths. Somehow this man, this *stranger,* glowed like a beacon, hot and bright, and Cam, who had never done a dangerous thing in his life as far as he could recall, had finally found someone who wanted something from him that he wanted to give. He hopped off his stool and set his hand in Cort's larger one.

"Let's go."

CHAPTER FIVE

The Jameson has gone to your head, Cortland.

Not that they'd had all that much, and what they *had* drunk seemed to mostly burn away when their conversation - the longest and weirdest and *coolest* conversation of Cort's life - had turned to the crash. But what other explanation could there be for Cort suddenly finding himself in an elevator standing oh-so-close to Cam Seaver - the younger brother of a man Cort despised, and exactly the kind of entitled, rich-kid asshole Cort had always hated?

Except Cam wasn't like that at all.

Cort had come here tonight with only one item on his agenda - to find Cam Seaver and do some firsthand reconnaissance. All the evidence suggested that to find Damon, Cort needed to score himself an invitation to the Tyndalls' gala on St. Brigitte. But without his FBI connections or any social pedigree of his own, it meant cozying up to someone with an invite, or possibly blackmailing them. Using the very assholes who'd stolen Damon's life from him had seemed like poetic justice, and Cam Seaver was by all accounts the weaker link. So, he'd put together a folder on Cam with everything from Cam's impressive SAT scores to the kind of car he drove, but he'd known he'd need a lot more information than that. Tonight's goal had been to figure out what made the younger Seaver tick - what his strengths and weaknesses were.

Liking the guy - genuinely, down-deep, *liking* him – had not been part of the plan.

He'd been staring at Cam's picture for the past few weeks, but weirdly enough, Cort hadn't immediately recognized the man when he stepped into the ballroom. Maybe it was because the picture was a couple of years out of date, or maybe it was because Cort had been looking for Sebastian Seaver's kid brother - a short kid with dark hair and freckles.

What Cort had found, when a busty blonde near the door had been helpful enough to point him in the right direction, was definitely *not* a kid. Cam was all man, and gorgeous to boot.

His jaw was sharp as a knife, and the cleft in his chin was completely lickable - not a word Cort had ever applied to another man before. His eyes were pale enough to be noticeable from across the room, and his *lips*. Holy hell. Plump and wide, like a wet dream come to life. Yeah, Cam wasn't built like most of the guys Cort had dated, but there was strength in the line of his shoulders and the column of his back. At the bar, Cam had said he was a runner, and Cort could totally see it in the fluid movement of Cam's body and the way his pants hugged the contours of his ass. He'd never felt such an instantaneous attraction before, nor such a fucking inconvenient one.

Cort glanced at the man beside him as the elevator hit the roof deck. It appeared nobody else had the crazy idea to hang out on the roof this late at night since they had the elevator to themselves. Cam's visible tension was amusing and fascinating and arousing as hell, like everything Cort had learned about the man from the moment they'd sat at the bar, when Cam had engaged one of the cleaning staff in a long and cheerful conversation about her family back in Honduras *in fluent Spanish*. He'd quickly realized the Cam Seaver on paper couldn't hold a candle to the complex, fascinating man himself.

The doors opened, and Cort ushered Cam forward, placing his hand on the small of his back. Cam shivered at the contact, and Cort felt the same current flow through him. His dick thickened beneath the outrageously expensive suit he'd bought just for tonight, fast and painful enough to remind him how completely off-the-rails this evening had gotten.

He hadn't thought of Sebastian Seaver at all tonight, except when Cam was talking about his parents' deaths, and even then Cort hadn't felt the same burning anger, the same driving need to clear Damon's name that he usually felt when he thought of the crash.

He'd felt Cam's pain, confusion, and anger instead, every emotion clearly broadcast on the man's beautiful face.

So even though the trained investigator in him wanted to capitalize on the trust he'd established, to push for more information he could use later, Cort couldn't bring himself to do it. Some other part of himself, a part he barely recognized, compelled him to offer Cam something genuine, instead.

They walked through the small elevator lobby, then Cort scanned his hotel keycard and pushed open the doors to the outdoor pool deck. Though the air was cooler than it had been earlier in the day, it clung to his skin, heavy and damp, like the precursor to a thunderstorm. Even the street noise below was nothing but a distant hum, nearly drowned out by the soft gurgle of the water lapping against the edges of the pool. They were cocooned in their own little bubble. It was eerie but beautiful.

"Watch your step," Cort warned, as he propelled Cam towards the far side of the deck, near the high glass enclosure which provided a stunning view of the city. They looked out over the lights silently for a moment. Cam drew a little closer.

What the hell am I doing here?

But when Cam finally turned to him, those light blue eyes of his wide and anxious, and voiced the same question, "What are we doing, Cort?," Cort didn't make excuses, and he didn't turn to leave. Instead, he slipped off his own suit jacket and kicked off his shoes, setting them on one of the nearby lounge chairs, along with the hated FBI-issue smart phone from his pocket.

"Undress," he told Cam, whose gaze had focused on Cort's discarded belongings, as though he wasn't sure where to look.

Cam blinked at him, then looked around the empty space. "Undress. What, here?"

"Yeah, right here. Right now. You can leave the boxer-briefs if you want. I've been dying to see them anyway." He winked.

Cam shook his head like he couldn't believe this was happening, but fuck if he didn't start stripping. He began unbuttoning his shirt, his eyes focused on Cort the entire time, and when the shirt sleeve slipped off his shoulder, revealing his skin-tight t-shirt and tanned, toned arms, Cort stopped breathing for a moment. Would Cam show him the same trust if he knew who Cort really was?

God, tonight would go down in history as the stupidest

decision Cort had ever made, but he didn't care. He'd never wanted anyone or anything the way he wanted Cam Seaver. So, they'd have tonight, maybe. Just a few hours, until sanity was restored and he remembered all the reasons why he shouldn't like Cam as much as he did.

Then Cam took off his shirt, and once again, all rational thought fled Cort's mind. Cam glowed in the golden light, all sleek, smooth skin and firm, barely-defined muscles.

The man was gorgeous.

The nicely cut suit jacket and ass-hugging pants had given the impression of lean strength inside the crowded ballroom, but it was nothing to the way Cam looked in the ambient light: lean, golden, and gorgeous. Cort's mouth went dry. He quickly shucked his own shirt, socks, and pants, then crossed the short distance between them.

"Take them off," he said, hooking a thumb in the waistband of Cam's pants. His voice was thick with arousal, and he knew Cam heard it when he shuddered despite the warm air.

But Cam backed up a pace. "Tell me what's happening here first." Any effect from the Jameson had burned off long ago, and Cam was clearly back in control. For now.

Cort rolled his eyes and took a step forward. "We're stripping down next to a pool. I figured it was pretty obvious, badass. We're getting in the water."

Cam looked from Cort, to the water, and back again. Then he licked his full lips. "What if I don't want to?"

It gave Cort pause for thought. He had zero interest in forcing the guy into the water if he were genuinely afraid or didn't know how to swim, but... "You said you were a lifeguard," Cort remembered.

Cam raised one eyebrow. "Yes, I was. Swim team, too."

Ah. So not fear, then, but a challenge. Cort's pulse kicked up. "Then *get in the pool*, badass."

"I suppose you could make me." Cam licked his lips once again, a slow and deliberate stroke Cort could feel in his dick. "You're taller than me. Stronger, too."

"I could," Cort agreed. He stepped close enough for their chests to almost touch, and Cam's eyes flared with heat. This teasing - the war of words, and wills, and barely-there touches was torture of the particular variety Cort liked, and he loved that Cam seemed to like it too. "I could pick you up right now, push you against the wall, and make you do whatever I wanted. *Whatever the hell I wanted*, Cam, and I could make you like it."

Cam's breathing was erratic. "Then do it," he demanded.

Cort pursed his lips. He was tempted, fuck, he was so damn tempted. But something told him if he won the easy way, it wouldn't really be a win at all. So he shook his head slowly. "Not right now. Tonight, I want you to choose to do it. Do it because I asked you. Do it because I want you to, and because you want to please me."

Cam closed his eyes and inhaled deeply, bringing his chest in line with Cort's, then he opened his eyes and unzipped his pants, letting the expensive fabric pool on the concrete decking. His dick was already semi-hard and pushing at the red cotton of his underwear. Cort nearly groaned at the sight.

Cam's eyes flew open. "So now what?" he asked.

The heat in Cam's eyes was blinding, his jaw locked defiantly, but Cort had been trained to see beyond the obvious, and right now he could see the tension in the other man's face, in the twitch of those lips he couldn't wait to kiss.

Cam effortlessly conjured emotions in Cort - strange and awesome and totally unwelcome. Cort wanted to protect him and support him and —

Fuck. This wasn't supposed to go down this way. He

wasn't supposed to admire or respect Cam Seaver. He was the enemy, wasn't he? Or at the very least, a tool to be used to help Damon? Cam wasn't the only one outside of his comfort zone, and Cort wondered if he could handle it as well as Cam seemed to.

"What do you want?" Cort whispered.

Cam swallowed hard, like he was gathering courage, then leaned forward, pressing himself against Cort. "I... I want you to show me how you blow off steam. It's why you brought me up here, right?"

Cort smiled. God, the man managed to surprise him at every turn. The feeling of Cam's hot skin against his own was mind-blowing, and his body was absolutely primed to take Cam right here and now. But for some reason, his mind balked at the idea of Cam becoming just another in a line of hard, fast, nearly-anonymous fucks. He wanted to prove something to Cam, and maybe to himself, and to do it, he needed to regain just a little of his control.

So, even though his body was screaming for him to bend his head just slightly, to cup his hand around Cam's hard jaw, he didn't. Instead, he wrapped his arms around Cam's waist and lifted him, ignoring the man's shocked gasp, then carried him the few steps to the edge of the pool.

"Remember you asked for it, badass," he told Cam, and then he jumped, sending them both crashing into the warm, clear water.

Cort kept his hands wrapped around Cam until they hit bottom, then released him as they both bobbed to the surface a few feet apart and sucked in air.

"You. Asshole!" Cam sputtered, pissed off and gorgeous. Water droplets clung to his cheeks and spiked his hair, making him look like a startled kitten. Cort laughed harder than he had in months.

A large splash of water caught him full in the face,

choking him. "Oh, badass is taking his revenge!" he gasped, still laughing as another burst of water hit him. "Better watch out."

Cort coiled his muscles and lunged at Cam, ducking them both under. Cam came up coughing and spewing curses, and Cort braced himself for a frontal attack. But a second later, Cam had dived back under, catching Cort by the ankles and dragging him down.

The sneaky bastard.

They played like that for God-only-knew how long, neither of them willing to yield. They were more alike than Cort had anticipated.

When they'd both swum apart for a second to catch their breath, Cort remembered why he'd brought Cam up here in the first place. "You wanna see something cool?" he asked.

Cam raised one eyebrow. "Is this the part where you pull off your underwear?"

Cort laughed again - God, when was the last time he'd laughed so much? "Dude, when I pull them off, you'll be saying something a lot better than *cool*."

Cam snorted.

"It's another piece of random trivia for you to add to your stash. Watch," Cort said. Then he dived under the water and *screamed*, sending all the air in his lungs rushing to the surface in a cloud of bubbles.

When he resurfaced, Cam was watching him with a pitying expression. "You blew bubbles? Wow."

Cort grinned. "Come down with me this time."

When he dived the second time, so did Cam, watching him in the glow of the pool lights. Once again, Cort screamed, but this time he could see understanding dawn on Cam's face. They both surfaced again.

"You were screaming down there?" Cam said breathlessly. "It looked like you were, but I could barely hear it."

Cort nodded, wiping water from his eyes. "Water doesn't conduct sound the same way as air, so the sound doesn't travel above the surface."

"Oh my God. You're a science nerd?" He sounded shocked and more than a little impressed. Cort rolled his eyes.

"Sorry to disappoint you, badass, but that and baking soda volcanoes are about the extent of my scientific knowledge. This is typical kids' stuff. There was a pond down the street, and my brother and I—" Cort paused and looked away for a second. "My brother and I would sneak down there sometimes to hang out with the other kids. *He* was a physics geek."

"You have a brother, too?"

Cort nodded, easily treading water.

"Older or younger?"

Cort hesitated. He never spoke about Damon - not to his partner, not to his coworkers, not to anyone - and it seemed especially wrong to speak of him here and now. But it also seemed wrong to lie, or to use one of his million strategies for deflection, so he answered honestly.

"Seven years older."

Cam nodded, gliding a few feet away. "And you guys were close? What about your parents?"

Cort could tell Cam was thinking about his own parents and the dickwad of a brother he seemed pretty fond of, but Cam and Cort weren't ever going to have any kumbaya moments where they both reminisced about their awesome childhoods. "My parents are not something I discuss."

"Ah. Got it." Cam didn't seem disappointed or rejected or whatever, but somehow Cort felt like an asshole anyway.

He just didn't share this shit - *his* shit - with anyone except Damon, because Damon had lived it too.

Cam watched him silently for half a second, then swam closer. His pale blue eyes glowed with spooky intensity in the pool lights, and it almost seemed as if he could read Cort's thoughts. Then he smiled, and held out a hand. Cort reached out and grabbed it, and together they let the water claim them, sinking down to the bottom and screaming their heads off where nobody but the two of them could hear.

A few minutes later, they were floating on their backs, close but not touching, staring up at the stars - or the place where stars *would* have been on a less cloudy night. Cort had no idea what time it was other than *late*, and he was exhausted. Learning about Damon, dealing with Porter and Sean, everything had propelled him here tonight. But after the whiskey and the screaming, after learning way more about Cam than was good for him to know, his anger had evaporated, and he had completely lost sight of the plan that had brought him here. His mind was floating the same way his body did.

His hand bumped Cam's in the water, and without giving it a thought, he tugged until they were floating together, side-by-side. He shifted his head slightly and saw that Cam, too, looked more peaceful than he'd been all evening. Cam turned his head just a little and gave Cort a look both fond and affectionate - as if they'd known each other for a million years instead of only a single night, and Cam trusted him implicitly. A single thought swam into Cort's brain and took up residence.

I want to be worthy of that trust.

He instinctively backed away from the thought as soon as it formed in his mind.

It was wrong and stupid. He was loyal to Damon first, which meant he couldn't be loyal to Cam. This night had been a messed up, wonderful lie, but it would end the second Cam knew who he really was. He glanced back up at the sky, and felt the first few drops of cold rain hit his face. Their warm, drifting time was over.

He brought his feet down to touch bottom and turned, sheets of water sluicing down his chest with a loud splash. "Cam, I think—" he began, with every intention of calling a halt to this madness before he risked more than he was willing to lose.

But Cam surprised him once again. He stood up too, light and shadow playing across his face and the sleek expanse of his chest, and lifted strong arms to wrap around Cort's neck.

"It's crazy. It's stupid. This connection can't be real," he whispered, his voice mirroring Cort's own thoughts. "But for tonight, can we please do things the easy way and *not* think?"

He pressed his lips to Cort's collarbone, and the heat of his mouth made Cort shiver. Then he pulled back, his eyes finding Cort's like he was waiting for approval or maybe... *Jesus*. Permission.

Cort wrapped his arms around Cam's waist, locking them together in the waist-deep water. Cam's breath caught, and lust pooled in Cort's belly. He let his doubts and misgivings float off into the gently lapping water as he stared at Cam's mouth, slowly lowered his head, and decided for one night perhaps they both deserved the easy way.

His lips pressed against Cam's, and then Cam's parted, his tongue tangling with Cort's like maybe he thought Cort needed convincing. Cort sucked on his tongue firmly, making Cam moan, and then he was licking inside Cam's mouth tasting the smoky spice of the Jameson, and something even sweeter and more potent which was Cam's alone.

Cam's hands came up to grab at Cort's hair, locking them together, but then just as suddenly, he yielded, his lips becoming pliant under Cort's. The sensation was so heady that Cort broke away slightly, pulling his lips an inch away from Cam's to stare down at him. Both were panting, Cort was painfully hard, and he wondered if the easy way just might kill him.

CHAPTER SIX

Cort pulled open the huge metal fire door and ushered Cam inside the stairwell with a hand against his lower back.

"Oh my god, it's so cold," Cam complained. The change in air temperature was messing with his equilibrium, making his belly clench and his skin break out in goosebumps beneath the rough hotel towels they'd snagged from the pool area. Or maybe it was the man beside him who was causing that reaction? He had no experience to draw from when it came to this.

Not the attraction - *that* was familiar. Sex was familiar, too. Hell, even the reckless need to lose himself for a night, to get out of his own head, was familiar. But the enticing connection between them after a handful of hours, *that* was weird. And the kiss! Holy fuck, that kiss. Cort licking into his mouth, biting his lip… it had felt more like a possession than simple foreplay, and Cam had gotten off on it. That was new too. In fact, the way he was letting Cort take the lead in all of this was not just weird but *unprecedented*. Guys - including Drew - seemed to assume because he looked criminally young and preferred to bottom, he must there-fore be inexperienced and passive. He had no problem showing them they were dead wrong. So *why* wasn't he doing it now?

No thinking. Just for tonight.

"Come on, princess, no complaining." Cort grinned and shifted in front of him to lead the way down the stairs, a towel wrapped around his waist, a rumpled ball of clothing and shoes tucked under his arm, and his suit jacket slung over his shoulder. "I'm on the forty-seventh floor. We've got twenty million flights to go."

"Who are you calling *princess*?" Cam demanded, skip-ping down the stairs so they reached the landing half a flight down at the same time. He hip-checked Cort into the railing as he passed him. "I thought I was *badass*."

"Yeah, yeah. Hey! Hold up, badass," Cort said, grab-bing Cam by the wrist to pull him back up to the landing. "Don't run down the damn stairs when you're still dripping wet. You'll crack your head open."

Cam rolled his eyes, even as his pulse started to pound. Cort was still holding his wrist aloft, like he was proving a point. Cam dropped the clothes he'd been carrying to the ground and tried to jerk away, but Cort had leverage, so he couldn't. Cort's jacket fell off his shoulders in the tussle, and one of the shoes he'd been holding clattered down the stairs. Cort swore under his breath and dropped the rest of his belongings on the landing next to Cam's. Then he backed Cam against the wall and paused, looking down at him. It was so quiet their harsh breathing seemed to echo up and down the stairs.

"I'm not a kid and I don't need a babysitter, Cort," Cam told him.

"Yeah? Then act like it, before I spank that ass."

Oh. *Holy shit!* Cam felt those words go straight to his

dick, but he masked his arousal. "I'd like to see you try. I'm not into that shit. I don't need a… a *Master*, or whatever."

But Cort just grinned and whispered, "Hmmm. Your eyes tell a different story, baby."

Cort's voice was so deep, so hungry, Cam could feel the vibration in his chest and he sucked in a breath. *Baby* was just a *word*, one guys used all the damn time, and it didn't mean *anything*. Cam didn't *want* it to mean anything. Tomorrow, this would all be an amazing memory, and he was going to enjoy it while it lasted.

With his free hand, Cort skimmed down the plane of Cam's chest and then around his waist and down, cupping Cam's ass. "I think you like this a lot, don't you Cam? I think you want me to own this ass in more ways than one."

Cam wanted to shake his head, wanted to emphatically deny it, but he couldn't. It seemed like the kind of thing that *should* be wrong. He had never gotten off on power games before, but suddenly he actually was.

"You stay there," Cort told him, eyes flaring in a way that said Cam could back out if he wanted, but Cort really hoped he wouldn't. He lifted Cam's free wrist and pinned it to the wall, so both Cam's hands were joined above his head. Then Cort ducked his chin and claimed Cam's mouth again, forcing his lips open.

Cam's head went back an inch to hit the concrete wall, hard enough to pull a startled *mmmph* from him, although it wasn't painful. Cort immediately moved his head away, his lips glistening and green eyes glowing with arousal and concern.

"God, Cam. I'm sorry. Are you okay?"

Cam didn't answer in words. Instead, he leaned forward and pressed his lips to Cort's, trying to convey that he was more than okay, he wanted it - the roughness, the heat, the hands against the wall.

It didn't take Cort more than half a beat to catch on. "Oh, fuck. You want it hard, baby? Yeah? God, you're perfect."

He transferred Cam's wrists to one big hand and skimmed the other down Cam's smooth chest, flicking his fingertip over one flat nipple experimentally. Little jolts of electricity pulsed along Cam's skin, goosebumps rose on his arms, and he moaned, thrusting his hips forward into Cort's. Cort groaned in response, but shifted slightly to the side, denying Cam anything to grind against, all the while trailing his fingertips up and down Cam's chest, torturing him with sensation.

Sadistic bastard. And the more Cort drew it out, the more Cam lost track of reality, falling under Cort's spell.

He was on fire from head to toe, lust clogging his throat. His dick was rock hard, straining at the still-damp fabric of his boxers, and he needed *friction.* He pulled against Cort's restraining hand, but Cort merely squeezed Cam's wrists more tightly.

Fuck.

Cam bucked his hips harder, trying to break the hold, but all he succeeded in doing was making Cort lift his head and take a half-step backward.

"I said, you stay there, Cam." Cort's voice was a harsh, breathless, warning and his eyes were hard as jade as they stared down into Cam's.

"But I want—" Cam began, and then stopped, his mind flailing. He couldn't articulate what he wanted - it was way too huge. He wanted friction, Cort's lips back on his, Cort pushing him into the wall and making him take it. He wanted to *come,* goddammit, and he wanted Cort to lose his mind, but he didn't know *how* to give up control.

"I know," Cort said. His voice was soothing, and he leaned forward again, just a tiny bit, just enough to rock his stiffened cock against Cam's. Their twin moans echoed around the empty stairwell. "I know exactly what you need, but you need to trust me to give it to you. Can you do that, badass? Just for tonight."

Cam's breath stuttered. Could he? Cort rocked against him, his lower lip caught between even white teeth, not like he was tormenting Cam, but as if he couldn't help himself - as if he wanted Cam as much as Cam wanted him, needed Cam to say *yes* and trust him enough to yield control.

Just for tonight.

Cam took a deep breath, but it did nothing to calm him down. "Yes," he whispered.

Cort's smile was desperate and feral, making Cam's heart thump out an even faster rhythm. "Then leave these here," he instructed, squeezing Cam's wrists to the wall firmly, just once, before letting go completely.

Cam couldn't have moved his arms down in that moment even if he'd wanted to.

Cort ran his hands up and down Cam's arms gently, approvingly. "So hot. So fucking hot, Cam."

He nipped at Cam's chin and slid his mouth back along Cam's jaw, the scruff of his beard nearly painful against Cam's sensitized skin. Then he bit harder right on the hinge. Cam whimpered.

"You like it like this, baby? I'm gonna mark you up, make sure everybody who sees you tomorrow knows exactly where my mouth was, where my teeth were." His voice was a warm breath in Cam's ear, ghosting over his damp skin, making him shiver as if he was fevered. Then Cort's mouth moved to Cam's neck and sucked *hard*, hard enough to ensure more of those involuntary whimpers came from Cam's throat, before his tongue lapped over the place he'd sucked, soothing and arousing at the same time.

Cort's broad palms came to rest on Cam's chest once

again, then he dragged them down Cam's sides *oh so very slowly,* dislodging the towel wrapped around his waist and snagging on the band of his boxers, pulling them down over his hips. Cort adjusted his hold to squeeze Cam's hipbones *hard,* as he whispered, "I'm gonna leave my fingerprints on your skin, so every time you look in the mirror, you'll remember who held you, who owned you."

Cort's broad palms coasted around to cup Cam's ass cheeks, squeezing and molding the pliable flesh like clay, forcing the tight material of Cam's boxers to rub against his dick in a way that was almost painfully intense. "I saw you across the sea of people tonight, and I wanted you," he growled just before his teeth scraped Cam's collarbone. "I knew I shouldn't. I tried to tell myself I didn't come here for this. But then you talked to me. You made me laugh. And I could no more walk away than I could turn back time. I have never wanted anyone more than I want you, so how could I stop this, Cam? *How was I supposed to stop this?*"

Cam had never been so aroused in his life. He couldn't make sense of the words Cort was speaking, only the desperate lust thickening Cort's voice. He had to focus every shred of his remaining control to keep his wrists elevated, to hold his body motionless, to obey Cort's instructions. His balls were already tight and aching, his dick practically throbbing with every word Cort spoke. *He hasn't even touched my cock yet,* Cam thought desperately.

And then, as if Cort could read his mind, he bent and slid Cam's boxers over his straining erection and further down, until they joined his towel and the other clothes on the floor.

"Jesus, Cam. Look at you." The words were a reverent command, and Cam obediently looked down. His dick was so hard, upright and ready, it was nearly touching his stomach, and a bead of precum had formed along his slit.

Touch me, Cam wanted to beg, but before he could form the words, Cort's hand was back on his body, his fingertips coasting along the tops of Cam's thighs, moving in tiny circles closer and closer to Cam's cock. Cam had to bite his lip to keep from wailing.

Cort rested his forehead against Cam's, and together they watched as Cort's hand slid closer and closer, until finally he touched the base of Cam's cock and slid his fingers up to the head, swiping the moisture with his thumb.

"Is this for me, Cam? Is this for *me*?" Cort asked, his voice wrecked with arousal. He made sure Cam was watching - as though his eyes weren't already fixed on Cort's hand like a magnet on true north - and brought that thumb to his mouth. Cort groaned, a filthy, gritty sound torn from his throat. "You taste delicious, baby. And I need to have more."

He grabbed Cam's nearly-numb hands and pulled them down, pinning them to the wall on either side of Cam's waist with a hard look that clearly said *Keep them there*. Cam had no plans to move - the blood that had drained from his fingers while he held them up had all been diverted to his dick, and it wasn't coming back anytime soon.

Especially once Cort sank to his knees.

Fuck.

He put his hands on Cam's thighs, squeezing the muscles there, and leaned forward, licking up Cam's length with one broad, flat stroke of his tongue. Cam's head fell back against the wall. The sight and sensation simultaneously were sensory overload - too much for him to handle without losing his mind.

But Cort wasn't satisfied with that, of course. He gripped Cam firmly around the base of his cock. "Look at me. Watch me on my knees for you," he commanded, and

Cam's head swiveled down automatically, obeying the command without ever consulting his brain.

His eyes locked with Cort's fiery green ones and Cort licked his lips before taking Cam's cock in his mouth, swallowing him down in one swift movement. Cam's howl rang off the walls.

Cort moved his mouth away and glared up at Cam, the fingers of one hand clamping hard onto Cam's thigh. "Quiet."

"I can't… I can't help it," Cam panted. "Cort—"

But Cort was implacable. "One more noise, and this is over." He sounded honestly regretful as he leaned forward and trailed his nose up Cam's cock. It was only the lightest of touches, the barest tease - enough to make Cam insane. "I don't want that, baby. And I know *you* don't. You want to make me happy, right?"

Rational thought was so far beyond Cam's power in that moment, he might have agreed to *anything* to get Cort's mouth back around his dick, but the truth was, he *did* want to make Cort happy, as messed up and crazy as it was to feel that way about a guy he'd just met. He had no defenses left.

"Yes," he breathed.

Cort's answering grin was as bright as a flame. "God, I have never, ever wanted anyone like this," he confessed. "I'm going to take such good care of you, Cam. I've got you, baby."

And damn if that thought didn't worm its way into Cam's chest and attach itself dangerously close to his heart.

But Cam didn't have time to even think about it, because Cort's mouth was back, sucking him down deep. One large hand wrapped around the base of Cam's dick to provide the perfect counterpoint to his mouth, while the other reached further back, to gently play with Cam's balls.

The sight of such a powerful man down on his knees, all that strong will and leashed power focused on Cam's pleasure, those burning green eyes staring up at him, was the hottest thing Cam had ever seen. This was his every fantasy come true, but better, *more*, because he'd never known to wish for this. He wasn't just powerful, or cherished, but *necessary*. Like he, Cam Seaver, was integral to Cort's survival somehow.

The very idea made him want to moan, to cry out in pleasure, but the weight of Cort's stare kept his teeth clamped and his throat closed. *You want to make me happy, right?* He really, really *did*.

Cam was only dimly aware of Cort pulling down his own underwear one-handed and jacking himself frantically. Tongues of flame were dancing up and down Cam's spine. He wanted to grab Cort's hair, wrap those long golden strands around his hands, but he forced himself to sink further against the wall and take it, over and over and over, accepting everything the way Cort wanted to give it to him.

He was shocked he'd held out so long against this onslaught.

But then Cort pulled away. "Say it," he demanded, his voice like gravel while his hands still jerked them both. "Say you want me to own you."

"C-Cort," Cam whispered, his hips were bucking and he couldn't control himself. He was close. So, *so* close.

"Yes, baby. I'm right here. Say it. Say please."

What? What the hell was he... *Oh, right.*

The very idea made Cam's stomach flip. But they were only words, right? This was a game? He wouldn't make this out to be more than it was, attach importance to something that wasn't. It would change nothing. He could say it, and...

"I want it all," he whispered. "I want you to own me. *P-please.*"

"Fuck, yes," Cort growled, then he swallowed Cam down to the root again.

A small cry escaped from Cam's throat then - a cry of absolute surrender. Surrender to this man and the incredible pleasure which was beyond anything he'd ever experienced before.

"Oh fuck, yes. Yes. Cort!" he cried. He came in pulsing waves, and Cort drank it all down. Then Cort jacked himself off and spilled on the floor with a hoarse cry while Cam could only watch with wide, unfocused eyes.

Jesus. Fucking. Christ.

Cort pulled up his boxers and swiped at the mess on the floor with a towel. Then flopping onto his ass, he pulled Cam down to straddle his lap. Cam buried his head in Cort's neck, and the two of them remained sitting for a minute, or an hour, who the hell knew, while their breathing calmed and their pulses steadied.

Two thoughts occurred to Cam, one immediately after the other. First, it was really freaking cold in here. And second, he was *naked* in a *public* stairway, and literally *anyone* could come along and find them like this.

He sucked in a breath and pushed himself up and off Cort's lap.

"So, fun time is over, hmm?" Cort asked. He shifted to lean his back against the wall and folded his arms over his chest, his legs still splayed out in front of him and still naked apart from the plain black boxers molded to his thighs. Cam looked away and began scrambling for his clothes.

"I… it's just, anyone could come and see. I don't want to have to explain what we're doing here," Cam said. And wasn't *that* the damn truth? The shit he'd just said to Cort, for God's sake! *Was* there even an explanation, beyond the whiskey they'd drunk and the complete lack of judgment Drew was always accusing him of?

So, why the *hell* did he want to do it again?

Cort nodded, but made no move to get dressed, while Cam hopped around, pulling his suit pants back into place and throwing on his shirt. "I need… I mean, I should probably get home. It's late?"

Could he be any lamer? He could feel the blush creeping up his cheeks.

Cort snorted and heaved himself to his feet with a sigh, stepping into his pants and grabbing his remaining clothes into a bundle. "You can use the bathroom in my room if you'd like," he offered, but his voice was closed off, cooler than it had been all night. A perfunctory offer. He knew Cam would say no.

Cam closed his eyes and sighed, raking a hand through his messy, damp hair. Just because *he* was freaking out, that was no reason to treat Cort like a leper. He'd never found anyone as easy to talk to as Cort. He wanted to get to know him.

"Yeah. Yeah, I'd like to," Cam said. He opened his eyes in time to see shock, surprise, and a trace of uncertainty flit across Cort's face. "Unless, maybe it's not a good idea?"

Cort smiled, that lopsided smile that did crazy things to Cam's inside. "Define good?"

Cam laughed, and when Cort held out a hand to him a moment later, he didn't hesitate.

***

"OH. My. God. Tell me that's not the sun already," Cam said, grabbing the spare pillow from the unused side of the bed and burrowing his face into it.

Cort, who had been watching the sunrise for at least an hour, stroked his hand up from Cam's hip to his rib cage. He laughed softly, but he could sympathize with Cam's feelings because he wasn't ready for the sun to rise either.

He'd hardly slept after they'd made it downstairs the night before, not even bothering to shower or change before stripping off their clothes again and climbing into bed, spooning into one another. The combination of stellar orgasms and a million shots of Jameson had relaxed them both to the point where they hadn't needed to talk or overthink things further, but while Cam had fallen asleep quickly and deeply, Cort had lain awake for most of the night.

They'd shared a pillow.

And that wasn't the most intimate thing they'd shared.

The whole night had been like something from a dream, a slice of a parallel universe that had been cut out and inserted into this one. It had been phenomenal – everything he'd ever wanted yet never dreamed he'd be able to find. It was also the cruelest trick he'd ever played on himself, because he still needed to find his brother, Damon, the man Cam thought had caused his parents' deaths. There was no way Cam would help him. And Cam would never look at him the same way after he learned the truth.

"If I'm going to contemplate this day," Cam mumbled into the pillow. "I need *so* much caffeine. Like, ungodly amounts."

"Ungodly, huh?" Cort leaned more fully into Cam, running his nose along the column of Cam's neck, loving the way the man shivered.

"I suppose there are other ways to wake up," Cam allowed, pushing his ass back into Cort's groin. Cort's breath caught and he moaned.

"Only one tiny problem with that," he said, biting Cam's shoulder. "No lube."

It was Cam's turn to moan, but he shoved the pillow away from his face and turned to grin at Cort. "Well, fortunately for you, I'm endlessly creative, and I'm almost certain I can think of a way to make do."

Cort laughed out loud, stroking his finger down Cam's cheek. "I believe you can, baby."

His laughter died the second Cam reached for him, stroking his palm along the ridge of Cort's very interested dick. "*Fuck*," he groaned.

Cam laughed. "I'm feeling like this would be better in the shower."

"I'm feeling like I can't imagine how this *could* be better," Cort said, flopping onto his back and letting Cam balance above him. He wrapped his arm around Cam's neck and pulled him down for a kiss, but Cam tried to twist away.

"Gross! Cort, my breath is…"

But Cort didn't give a shit about morning breath. He lifted his head and met Cam's lips, parting them with his tongue, desperate for whatever pieces of Cam he could keep. He couldn't believe how quickly he'd fallen for the guy. Twenty-four hours ago, he'd thought Cam was his enemy. Twenty-four hours from now, he was positive they'd be enemies for real, and there would be nothing he could do to change it. Damon had to come first. But perhaps he could have just a few more minutes.

Cort rolled, pushing Cam onto his back, loving the way Cam's legs automatically parted, making room for him. He braced himself, palms to the mattress, and stared down into Cam's eyes.

"Cam, I…"

From the heap of clothing on the floor, a phone began to

ring. Cam closed his eyes briefly and swore under his breath.

"Sorry. Shit. That's my brother's ringtone. Just gimme a minute, okay?"

He squirmed out of bed, and Cort flopped onto his back, staring up at the ceiling. He wasn't sure exactly what he'd been about to say, but it was probably for the best that they were interrupted.

Too much, way too fast.

Cam grabbed his phone a second after it stopped ringing, and immediately hit redial.

"He never calls me, ever. So, I kinda need to take it."

Cort nodded, watching Cam as he waited and waited for his brother to answer. Apparently, the asshole was messing around or something, because Cam tried calling him three times, yet he didn't pick up.

"I mean, he's probably fine, right?" Cam said, frowning. He came to sit on the edge of the bed cradling the phone in both hands. "Like maybe he called me by accident, or…"

Cort pushed himself up to sitting. The moment was lost. He was fairly certain he could get it back easily, just by kissing Cam, but he wasn't sure whether he should, or even if he wanted to.

"Probably," he agreed.

Cam turned and looked at him, then back at his phone, disappointment evident in the slump of his shoulders. "Or maybe I should get going and, uh, check on him," he said quietly.

Cort wondered if Cam wanted him to argue. He wouldn't.

"I should probably go, too. Do some… stuff," he said instead. Stuff like hitting the liquor store and wishing his own brother would call.

Cort stood up and stepped in front of Cam, pulling the

man to his feet and kissing him with every ounce of the happiness and need he'd begun to associate with Cam. "This has probably been the best night of my whole life," he told Cam simply. "Believe it." He rested his forehead on Cam's for a second, cursing his dumb luck and Cam's, then he pulled back. "I'll see you around, Mr. Seaver," he said, then he walked into the bathroom.

When he turned to close the door, he saw Cam standing silently, watching him.

CHAPTER SEVEN

August could be a bitch of a month in Boston. Tourists thought of Massachusetts as the land of apple cider and snowfall, but Cam had lived there his whole life and knew very well that walking down the street could feel more like *swimming* when the epic humidity of summer hit, which was why he was kicking his own ass as he ran down the block toward the Union Park brownstone his brother called home.

The good news was, he'd sweat out the last remaining drops of the alcohol he'd consumed the night before at some point along the four-mile run from his place in Cambridge. The bad news was, without the lingering, memory-dampening effects of a hangover to distract him, he felt like an even bigger idiot about the events of the previous evening.

He leaned against the short, wrought-iron gate in front of Bas's building and panted, sucking down the last few drops of water from the bottle he'd carried.

Not that he blamed his behavior yesterday on alcohol entirely. Yeah, maybe at first the alcohol helped to make him a little less awkward, a little more accepting, but everything after that had been totally him, from the hot-as-hell control thing to the total fizzle-out at the end.

The gate squeaked as he pushed it open and walked up the path.

God, but the control thing had worked for him in a major way. He'd known people who really got off on that kink, who worked the dynamic 24/7, yet while he'd always been sorta you-do-you about the whole thing, he'd never truly understood the appeal. But for him last night, it hadn't been about the nurturing and constant focus his friends loved so much, it had been one hundred percent about the power exchange, about giving control over to someone he trusted. Cam couldn't remember anything as good, ever.

It had been glorious, but scary, too, because it was the kind of thing he could quickly become addicted to. Cam got the feeling Cort didn't do permanent, and Cam wasn't exactly free of baggage. Case in point, one messed-up, reclusive brother who was apparently hacking the government.

He removed Bas's key from the zippered pocket of his shorts and contemplated the heavy wooden door. He could knock and give Bas enough time to pretend to be sleeping or showering, or he could walk straight in and see how Bas was *really* doing. Weighing the key in his palm, thinking of his conversation with Drew last night and the unreturned calls this morning, he knew he'd choose option B. He needed to see how bad Bas really was. So, he unlocked the door, taking care to make enough noise that Bas could dive for cover if he was naked or whatever.

He needn't have worried.

The air inside the apartment was blessedly cool - almost too cold against Cam's damp skin, and though the sun was raising rippling heat waves from the pavement outside, inside it was dark as a tomb. Sitting on the red sofa, not bothering to stand or even turn his head - *and Jesus, I could be an ax-murderer for God's sake* - was his brother. Cam's eyes popped open in surprise at the sight.

Bas hadn't been right since the crash - losing Amy, losing their parents, it had sent him into a tailspin. During the first couple of months, Cam had thought maybe things would be okay. And then the stupid NTSB report had come out, giving Bas somewhere to focus his attention, and any gains he had made vanished in an instant.

But he hadn't been this bad.

Sebastian was wearing a pair of baggy, gray cutoff sweatpants and a sleeveless white t-shirt which hung from his thinning frame, both of which looked far too broken-in and wrinkled to be clean. His thick brown hair, usually carefully styled back from his face, flopped in greasy, life-less waves above tired blue eyes. His normally tanned skin seemed four shades too pale, and he stared at the flat-screen television on the wall as if it was somehow speaking messages directly into his brain.

Cam felt a hum of unease at the base of his skull.

The screen was paused on a television interview which had taken place shortly after the crash. A witness had come forward who'd been drinking with the pilot responsible for the accident, a redheaded man maybe around Cort's age. No doubt he'd been seeking his fifteen minutes of fame, and had done a tell-all interview with some bottom-feeder of a tabloid show. It had been short on details and long on spec-ulation, just enough to fire up imaginations and send the media - and Sebastian - out sniffing for blood.

"What are you doing?" Cam asked.

Bas turned his head slowly, reluctantly, fighting the magnetic force of the on-screen images. He looked confused to see Cam there, but then his expression cleared and he became animated.

"Oh, Cam! Just the person I needed. Look at this man! Who does he look like?"

Cam blinked. "I dunno? The guy from Grey's Anatomy?"

The glance Bas turned on him was wild-eyed and impatient. "No, someone we know. Someone we've met before."

"Nobody I know," Cam said, giving the television another passing glance. "Bas, we need to talk. This shit you've been pulling has to stop."

Bas shook his head. "This is the key, Cam. The key!" He grabbed the remote from the coffee table and flipped to a different stored video, this one of Cam's college graduation. He pushed Play.

"I know I've seen this guy somewhere."

"The guy in the interview? Bas, that's hardly likely. He looks like a lot of people." Cam was trying to be patient, but failing. Bas needed to listen to him.

Instead, his brother chose a different video. A TZT-online-news clip about their parents' funeral. Cam sighed as the reporter recounted the tragedy with barely-concealed excitement. Even a year later, that thread of satisfaction some people enjoyed when talking about the death of an attractive, rich couple and a young, beautiful, wealthy woman drove him bonkers.

Cam grabbed the remote from Bas and paused the video, then took a seat on the edge of the sofa and forced Bas to look at him.

"Bas. Talk to me. Have you been hacking government systems in a reckless and obvious way? Is… is this a cry for help? Do you want to get caught?"

Sebastian rolled his eyes impatiently. "I don't know what the fuck you're talking about, Cam."

He reached for the remote again, but Cam laid a hand on his wrist. "Being serious here, Bas."

Bas rolled his eyes again. "I know you are. You *always* are, Cam. Speaking plain facts without emotion. It's what you do." The bitterness in his tone was like a punch to Cam's chest.

"What's that supposed to mean?" Cam demanded, but he knew. He'd talked more about his parents during the past few days than he had in the whole of the past year, but the constant comments about it were really starting to piss him off. Was he supposed to talk about his parents all the time? Parade his emotions around on his sleeve?

God.

Bas opened his mouth like he was about to say something, but thought better of it. "Get out of here, Cam. I'm busy."

Cam stood. "Busy? Busy with *what?* When was the last time you came into the office?" Worry and frustration - with Bas, with Cort, with his whole screwed-up life made his voice unnaturally high-pitched. "David is working on the new release without you. Margaret is worried. Uncle Shaw is determined to step in and take over from you."

"We don't need *his* help," Bas muttered, spearing Cam with a glare. "Absolutely not."

Cam had been on the exact same page when Uncle Shaw had broached the idea, but now he found himself chafing. How dare Bas have an opinion about *this*, when he refused to have one on anything else?

"I could use the help," he taunted his big brother instead. "You're obsessed with finding someone to blame, obsessed with the past, but it won't bring anybody back, Bas."

"You think I don't know that?" he demanded.

"Well, then *why?*" Cam said, throwing a hand up in the direction of the television. "Why spend your whole life communing with the dead when I am *right here* and I need you?"

Cam snapped his jaw shut. He couldn't believe the words that had tumbled from his lips. All that openness with Cort last night had made him spill his guts in a way he would *never* have dreamed of a couple of days ago.

"Cam," Sebastian began in a placating tone, but Cam shook his head. Enough with the emotional rollercoaster. He wanted nothing more than to run himself to the point of epic exhaustion, and sleep through until the time came on Monday when he *had* to get up and deal with his life.

"Never mind," Cam told him. "Don't do me any favors." He turned to leave. "Just make sure you eat something, okay? You look like a skeleton."

He glanced up just once before he left, but when he did, Sebastian's slack-jawed attention was fully focused back on the paused television screen.

CHAPTER EIGHT

By the time his alarm blared on Monday morning, Cort had already been awake for hours, staring at the tiny fissures in the plaster ceiling above his bed and contemplating his life choices. He sucked in a breath, let it out in a sigh, and rolled over to grab his phone from the nightstand. The stupid thing played an obnoxiously peppy song - like *Happy Birthday* with maracas - and he never could figure out how to change it, but at least it meant he always leapt out of bed immediately at seven a.m., wide awake if somewhat annoyed.

Today, though, he flopped back on the bed after silencing the alarm, and debated throwing the damn phone out his second-story window to shatter on the asphalt below. There had to be *some* silver linings to being *thisclose* to unemployment for the first time in his adult life, goddamn it. He had a *right* to lie in his bed, still stinking faintly of chlorine because he hadn't bothered to shower all weekend, and he didn't need an alarm going off every morning to remind him he had no job to go to. Since he was unlikely to get his job back at all, he probably didn't need the FBI-issued piece of crap any longer anyway.

He stood up and stretched, tossing the phone onto his dresser next to his wallet, then picked his way through the living room to the little kitchen. His foot swiped a mostly-empty bag of chips sticking out from beneath the couch, sending dull yellow crumbs scattering across the floor, and he grimaced when he accidentally stepped on some, grinding them into the area rug in the center of the room. In the kitchen, he set the kettle on to boil, then turned to stare in disgust at the wreck of his apartment.

The folders of notes piled haphazardly, clothing thrown over chairs, and paperbacks stacked sideways and double-banked on the cheap bookcase didn't bother him at all, though he'd pissed off enough roommates over the years to know he was no picnic to live with. The other stuff, though, all the signs of the weekend-long pity-party he'd thrown himself, bothered him immensely. He had no reason to feel sorry for himself, after all. The food strewn on the coffee table, the mugs of half-drunk coffee and dirty dishes he'd accumulated over the past few days, the stale scents of beer and unwashed human - all that shit reminded him a little too much of some of his childhood homes, and the kind of person he'd sworn he'd never become.

And all this because Cam Seaver tied you up in knots. It was shameful, it really was. He grabbed a garbage bag and broom, and began systematically tidying the living room while he waited for the water to heat.

What else did you expect would happen on Friday night? he asked himself for at least the hundredth time in two days. And just like every other time, he had no good response. It was a foregone conclusion that Cam was going to learn the truth about Cort, that he'd feel like an ass when he did, and that Cam would never want to speak to him again.

So why did he regret that everything was going to plan?

Cort hadn't expected the guy would make him laugh so much, or that Cam's trust in Cort would make him want to confide in Cam, too. He'd never figured the kid in the surveillance pictures would be very much a man, and the hottest one Cort had laid eyes on in a really long while. Blowing the guy in a stairwell, of all places, hadn't been part of the plan. Neither had the way Cam responded to his dominance.

Shit. Just thinking about it had wound him up again.

But the surprise of the connection and the hot sex were nothing compared to the shock of finding he honestly *liked* Cam Seaver. For a minute there, he'd been second-guessing his careful plan, thinking about coming clean to Cam and asking for his *help* instead of forcing his hand. A guy who could be loyal to a dickwad like Sebastian Seaver would understand Cort's loyalty to his own brother, right?

As the kettle began to whistle, he threw the last of his trash into the garbage bag and made himself a cup of pour-over coffee, tapping his fingers on the counter as he waited.

So, yeah, on some level he'd known all evening long, even as they'd played games at the bar, traded secrets at the pool, and shared their mind-blowing exchange on the stairs, that once Cam found out who Cort actually was and why he'd come to the fundraiser, they'd be headed for disaster. But Cam *hadn't* found out, and things had ended anyway. The air around them had barely cooled before Cam was grabbing Sebastian's call — an epic reminder from the universe of why they could never be together. And Cam hadn't said a word to stop Cort from walking away, either. It was as if he recognized some essential lacking element in Cort's makeup - probably the same thing that had made him disposable to everyone but Damon since the day he was born.

He sipped his coffee, grimacing slightly at the bitter burn in his throat.

Whatever. Two days of wallowing was two days too long, and he had a job to do.

A job that still involved him confronting Cam Seaver and making some carefully-worded demands.

Cort ran a hand through his messy hair, then took his coffee to the sofa and sat down, toying with a pen on the coffee table and contemplating the files in front of him. Though he could practically recite all the information by heart, he grabbed the top folder from the stack anyway - the file on his brother - and looked at the picture he'd carefully clipped to the top of the page, needing to remind himself of exactly why he'd targeted Cam Seaver in the first place, why he couldn't afford to show the man any weakness.

He winced. Any *more* weakness.

Nineteen-year-old Damon Fitzpatrick stood in front of the Dempseys' one-story house, his broad shoulders hunched, brow furrowed, eyes staring straight ahead as though he was anticipating a fight. His hair was still blond, not yet the all-over gray Damon had acquired in his early thirties. Meanwhile, beneath his right arm, was a scrawny twelve-year-old Cort wearing a t-shirt two sizes too big, and looking up at Damon as though he was magic.

Cort snorted. In a way, his brother *had* been magic, especially when Cort was younger. From the first moment Cort had been placed with the Dempseys, eight years old and way more pissed at the world than a third-grader should have any reason to be, Damon had taken care of him. Seven years older and already wise to the way things ran at Craig and Rhonda Dempsey's house, Damon seemed to feel like it was his mission to keep Cort safe. No food in the cabinets or the fridge? No worries, because Damon would find some. The guy who lived across the street, in the house with the boarded-up windows, was eyeing Cort in a way that made Cort squirm? Not a problem, because Damon would get him to stop. If Cort was sick, injured, confused, or sad, Damon had always been around to help. And when Damon's friends asked why little Cort was always hanging around, Cort remembered the happy thrill he'd get when Damon would give his friend a killing look and reply, "Because he's my *brother*, that's why."

It wasn't until Cort was sixteen or so that he'd realized exactly how much Damon had sacrificed to take care of a kid who was no blood relation - the junk food that miraculously appeared when Craig and Rhonda failed to do any shopping was stuff Damon had *stolen*, the reason Randall from across the street had disappeared was because Damon had *beaten him* within an inch of his life, and the only reason Damon had stayed in the house after he'd turned eighteen and was phased out of the system, was by working out a deal with the Dempseys where he would pay an exorbitant monthly rent to continue living there - a rent so high Damon couldn't afford to go to school.

After that, there had been arguments aplenty, about how Cort was practically an adult and perfectly capable of taking care of himself, *thankyouverymuch*, and how Damon's decisions were none of Cort's business, so he should keep his damn mouth shut. But in the end, Damon had stayed in Johnsville, working as a mechanic at the tiny regional airport, until the day Cort turned eighteen a month after his high school graduation. And then, while Cort had secured a partial football scholarship to Northeastern, and moved on to various assignments with the Bureau, Damon had kept his mechanic job and studied for his degree at night, before training to become a pilot and getting a job at a charter airline service. It hadn't been a painless process, not for either of them, but as Damon used to say, "Hard and easy don't matter when there's no Plan B."

Cort sipped his cooling coffee and flipped the page, feeling a familiar rage churn in his gut as he pulled out the official report of the plane crash where Damon was believed to have died thirteen months previously, along with Levi Seaver, Charlotte Seaver, and Amy McMann. Pilot error, the official cause said. *Damon's* error.

Examination of the airplane by an FAA inspector reveals fire damage in engine compartment. Fuel control feed lines and return lines found to be loose at rear engine fittings above the starter adapter. Probable cause of incident: Loss of engine power caused by failure to properly secure fuel control lines. Maintenance records show the pilot, Damon Fitzpatrick, had replaced the plane's starter adapter eight hours before the incident. Witness reports indicate the pilot had been drinking heavily during the hours before the flight. Heavy fog likely an additional contribution to the incident.

It was all neat, tidy, and official-looking to anyone who didn't know Damon, who didn't understand how fastidious and responsible he was. It had been especially convincing to Sebastian Seaver, who'd been looking to point fingers. Cort sure as hell understood the impulse to handle grief by becoming angry and casting blame - he was a gold-medal all-star at that shit. But Sebastian Seaver hadn't merely vented to his friends or talked to his grief counselor, he hadn't had a few too many drinks and thrown out a few careless words at a bar. No, when Sebastian Seaver had read the NTSB report and gone off the deep end, he'd done it on the public stage. And for a Seaver, for *American royalty*, that was a *very* big stage. *Grossly negligent*, he'd called Damon in one article. *Murderously incompetent,* were the words he'd chosen for a television interview. And when the sympathetic host had shaken her head and asked what Sebastian would say to Damon Fitzpatrick if he could have the opportunity, he'd looked directly at the camera and said, "I hope he and his entire family rot in hell." Naturally, reporters had jumped on the story, digging into every aspect of Damon's private life. And the bastards hadn't cared about the innocent people who'd been caught in the crossfire.

It was how they'd found Damon's asshole of a father who, for the right price, had been happy to dish about Damon, along with Chelsea, the twenty-year-old sister Cort was positive Damon had never known about, and her three-year-old daughter Molly.

Cort tapped his pen against his thigh and turned the page again. Damon had never talked about his life before the Dempseys, even to him. Since the bits and fragments Cort recalled about his own life before foster care generally turned his stomach to think about, and he wasn't one to share personal shit at the best of times - *did Derrick Green even know Cort was once in foster care?* - Cort had understood this. But it meant he had to wonder whether Damon had ever known his father had sired another child. Given the way Damon had protected *him* all these years, he was pretty sure the answer was no. The idea that Chelsea and Molly would never know Damon was just one more level of loss, added to Cort's already overwhelming grief over his brother, whose remains had never even been recovered from the mountain, for the love of God, and anger at the way Damon was being demonized by Sebastian Seaver's pet reporters. Cort's own overtures towards the girl had been completely rebuffed, and he had felt more alone than ever.

And then, just six months ago, the first package had arrived.

A random box of Twinkies arriving in the mail might not be a heart-attack-inducing moment to anyone else. But for a kid who'd never had a birthday cake until his teenaged brother had stuck a candle in a Twinkie one time and told him to make a wish, receiving the box of treats *on his birthday* was like receiving a message from beyond the grave. Cort had never told anybody about the Twinkies, so what the hell could this mean but Damon was still alive?

Then, newspaper clippings began arriving. Old-school, the way Damon knew Cort did things, no computers involved. Roughly once a month to begin with, but at other times more frequently, once or even twice a week. Cort had collected articles which ran the gamut from fluff pieces on the rise and fall of Levi Seaver, to business reports about Seaver Tech stock having plummeted before Sebastian Seaver took over the development reins and Camden stepped in as president.

He'd pored over a picture of Cam and Sebastian at their parents' funeral, flanked by Senator Emmett Shaw and his entourage. He'd encountered dead-end after dead-end trying to trace the witness who'd seen Damon drinking before the crash. He'd slogged through multi-page articles cut from tech journals reporting on new technologies, and rolled his eyes at political pieces on special interest lobbies and military spending. He'd pored over every article as though they were fragments of a puzzle, trying to figure out the hidden meanings, trying to twist them into a clear picture of whatever Damon was trying to tell him, but only one consistent theme had emerged: *Seaver, Seaver, Seaver.*

What he'd found during his investigation was that Cam was at the helm of the company, while Sebastian had become a near-recluse who disappeared for weeks at a time, only emerging to continue dragging Damon's reputation through the mud at every opportunity, or hack government computers without repercussions.

It had been an easy leap from there to see what Damon

was pointing out. If Damon himself hadn't caused the accident by failing to inspect the engine, *someone else must have sabotaged the plane.* Who would profit from the death of Charlotte and Levi Seaver?

Sebastian and Cam.

Cort had pretty much ruled out Cam even before his dick had become involved Friday night, and nothing about his quiet strength or reluctant assumption of authority suggested he could have set the events in motion that killed his parents. So, Sebastian must have been involved.

And wouldn't Cam love to hear that, coming from Cort?

Cort squeezed his eyes shut at the idea of causing Cam that much pain. And he would never believe it, not until Cort had concrete proof, so Cort would wait to share that information until Cam could easily draw his own conclusions.

Not for the first time, he wished he could call Damon and consult his brother.

It wasn't lost on him that Damon hadn't called to ask *Cort's* opinion on the case over all these months, or to chat about Cort's life and mental state. And he recognized that he was essentially duplicating Damon's work, double-checking all the conclusions Damon had already come to. Why couldn't Damon call him, even anonymously? Why not send a letter of explanation? Why wait until nearly six months after the accident?

He shoved the papers back in the folder along with all the newspaper clippings which had fallen out, before placing the whole stack of folders into his briefcase. He took his coffee cup to the sink and washed it carefully - *look at me, being responsible and not pitiful!* - and then headed for the shower.

He had had no clue what his brother was doing, but he knew Damon was smart, and would have faith in Cort's loyalty. So Cort had set up a facial recognition scan and waited patiently for months, until the previous week when pieces began to fall into place.

The first, another anonymous envelope, had arrived on Monday containing an outdated travel brochure from a tiny island called St. Brigitte. Google told him the island was once semi-private, but now owned entirely by the Tyndall family, who used it to host enormous fundraising galas like the ones the Seavers always attended. And a quick (nausea-inducing) glance at a well-known Boston society blog had told him the next such event, the Tyndalls' end-of-summer party, was coming up.

The second breakthrough was on Friday morning, when Damon's face had been captured at the largest commercial airport near St. Brigitte. Damon would be on the island, Cort had no doubt, so he needed to get there too. And whether Cam liked it or not, he would be Cort's ticket.

Cort took the fastest shower known to man then threw on a suit and tie. He grabbed his phone, wallet, and lucky quarter from the dresser, collected his briefcase from the coffee table, then headed for the door before he could reconsider his plan. Damon was counting on him. He would not betray his brother's trust for a love affair which could only end in tragedy.

CHAPTER NINE

"You've got lunch with Trillian in R&D, followed by a two-thirty call with Devon Marks from Philadelphia about the issues with the Genysys launch – I've set up a highlights file on the server, but just so you're aware, Devon assumes you've spoken with Sebastian at length on this issue and are speaking on his behalf." Cam's administrative assistant, Margaret, glanced up from her tablet and appraised him over the top of her reading glasses.

"And then at four-thirty you're meeting with Colleen from Finance. Shouldn't take more than half an hour."

Cam nodded robotically, tidying up his desk

"Then tonight, the aliens are coming. I'm unclear about whether it's a full-scale invasion, or they just want to take you back to their pod for further study. Shall I put *that* on your calendar?"

"Of course," Cam replied automatically, barely hearing her. "Sounds great."

Margaret set her tablet down on the desk, knocking his stapler askew, and Cam glanced up to find her sitting back in her chair opposite him, staring at him.

"Is there a problem?" he asked.

Margaret pushed her glasses to the top of her head, mussing her gray hair. "I think that's my line, Mr. Seaver."

Cam rolled his eyes. "Cam, Margaret. *Camden.* Mr. Seaver was—"

"Your dad," she finished impatiently. "Yes, I know. I worked for the man for twenty-seven years, Cam. It's also *you.*"

Right. Yes. In the most technical sense. But in his father's old office, it didn't feel right.

He cleared his throat and waved a dismissive hand through the air. "Everything's fine. I've already started going through the designs Pam sent over, and should have them all approved by lunchtime."

Margaret nodded. "Of course you will. You always get things done."

It was a simple statement, but the way she studied him after she had spoken suggested she knew how much he needed to hear it.

"Have you slept?"

He forced himself not to roll his eyes again.

"Of course." *A few hours Saturday night, a couple last night.* "And I ate all my vegetables and brushed my teeth, too." *And drank my weight in alcohol, had sex with a total stranger in a stairwell, and went back to his hotel room and slept better than I have in a year.*

Margaret was completely unperturbed by his snark. "I ask because you look like you were ridden hard and put away wet, as my granny used to say."

"No. I'm fine." He moved Margaret's tablet forward an inch and put his stapler back into position.

"You could call Doctor Meredith," she reminded him, and Cam sighed.

"Margaret, I promise I don't need an emergency session

with my therapist. I had way too good a time at the gala Friday, drank a little too much, stayed up too late, and it's taking me a while to recover. Otherwise, I'm fine."

"You're sure?"

"Positive." Cam lied emphatically.

Margaret's glasses slid down an inch as she nodded, and she grabbed her tablet from the desktop, tapping a few boxes. "Alright, then. Drew called and asked if you were free for coffee around ten today."

Cam looked up sharply. "And what did you tell him?"

"I said that I wasn't sure of your schedule, though he was very insistent."

Shocker. Cam had ignored seven calls and three dozen texts from an increasingly-irate Drew over the weekend, but of course the man knew exactly how to find him at work.

He didn't have the focus to deal with Drew this morning, not after the long and sleepless weekend he'd had. And though he had a million *real* things to worry about, he'd be lying if he said it wasn't memories of Friday night that had kept him awake. His instincts had told him Cort was with him every step of the way, his green eyes locked on Cam, glowing with arousal, but the way Cort had walked away called those instincts into question. Had Cam talked too much? Were his abs not toned enough? Should he have volunteered a little less about what a total nerd he was? Was it weird and disgusting how much he liked it *rough*, and wanted to be *dominated?*

He *hated* questioning himself this way.

Any way you sliced it, he had nobody to blame for his misery but himself, and the last thing he needed was Drew McMann driving that point home.

"Right. Well, when he calls back, you tell him I already have a meeting scheduled after all."

"Alright," Margaret said dubiously.

"Margaret," he warned, sitting forward in his chair. "Seriously. You are my only hope. Do not fail me in this. You just went over everything on my agenda today, and the last thing I need is Drew barging in and making himself at home in that chair while he tells me all the ways I could be doing things differently and therefore better."

She raised one eyebrow and pursed her lips. "You should tell him that."

Cam snorted. "*Right*. Tell him to mind his own business and stop trying to tell me I'm incompetent. That'll go over well. Do you do family counseling as a side job?"

Margaret threw up her hands in defeat. "You three boys will be the death of me. I watched you all grow up together, thick as thieves, and now I'm seeing you tear each other apart. *You* are so convinced you don't deserve your job, you won't look up and see exactly how well you're doing and how valuable you are. *Drew* is so devastated about Amy and Bas and his parents' divorce, he's determined to take care of everyone he has left, even if he smothers you all to death in the process. And *Sebastian...*" She hesitated.

"Oh, don't stop now," Cam told her, folding his arms across his chest. He smirked. "This I want to hear."

"Fine," she said, raising her chin defiantly. "Bas is so damn guilty he *lived*, he's determined to kill himself one way or another."

Direct hit. Cam's stomach bottomed out and his smile died immediately.

Margaret closed her eyes and gave a slight, rueful shake of her head. She stood, clasping her tablet to her chest, and picked up his empty coffee cup. "I'll get you more coffee Mr. Seaver," she said softly.

Cam nodded, accepting the peace offering. All the coffee

in Boston wouldn't bring the world into focus today, but he'd give it a decent try.

He tried to focus on the new designs for their virtual reality program which could help pediatric neurosurgeons, but a commotion out in the lobby caught his attention. Margaret was talking to someone out there – through the open door, he could hear a deep voice arguing in counterpoint to Margaret's sweet soprano. He checked the time on his phone. *Nine forty-five.* Probably Drew, goddamn it, not bothering to call back to check and simply assuming Cam was free.

He hesitated, girding himself mentally. If Drew was so worked up he was harassing Margaret, Cam shouldn't put off this meeting any longer.

Polite but firm NO. Polite. Firm. NO.

"Margaret, send him in."

Her head appeared in the doorway, and she frowned. "But Mr. Seaver, he doesn't have an appointment."

Cam sighed and minimized the design specs on his computer. "I know. And he really should, but it's okay. Maybe offer him coffee so he's not quite such an asshole while he's here."

"I'm hardly ever an asshole," the voice in the doorway joked, and even before he turned, Cam's heart gave a traitorous leap.

Cort stood in the doorway next to Margaret, looking better than Cam had allowed himself to remember. His longish golden hair was slicked neatly back, and the well-cut navy suit emphasized his broad shoulders and lean waist, but it was his face with its intense green eyes and secret smile which had Cam entranced.

"Mr. Seaver, this is highly irregular," Margaret complained. "I'll get Mr. McMann down here immediately."

Cam pulled his gaze away from Cort and raised an

eyebrow. She seemed flustered, and Margaret was hardly ever flustered. What in the world would they need Drew for?

He stood and walked around his desk. "That won't be necessary, Margaret," he said, coming to take the coffee from her hand. "Cort and I have already met."

Her brow puckered. "You've met?" she said, wide-eyed with confusion. "But… Are you sure? Mr. McMann sent out a memo."

Cam blinked. Drew had sent out a memo about Cort?

Cort cleared his throat and drew Cam's attention once more. "I'm good, Margaret," Cam told his assistant, ushering her out through the door. "Do not call Drew. My earlier instructions still apply."

"Yes, Mr. Seaver," she sighed, and he shut the door behind her.

Cam took a second to compose himself before he turned around to face him. *Cort had found him.* Cam had no idea what it meant, but his heart was pounding unsteadily and he felt hope bloom in his stomach. Perhaps Cort wanted more than one night, and Cam would have a chance to redeem himself. Maybe he ought to have a little more faith in himself, in other people, and trust his own instincts.

"So, I guess you weren't a figment of my imagination, huh? I wasn't sure after Saturday morning. I didn't get your number." Cam turned and leaned back against the door, unable to stop himself from smiling. Cort was close by, a few feet away, and the same electric current which had zapped between them on Friday crackled. *Didn't imagine that zing. Nor the way he smells of oranges and Christmas, either.*

Cam's body reacted to the scents almost instantly, his stomach heating, tightening, clenching. *Down boy.*

Cort looked him up and down, his lips pressed together as if he was fighting memories too, but he wasn't smiling this time. His eyes looked troubled, and he didn't seem to have had any more sleep over the weekend than Cam. "No, it was definitely real," he said, but then he looked away. "But we need to talk."

Cam frowned. God, he was beginning to hate that phrase. Nobody ever said it when they had good news to relay. Plus, Cort's voice was off. It wasn't warm and deep, but crisp and businesslike. For the first time, Cam noticed Cort was carrying a briefcase. Instinctively, Cam pushed off the door and walked back around his desk, needing the physical distance.

He wants something from me.

Of course he does.

Bone-chilling cold replaced the heat he'd felt earlier, and he heard the voice in his head, taunting him. *Did you really think he was interested in you? Grow up, Cam.* Cort was gorgeous, daring, witty, sexy-as-hell. All the things Cam *wasn't.* As quickly as hope had bloomed in his chest, it now withered.

"How may I help you, Mr. Cortland?" Cam asked as he took his seat, scooting his chair under the desk. He schooled his features in much the same way he did when talking to the board or the media. He gestured to the chair in front of his desk that Margaret had recently vacated and scooted his stapler a mere quarter-inch to the left.

Would Cort blackmail him? Recalling everything he'd divulged Friday night, the things they'd done together, the pain in his heart and the shame in his gut were almost paralyzing, but one worked to cancel out the other. He couldn't sink into the floor while adrenaline was buzzing through his bloodstream.

Cort seemed slightly startled by his businesslike tone, but recovered quickly. He strolled toward Cam's desk and Cam watched as he took his seat. *I will not notice the size of his shoulders, or his thighs, or the way he moves from his hips like a wave rolling over the beach.*

How could he be scared, pissed, and turned on all at once?

"Actually, I think the better question is how may I help *you*?" Cort set his briefcase on the floor.

"Oh, dear God. You sound like a bad salesman or a politician," Cam blurted. "I'm not contributing to your campaign, but I'd be delighted to tell your constituents, your oral skills are absolutely incredible."

Cort laughed, and then stopped as though he'd surprised himself.

Cam remembered him doing that the other night. It had seemed so cute at the time.

Cort sucked in a breath, and Cam dug his fingers into his thighs beneath the desk. Whatever Cort was going to say was gonna break him, he could feel it. "I didn't introduce myself fully the other night. I'm *Agent* Kendrick Cortland."

"Agent. Like, Secret Agent?" Cam's heart raced.

"Like, FBI Agent." Cort reached into his jacket pocket and produced a business card which he slid onto Cam's desk. Cam didn't even glance at it as his stomach somersaulted.

Liar! he wanted to scream. But no, Cort hadn't lied at all, had he? He just hadn't told the truth. He'd let Cam spill all his secrets, like the most trusting idiot on earth, and hadn't given a single piece of information on his own life. Hadn't volunteered he worked for the FBI.

And then realization struck.

The FBI, who might be investigating Bas for hacking a server. His mind churned trying to recall exactly what Drew had said the other night, how much Cam had revealed to Cort, and just how thoroughly he might have screwed up Bas's life. Cam had wanted one night of *easy,* but he'd forgotten the simple truth - nothing in life came easy. There was always payment required.

"Alright," Cam said, striving to sound bored even as his heart was beating out of his chest. "And?"

"And—" Cort toyed with Cam's stapler, twisting it over and over in his hand - those hands which had been *on* Cam just two days ago. Cam shuddered. "I think you're already aware from the letter we sent, there are some concerns about illegal activities. Your brother didn't answer our request for an interview."

"I heard about it from our legal team. I understood the FBI had chosen not to pursue an investigation."

Cam stared at Cort who didn't meet his gaze. His jaw was hard. "The FBI chose not to pursue an investigation *at this time*." Cort's eyes flitted to Cam's. "It's always subject to change."

And here it came.

"Ah. So, what is it you want?"

Cort shrugged, his voice tight. "It's simple, really. We'd like your assistance with a different investigation." He set Cam's stapler down exactly where it had been and bent to retrieve a single paper from his briefcase. "Do you know this man?"

He set a photograph on the desk in front of Cam. It was a shot taken from above, like through a surveillance camera. It showed a man with shoulder-length blondish-gray hair and a scruffy beard, dressed in cargo shorts, flip flops, and an old-school heavy metal t-shirt. He was completely unfamiliar.

Cam shook his head. "Should I? He looks like a surfer. One with dubious musical taste."

Cort's head shot up. "Hey, Slayer is good shit."

"If you say so."

"I do."

"Then *you* have dubious musical taste, too." Cam snapped, sitting back and crossing his arms over his chest. The effort of holding himself steady, of distancing himself from Cort, was physically painful. "What does this have to do with Seaver Tech?"

"Not a thing," Cort told him. "The assistance we need will come from you, personally."

There was *nothing* sexy in the way Cort's voice had dropped at the end of that sentence, and Cam did *not* feel an answering tug in his dick. "I'm not sleeping with you," Cam blurted. He could feel the blush spreading over his cheeks, even as Cort shook his head.

"That's not what this is about," Cort said. His eyes were hot on Cam's, and Cam wanted to ask what *Friday night had been about*, for God's sake, but he wouldn't. He had *that* much pride, at least.

Cam licked his lips. "Start talking, then. And be specific."

Cort nodded and tapped the picture. "This image was taken at an airport in Barbados, and we have reason to believe the subject was headed to a small Caribbean island called St. Brigitte." He lifted his gaze to Cam's. "We need access to the island in order to find this man and question him. We can't alert the Tyndalls without arousing suspicion, and the subject is a flight risk."

"Is he dangerous?"

"He has never harmed anyone in his life," Cort said, with so much conviction Cam stared in surprise.

Cort cleared his throat. "We need your help to get an investigator on the island during the Tyndalls' party this weekend. Only to question him."

Cam frowned. "Did you overhear my conversation with Drew the other night? I told him, and Lydia Tyndall, I'm not going."

"I was slightly distracted Friday night," Cort admitted. "But you might want to reconsider."

Jesus Effing Christ. The whole world was conspiring to get him on that damn island, when the very thought of flying in a small plane - the only type which could fly to St. Brigitte - made him break out in a cold sweat.

And yet, Cam had to consider it for Bas's sake. His brother was so emotionally on-edge right now, so close to a total meltdown, Cam couldn't afford to take any chances. He couldn't dodge the feeling that Bas must've been *trying* to be caught, as though maybe guilt was steering him in a whole new twisted direction. Was an FBI investigation - even one Drew felt wasn't a big deal - the straw that would finally make Bas crack?

Still, he wasn't going to fall in line without more information. "I'm going to need more specifics than that," Cam argued. "The FBI doubtless has planes to fly you there."

"Yes, but no authorization to land without giving the Tyndalls a reason."

"And that would alert this guy?" Cam gestured to the photo.

"Yes."

"So you not only need me to get you there, you need me to give you a cover story."

Cort nodded slowly. "I'll need to go as your date."

And suddenly the entirety of Friday night made sense. Cort had wanted to ensure people saw them together, to make the ruse less obvious, and maybe to make Cam more amenable. Anger and disappointment churned in his gut.

I trusted you! he wanted to scream.

He needed to get Cort out of his office before he did something completely inexcusable, like cry.

Cam stood, signaling the meeting was over. "I'll have to talk to my attorneys, Mr. Cortland. I mean, *Agent* Cortland.

I'll get back to you." His hands were clenched into fists down by his sides, and it was too much to expect of Cort not to notice.

Cort glanced at Cam's face and hesitated for a moment before shaking his head. "Time and secrecy are crucial here. Nobody can know about this besides the two of us. This offer is off the table once I leave this room." He paused, then continued in a rush. "The choice is yours, Cam. I- I can't say for sure whether we would choose to pursue a case against your brother even if you decided to say no." He looked at Cam, really looked at him, as he had two nights before. "But I am begging you, please, to say yes."

Cam turned away and looked out the enormous window behind his desk. Boston was shimmering in the morning sunlight, but he could barely see it. Neither choice was good. Or, no, neither choice was *easy*, he realized ruefully. *Decide quick, Cam. Your fear, or your brother's life?*

"And you can guarantee if I agree, Bas won't be prosecuted?"

"It's not a get out of jail free card. But I can assure you he won't be prosecuted by the FBI for this particular crime, no."

The logical part of Cam's brain - the part which was shoved back into the tiniest corner of his mind whenever Cort walked into the room and Cam's dick took over - reminded him the smart thing to do would be to call Drew. Was this whole scheme even legal? But it would mean admitting the guy Drew had seen him chatting with on Friday night had been conning him all along.

And really, how amazing would it be if he *could* get to St. Brigitte? He'd prove to Drew he *wasn't* weak. He'd do his duty as a Seaver and a representative of Seaver Tech, and would show up at the gala with Cort as his arm candy. He could take control of this situation, redeem it completely. All he had to do was… fly.

The very idea made him nauseous.

Still, he turned to Cort and nodded once, firmly. "Fine, then. We'll do this your way."

Cort blinked, almost as though he hadn't expected Cam to agree, but he recovered and nodded smoothly. "Alright, good. That's very… good."

"I'll have my assistant make the arrangements and email you about the dress code," he said, grabbing Cort's business card from the desk for the first time.

"Dress code," Cort echoed. "Right."

"We'll leave on Friday afternoon, since the first cocktail reception is usually in the early evening." He grabbed his phone and entered Cort's contact information, making a note to have Margaret check the schedule of events for the party. "If you're going to be my date, we'll need a cover story. Who you are, all that sort of thing. You can email or text me whatever you come up with."

"I don't text. Or email."

Cam glanced down at him. "You do if you're going to be my date."

Now Cort scowled. "Can't we talk on the phone?"

Cam snorted. "No. We're not at that stage in our relationship yet."

"I've had your dick in my mouth," Cort reminded him angrily.

"That was before I realized you were sucking me off for a *purpose*, Cort. You're very dedicated to your job," Cam sneered. "Your superiors must be so proud."

Cort flushed and got to his feet, storming around the desk. "That had nothing to do with this."

"Oh, no? Well, I think you'd have to agree, as circumstantial evidence goes, it's pretty freaking strong. What's your *expert opinion* on that, *Agent Cortland*?"

Cort crowded him against the window, and Cam's hands flew to his sides as Cort crushed their chests together. "My expert opinion is… you need to be taught some manners."

Cam's breath caught, his anger forgotten for a mere second under a tidal wave of lust. *Yes, yes, yes!*

"No," he said, pushing Cort back a step. "This… thing," he gestured between the two of them, "is not happening again. It's non-negotiable."

"This… *thing*," Cort drawled. "Like when I ordered you to keep your hands against the wall, and sucked you off in a stairway? In a stairway where *anyone could have seen us*, Cam, and you got off on it completely? Like me making you come so hard I can still taste you on my tongue? Is *that* the thing you mean?"

Cam ground his teeth together. "I mean Friday night's *momentary lapse in judgment*, which is probably how I'm going to characterize my entire interaction with you."

Cort smiled, hands on his hips. "You say the sweetest things."

But Cam wouldn't let him pass this off as a joke. His voice was controlled and deadly serious when he spoke. "Friday night, I thought you and I had something special. Obviously, I was dead wrong."

Cam swallowed, his throat suddenly dry, as he watched Cort's eyes track the motion. "I understand now that I was an idiot," he whispered. "I knew better, and I fell for the delusion anyway. I won't make excuses. I shared things, *personal* things I had no business sharing. That was *my* mistake. I own that. But I am not going to make the same mistake twice. I don't know a thing about you, and I don't want to, because I sure as hell am never going to trust you again. Do you understand?"

Cort blinked and his jaw worked. There would be no more commands, no more submission.

"I didn't lie to you. I made sure I didn't lie to you," Cort told him, and it sounded shockingly like an apology, but it wasn't good enough.

"That's tremendously comforting. You misled me, and I won't pretend to understand why or what you thought you'd accomplish by getting me to have sex with you—"

"I told you," he interrupted gruffly. "That *wasn't* part of the plan. I got caught up in things just like you did."

Cam shook his head. How gullible did the man think he was, anyway? "And I told *you,* I don't trust you. So, here's how this is going to work. I agree to your stupid blackmail bullshit, and we are going to the damn party." He swallowed down the bile rising in his throat at the thought. "You will be my date, I will take you to the island." He paused. "Do you understand? You *win.* You got what you wanted from me - you made me look like an idiot *and* you got me to agree. So you don't need to con me anymore. Don't pretend to be my friend or to have any interest in me beyond what I can do for you. In fact, for God's sake, don't talk to me at all."

He stepped away from Cort - from the overwhelming heat and presence of the man - and walked to the other side of the office, throwing open the door.

"Margaret," he called to his assistant. "Change of plans."

CHAPTER TEN

Cam walked out to the subway on Monday evening, clutching his phone in his hand. He'd received a terse email from Margaret - who was likely still annoyed Cam had done a complete one-eighty on his plans for St. Brigitte and refused to explain the change - saying he needed to follow up with Cort about his tuxedo. Of all the stupid, domesticated bullshit things to have to text about.

He pushed his way through the barrier and found an empty spot against the grimy wall on the platform.

[Cam:] *Agent Cortland, my assistant Margaret asked me to inform you that she emailed you a copy of the weekend itinerary earlier today and you didn't reply. If you'd like her to provide you with a tuxedo, which is required for Saturday night, please reply to her with your sizes.*

There. He praised himself for being businesslike and not allowing the anger and hurt still competing in his brain to spew out onto the screen. Dealing with Cort would be like dealing with a member of the board from now on. Polite and remote.

[Cort:] *i got her email told you earlier today i don't text hate typing from my phone my fingres are too big*

It was not cute. It was *not* cute.

[Cam:] *Sounds like a personal problem. Do you need the tux?*

[Cort:] *yes pls i will send the infod*

[Cam:] *Jesus, this is painful. Did you know if you turned your phone to the side, the keyboard is larger?*

[Cort:] *Oh. This is much easier.*

[Cam:] *Welcome to 2017. It's almost over.*

[Cort:] *whatever.*

He would not be swayed by the fact text-Cort was every bit as sweet and funny as in-person-Cort, without the same electric intimidation factor he had in real life.

I hate him, Cam reminded himself firmly. *Hate.*

The hate carried him home and stayed with him as he forced himself to eat a lackluster dinner. He settled himself on the sofa with a new mystery novel, but couldn't force himself to concentrate.

He was hurt, seriously hurt. It was partly wounded pride, but it felt like more. He felt stupid, like the control he thought he'd been giving Cort had never really been his to begin with.

His phone buzzed from the side-table.

[Cort:] *Patriots pre-season is on. Are you watching?*

Cam ignored him. Whatever trick Cort was playing now, he could play alone.

[Cort:] *Never have I ever seen a red sox game*

[Cam:] *I'm not playing this with you*

[Cort:] *Your excitement is palpable. CONTROL YOURSELF.*

Cam found himself smiling and forced his lips to frown instead. God, why was he so weak with this guy?

[Cort:] *I'm not much of a baseball fan personally. I used to watch football every week with my brother.*

[Cam:] *I think you've forgotten how to play this game*
[Cort:] *Nah. If you're talking to me, I'm winning.*
Cam rolled his eyes. *Yeah, right.*
[Cam:] *Are you drunk?*
[Cort:] *No. Why?*
[Cam:] *Good night, Cort.*

———

CAM STARED at his phone as it buzzed on Tuesday evening. He'd just sat down to re-watch an old season of Leverage, and was massively annoyed with himself. Cort hadn't texted all day - which was great, totally great. Exactly what Cam had wanted. They'd do the thing this weekend, and then they wouldn't ever talk again, which was exactly how…

[Cort:] *Okay, new game. You ready?*

Cam's heart did not start to beat faster at the knowledge that Cort had been thinking about him. It didn't. It was probably the extra caffeine he'd had this morning.

[Cam:] *Will it matter if I say no?*

[Cort:] *Two truths and a lie. I'll go first.*

[Cort:] *I know all the verses of The Star-Spangled Banner*

[Cort:] *I have seen every episode of Baywatch*

[Cort:] *I really hate when you're all bitchy and silent during these convos*

Not charming. Or cute. He *didn't* love how random Cort was, or seeing the man drop his guard this way. He *didn't* like the way Cort constantly surprised him and charmed him without *trying*, without puzzling out the things Cam wanted to hear.

[Cam:] *You know how this works, right? Two of those things are supposed to be true and only one is supposed to be a lie?*

[Cort:] *Yep. The instructions are in the title, badass. I get it.*

Cam snorted. He hadn't even been going for bitchy and

silent, more like annoyed and scared shitless. He didn't need to know Cort any better. He didn't need to like him any more than he already did, when he knew he couldn't trust him.

[Cam:] *Whatever. You're an FBI agent. Maybe they make you memorize the anthem. Baywatch is a lie.*

[Cort:] *Nope.*

[Cam:] *I call bullshit.*

[Cort:] *Ha! One of the houses I stayed at while I was a kid had a TV that only played videos. Like on tapes. And it was either that or Cop Rock.*

[Cam:] *I don't know what that is?*

[Cort:] *Google it. I'll hold.*

[Cam:] *God. I would have chosen Baywatch too. There were hot people, anyway.*

[Cort:] *There was this whole shark storyline. People died. You should watch it.*

[Cam:] *I'm not watching Baywatch.*

[Cort:] *You're totally gonna go watch Baywatch.*

Whatever. David Hasselhoff was kinda hot in a bossy way, which got Cam thinking about all kinds of things he really didn't want to be thinking about, and...

[Cort:] *And for the record, the lie was me not liking when you're bitchy. I like it a lot. It totally turns me on.*

What the hell was Cam supposed to do with that? He didn't want this. He didn't trust this.

[Cam:] *Good night, Cort.*

And okay, so maybe he might have checked whether there were any old episodes of Baywatch on Netflix.

CAM WOKE up on Wednesday morning, a little hungover from a restless sleep and trippy dreams. He'd found episodes of Baywatch to stream, and he wasn't exactly proud of it, but that guilty pleasure had nothing on the dreams that had followed. He knew exactly what Cort looked like dripping wet and barely dressed, and so maybe it wasn't *entirely* bizarre when in his dreams, The Hoff had suddenly morphed into Cort, running down the beach with that weird torpedo thing under his arm, broad chest gleaming in the sun. But waking up with a hard-on for the guy who'd been a one-night mistake was lowering.

Cort didn't *really* like him. Cam wasn't sure exactly what game he was playing, but it was time to regain control.

[Cam:] *Do you have any food allergies?*

[Cort:] *Nope. Do you?*

[Cam:] *No. I'm only asking so I could let the Tyndalls know.*

[Cort:] *You don't need to make up an excuse to text me, badass.*

[Cam:] *Or maybe I wanted to poison you. Maybe you'd deserve it.*

[Cort:] *There are much more effective ways to bring me to my knees. Wanna hear them?*

[Cam:] *Fuck off, Cortland.*

[Cort:] *Knew it.*

Well. That had gone about as well as Cam could have expected.

He went to work, determined to do his *job*, to focus on the things he could control. But he couldn't deny the way his stomach flipped when his phone buzzed later that morning.

[Cort:] *So, how's work going?*

[Cam:] *Fine.*

[Cort:] *I'm kind of off this week. Bored.*

[Cam:] *How can I sleep safe at night knowing the FBI is missing its best agent?*

Bored. Cam almost couldn't conceive of Cort, all two-hundred-pounds of exasperating, panic-inducing wet-dream, sitting around bored. He frowned as he propped his feet up on his desk and stared out of the window at the cloudy gray sky.

What did Cort do for fun? Who else did he have in his life?

And why the hell did he *care* when he was supposed to be putting the man out of his mind?

When Cort didn't reply after a moment, Cam frowned at the screen. Perhaps his message had been a little nastier than he'd intended.

[Cam:] *Why aren't you chillin with Baywatch? How can you call yourself a true fan?*

[Cort:] *Do they have those movies on Netflix?*

[Cam:] *No.*

[Cam:] *Maybe.*

[Cam:] *I wouldn't know.*

[Cort:] *Oh my God. You watched them. You DID. Just when I thought I couldn't like you more!!!*

Cam rolled his eyes and fought the warmth creeping up his neck. Only words. They were only words, and Cort didn't mean them.

So why was the man still texting? Why was Cam still responding?

[Cam:] *Don't you have some other poor guy you can con into liking you, Cort? Surely I'm not the only one.*

[Cort:] *It wasn't a con.*

[Cam:] *What would you call it?*

Cam waited a long time, watching the three little dots next to Cort's name circle and circle and then disappear. He shook his head. He shouldn't be disappointed. He *wasn't* disappointed.

[Cort:] *Already told you. I would call it the best night I've ever had.*

[Cam:] *Because you got me where you wanted me.*

[Cort:] *Because it was real, even though it wasn't supposed to be.*

Cam did not have the capacity to handle this. His stupid, traitorous heart leapt at the words.

[Cam:] *Wow. I'm all aflutter. I bet you say that to all the guys you fuck for information.*

[Cort:] *Jesus. I think you're just trying to convince *yourself* now.*

Ding ding ding. Give the FBI agent a prize. It was disturbing that Cort could read him so well. It was even more disturbing that Cam wasn't having an easy time convincing himself. It had to be an act, but Cam couldn't figure out why, or what the endgame was.

[Cam:] *You're right. I'm deluding myself.*

[Cam:] *I mean, I'm kind of the total package - sexy, rich, daddy issues. Makes sense you'd go for me.*

[Cam:] *Who *wouldn't*?*

[Cort:] *Keep being snarky, badass. Remember what it does to me.*

[Cort:] *In fact, since I'm here all alone, I'm gonna re-read your sassy texts and have a private moment.*

Cam rolled his eyes. *Infuriating man!*

[Cam:] *Trying to work here.*

[Cam:] *Cort?*

[Cam:] *Cort, I swear to God, you'd better not be jerking off to my bitchy texts.*

[Cam:] *You. Make. Me. Insane.*

It was after seven o'clock and Cam had been fighting a losing battle against texting Cort again... or, *okay,* he'd actually been brainstorming stupid pretexts for messaging the man... when his phone buzzed in his hand.

[Cort:] *Okay, five questions.*

Cam waited a full two minutes, just staring at the

screen, before replying. Not that Cam was playing mind games or anything, because that would be *wrong*.

[Cam:] *Another game?*

[Cort:] *Nope, not a game. We just ask each other five questions. You have to answer honestly.*

[Cort:] *First person who refuses to answer loses.*

That didn't sound completely terrifying whatsoever.

Cam set his jaw. Hadn't he given Cort enough honesty already?

He stared at the phone in his hand, feeling as though he was standing on the ten-meter diving board back in high-school. He'd only ascended that platform once, on a dare, and from the ground it hadn't seemed scary at all. He was co-captain of the swim team, not afraid of water or heights, so *no big deal, right?*

But when he'd climbed to the top deck, reality had set in. He'd been around divers enough to know that breaching the water from that height *hurt*. You had to break the surface with your palms so you wouldn't brain yourself by smacking your head against the water, but they said even then, you'd feel the impact all the way up your spine, in every one of your muscles. It would be painful and disorienting.

The payoff was a massive adrenaline rush that made you feel like you could conquer the world, but first you had to survive the jump.

[Cam:] *Not interested.*

[Cort:] *We're pretending to be dates on Saturday. We should know some basic shit about each other.*

[Cam:] *God.*

[Cam:] *Did you not get enough of my sass to finish the job this afternoon?*

[Cort:] *Oh, no, I had plenty. And for round two, I remembered us on Friday night. Want to hear?*

[Cam:] *Ugh. No. I just ate.*

[Cort:] *You may not understand how honest answers work here, badass.*

[Cort:] *But I'm gonna go out on a limb and trust you.*

[Cam:] *What's that like?*

[Cort:] *Enough snark. I will even be the bigger person and let you go first.*

Fine. Clearly Cam was as susceptible to dares as he had been at seventeen. Whatever. If Cort was the water he had to break against, then so be it.

[Cam:] *Awesome. I will win this game right now.*

[Cam:] *Tell me about your childhood.*

[Cort:] *That doesn't count. Not a question.*

Cam smirked and felt the rush of victory. He hadn't expected Cort to answer.

Maybe he'd hoped, but he hadn't expected.

He could totally handle this.

[Cam:] *OMG, I can taste victory already. FINE. You said you watched Baywatch in one of the places you stayed growing up. Why were you staying someplace other than your home?*

[Cort:] *I was a foster kid. I didn't have a permanent placement until I was 10.*

Oh-kay. So that was new. Cam frowned at his phone. A foster kid. Cam remembered him mentioning his brother, saying his parents were something Cort wouldn't discuss. How bad had it been for him?

His heart squeezed in sympathy, even as he rolled his eyes at himself.

That doesn't excuse his behavior. It doesn't. I would have helped him without the blackmail. I trusted him and he should have trusted me, too.

Except, maybe for a pair of idiots who hated trusting people, this was the only way it *could* have gone down.

He took too long to reply, and then Cort was writing again.

[Cort:] *Stunned you, huh? That's okay. My turn. Do you like pineapple on your pizza?*

[Cam:] *No. And you're an idiot because we already discussed this on Friday.*

[Cort:] *I remember. Just an honesty check, Seaver. Your turn.*

[Cam:] *Rolling my eyes so hard right now.*

Cam licked his lips. He wanted to know so many things Cort wouldn't volunteer, like *What were you* really *thinking Friday?* and *Where the hell do you see this going?* and *Why are we doing this?* But he knew Cort probably didn't have any better answers to those questions than Cam, so he went with the more straightforward question.

[Cam:] *What's your brother like?*

Now it was Cort's turn to take an unnaturally long pause, so long Cam debated withdrawing the question, maybe giving him an easy, food-related out. But Cam really wanted to know the answer, suddenly. He wanted Cort to share, and Cort had been the one to start this in the first place, so…

[Cam:] *Oh, forfeiting already?*

[Cort:] *No. Jesus. It's just hard to figure out what to say. How would YOU describe YOUR brother?*

[Cam:] *Tall. Genius. Occasional Asshole. Hates onions.*

[Cort:] *Okay. Damon's big, loyal, long-haired, loves anything with an engine.*

[Cam:] *You make him sound like a dog.*

And in a way, it made sense, because Cam sorta thought of Cort that way. Determined, playful, loyal to a fault. But Cort would never allow anyone to leash him.

[Cort:] *Hush. Apple juice or orange juice, pick only one. And be aware this says a lot about you as a person.*

[Cam:] *Apple. You're crazy.*

[Cort:] *Apple lovers are minimalists and romantics. Orange lovers are risk-takers who secretly crave attention. Wanna know mine?*

Not charming, *not* charming. It was strange and silly and…

Oh, alright, fine. It was really fucking charming.

[Cam:] *I already know. You even smell like oranges.*

[Cort:] *I do? Weird. Very cute that you remember what I smell like, though.*

[Cam:] *Only because it bugged me.*

Such an obvious lie, Cam knew Cort would recognize it a mile away. Moreover, he knew Cort would see the pitiful truth Cam had just revealed, and how much his feelings were involved.

[Cam:] *I just remembered I need to do my marathon training in the morning. Going to bed. Goodnight.*

TEN MILES under his belt before the sticky-tar humidity rose up from the pavement to swamp him Thursday morning had Cam in a fine mood. He stopped for a water break before crossing the bridge back into Cambridge. He was in control. He would apologize to Cort for ducking out - which hadn't been cool - and he'd return them to the light-hearted banter they'd enjoyed earlier in the week.

Cort was right. If they were pretending to be together on Friday, they shouldn't be at each other's throats, but they didn't need to become best buddies. He was going to message Cort to say so, when his phone buzzed from inside his armband.

[Cort:] *Done running?*

[Cam:] *Hey, sorry about last night. Have to go to bed early to wake up early.*

[Cort:] *That's fine. For the record, I won.*

Cam scowled. *Won?* Like it had really been a contest? Whatever.

[Cam:] *No way.*

[Cort:] *You forfeited.*

[Cam:] *No, I delayed play. Different thing. Look it up.*

[Cort:] *You ran from our convo like a chicken at a fox convention.*

[Cam:] *What the hell does that even mean?*

[Cort:] *It's an expression. It means you ran because you didn't like admitting how attracted you were to me.*

[Cam:] *I needed to sleep.*

[Cort:] *That dog won't hunt.*

CAM SCOWLED DOWN at his phone, ignoring the curious glances of the other early-morning joggers. He stood with his back against the bridge railing, almost oblivious to the sun rising around him and the smell of coffee which always seemed to pervade the streets at this hour.

Cort thought he'd run away, just like Drew did.

Well, two could play at this game.

[Cam:] *Whatever. What's with the dogs and chickens? Where the fuck did you grow up?*

[Cort:] *Lots of places.*

[Cam:] *Like?*

[Cort:] *Like, lots of places. I don't remember them all.*

[Cam:] *Fine. We're done now.*

He clicked his phone screen off and resumed walking, unaccountably annoyed. Cort wanted to start this shit, but wouldn't finish it. He wanted Cam to take all the risks and take none himself.

Not. Happening.

[Cort:] *Are you pissy?*

[Cam:] *No.*

Not that he planned to admit, anyway. But he couldn't help adding, a second later:

[Cam:] *But for the record, I won.*

The next text came five minutes later, after Cam had walked over the bridge, bought himself a coffee, and turned onto his own quiet street. Maybe Cort had been in the shower, or working out, or making breakfast, but Cam *knew* in a way he couldn't explain even if he wanted to, Cort had been staring at his phone screen for a long time... and maybe thinking about diving.

[Cort:] *I spent the longest in Johnsville. It's where I graduated high school. I lived there 8 years.*

Cam sighed out loud and closed his eyes right there on the sidewalk. There were facts in that text, and Cam knew they were real and true, but they weren't the whole story. Cort was sharing them because they were playing a game and he hated to lose, but Cam didn't want to get information that way.

[Cam:] *Listen, don't start these convos if you don't wanna share, k? You don't owe me a thing and I don't pry.*

[Cort:] *Sometimes I want to share, Cam. It's just not easy. I'm out of practice, maybe.*

Cam got it, maybe better than Cort could imagine. So maybe he was talking to them both as he typed:

[Cam:] *Never gets easier if you don't try.*

[Cam:] *Anyway, enjoy your vacation.*

[Cort:] *Will do. Starting a new hobby today.*

Cam let himself into his building and stomped up the stairs to shower, wondering.

What if *trust* was the hard surface that could break him? What if Cort was the *payoff* he'd get if he did?

A little later that morning, Cam's phone buzzed again as he was signing his name to approximately a thousand thank you cards which Margaret would send to generous Safe-Water donors later that day. He threw his pen down on his desk and snatched up his phone to see what new things Cort had shared.

[Cort:] *How many times do I have to shoot this thing before I get paid?*

[Cam:] *What?*

[Cort:] *This malevolent little fucker popped up in front of me and I shot him. Where is my money?*

[Cam:] *Cort? Are you seeing things? Do I need to call someone?*

[Cort:] *Funny. This shit was YOUR idea, Cam. Now I'm gonna get killed and you're not even helping.*

Was he drunk? Cam's heart sank. Was Cort having a psychotic break, and all of this clearly-uncharacteristic sharing had been some type of symptom?

He rolled his eyes at himself. Fine. Not likely, but was it possible?

[Cam:] *Okay. Text slowly. Use small words. What is going on right now?*

[Cort:] *Ah, God! It's happening! I'm dying. Everything's gone gray. Goodbye Cam! Goodbye. Remember me fondly.*

[Cam:] *WTF?*

[Cort:] *Okay. Crisis averted. I've respawned. Now, how the hell do I get paid?*

[Cam:] *Oh. My. Fucking. God. Are you playing a game right now?*

[Cort:] *Uh, yeah. Obviously. League of Legends. It's the one you mentioned the other night, right?*

[Cam:] *((headdesk))*

Not charming. Not adorable. *Gahhhhh!!*

[Cam:] *I have work to do.*

Cam's phone buzzed again while he was in his weekly board meeting, also known as the longest hour of the week. The urge to pull the phone from his pocket was almost overwhelming, but he refrained *like a grownup*. The second the first person began pushing their chair back from the table, he was reading his messages.

[Cort:] *Cam, quick question: Do I get more gold if I kill the dragon?*

[Cort:] *Okay, I'm gonna assume bigger target, bigger payoff. I'm going in.*

[Cort:] *Thanks a lot. I'm dead again. You are no help whatsoever.*

Cam rubbed a hand over his eyes.

Cort *was* a big, playful, shaggy dog. He was funny as hell, hot as fuck, and infuriating beyond belief.

[Cam:] *I was in a meeting with the board of directors and two congressmen.*

[Cort:] *Yeah, well, meanwhile I was DYING. Again.*

[Cam:] *Right. I'm sorry you died while I was just fucking around over here.*

Cam had walked the short distance back to his office before Cort replied.

[Cort:] *Forgiven. IF you tell me how to kill the dragon.*

[Cam:] *First of all, that was sarcasm. Second, why do you want to kill the dragon?*

[Cort:] *To get the GOLD, Seaver.*

Margaret poked her head into Cam's office.

"Everything okay, Mr. Seaver?"

Cam glanced up at her, perplexed. "Yeah, why wouldn't it be?"

"You were laughing out loud, all by yourself," she said, looking at him as if maybe he'd finally lost his mind.

And Cam had no explanation for that, since it was nothing less than the truth.

[Cam:] *You don't get gold for killing dragons, Cortland. And at your level, you can't do it without teammates. Who are you playing with?*

[Cort:] *Eh. Pretty sure they're middle-schoolers from, uh, Brazil? They speak Portuguese. I only understand the swear words.*

[Cam:] *JFC. You get gold from killing the minions. The dragon gives you a stat boost.*

[Cort:] *Oh. What about the big worm on the other side? Does he give me money?*

[Cam:] *NO! Stop! Don't go after Baron.*

[Cam:] *Cort? Don't go after the worm on your own. You'll die again. Get the kids on your team to…*

[Cam:] *You know what? Nvm. I'm calling you.*

CHAPTER ELEVEN

Cort smiled at his phone screen and cracked open a fresh bottle of beer. A few seconds later, it rang and he answered.

"You suck," Cam said by way of greeting, and honest-to-God, Cort's stomach flipped. He hadn't been lying earlier when he said Cam's bitchy tone, whether in text or speech, totally did it for him. Like pretty much everything that had happened since Friday night, it was fucked up but true.

"Is that any way to speak to a fellow gamer, Seaver?" Cort demanded.

Cam snorted. "I can't believe you actually bought League of Legends and started playing."

"Why not? My work laptop was just sitting here, and you said the game was good. You made it sound fun," Cort returned.

Cam went silent for a moment as though he wasn't quite sure how to take that, or how to reply. Cort felt guilt flare in his chest. *And whose fault is it that everything is strained now, Cort?*

Before walking into Cam's office on Monday, he thought he'd known exactly how their meeting would go down. He'd still been shocked at how hard it had been for him to sit in that chair, watching Cam's face veer from hope to crushing hurt because of Cort's words. He'd been stunned by how much his own heart had ached when Cam had said, *I thought you and I had something special. Obviously, I was dead wrong.*

It had been one thing to plan to hurt *a Seaver* - one of the rich, entitled assholes Cort hated. But it had somehow become a different thing entirely to hurt *Cam.*

Cam had agreed to get them to St. Brigitte, and Cort knew he should be satisfied with that, but it wasn't enough. He'd seen something in Cam's face on Monday that made him realize once again precisely what he'd be giving up if he let Cam walk away. The guy had been scared and hopeful, and he'd wanted to trust Cort.

And just like Friday night, Cort found himself wanting to deserve that trust.

He wanted Cam to smile at him again, joke with him again, confide in him again, see the sparkle warm his light eyes again.

Sex was firmly off the table, *fine.* He honestly wasn't thinking about sex right now… Or, okay, not *much.* He only wanted to regain what he'd thrown away. For himself, yeah, so he didn't feel like the world's biggest asshole, but also for Cam, because somehow, he'd come to realize Cam deserved at least that much. If he had to text or call Cam more than twenty times a day and show his ridiculously geeky, awkward side to achieve that, then so be it.

It was way outside Cort's usual playbook, but suddenly he felt as if he needed to change up his plays.

"I keep dying embarrassingly fast, though." Cort was kind of surprised by how much fun he'd found the game, his multiple deaths notwithstanding.

Cam cleared his throat. "Well, keep leveling up and we can play together sometime. I'll, ah, invite you on my team."

"Yeah?" Cort was absurdly pleased by this offer, a promise of time together even after the party this weekend. "We can do that. My Yoda you can be."

"Well, first rule you need to remember, young Padawan, is don't go after the big guys without your team."

Cort snickered. "You'd be surprised at how often I get told that, badass." Sean's words right before Cort had been escorted out of the FBI office came to mind. "Hard to find good teammates sometimes," he added quietly.

"Gotta give loyalty to get loyalty."

Ouch. "What happens when one of your teammates fucks up, though? What happens when they go off and do something stupid so the other team kills you?"

"Get better teammates," Cam said, so dryly Cort nearly laughed.

"Well, you could, but maybe it'd be better to keep the teammate you have and just, you know, trust they'll learn their lesson and not fuck shit up again."

Cam sighed, and Cort could hear the creak of a chair, as though maybe Cam was leaning back.

"Yeah, well. Problem is, they'd have to understand what they did wrong, Cort, and you'd have to believe they gave a shit about not doing it again. I don't know if that's possible."

Ouch, again. Cam's words cut like a razor and Cort sucked in a breath, twisting his beer bottle around on his desk.

"I don't *do* apologies, usually. I do whatever I have to do to get stuff done. But, I'm sorry I didn't tell you who I was on Friday night. At first it was only because I wanted to get to know you, so I could handle you more effectively, but then I started to like you." Dear God, he sounded like a high schooler, didn't he? He huffed. He'd rather walk on hot coals than spew this mortifying emotional garbage, but if this was what Cam needed from him, if this was what would put the spark back in Cam's eyes then *whatever*. "I wasn't thinking of you as an asset after that, I was thinking of you as an incredibly hot guy I really wanted to spend the night with."

Cam was silent for so long after Cort spoke, Cort had to check whether the call had been disconnected. But finally, Cam sighed.

"You don't usually do apologies and I don't usually do second chances," he said. "So, fine. I guess we'll both make an exception in this case. I'll see you tomorrow."

Cort clutched his phone for a long while after Cam disconnected, feeling as though he'd won something really important for the very first time.

CHAPTER TWELVE

Cam sat on his bed, staring at his phone. Nothing from Cort all day, which shouldn't have been unexpected. They would see each other at the airport in a little while anyway. Still, he debated messaging. Cort could reassure him like no one else.

How one man could fuck up his mind and calm it down at the same time was a mystery Cam couldn't solve.

He sighed and rolled to his feet, contemplating his suitcase. He'd packed his bathing suit and tux, but he'd hesitated before also packing his oldest, most comfortable t-shirts and a couple of fitted polos. He threw in a pair of Converse and some flip-flops, then zipped the case closed.

He grabbed his charger from beside the bed and hesitated, staring at the closed drawer of his nightstand. Condoms and lube? He shook his head.

Not this weekend, not gonna happen.

But he closed his eyes and quickly nabbed a few foil packets and a small bottle of lube and stashed them in his suitcase anyway, as if doing it blind meant he wouldn't have to acknowledge his own idiocy.

You want him. This doesn't have to be a big thing, dummy. Let things happen the easy way again... just this once.

Cort was an agent, and theoretically they were on opposite teams when it came to blackmailing Bas, but a thought had been niggling at the back of Cam's brain. Cort had told him flat-out that maybe they wouldn't have investigated Sebastian even if Cam had refused to go along with Cort's scheme. Was that his way of offering Cam an out, even while he manipulated him?

Or was Cam just desperate enough to want to believe it?

Which brought up the larger question of why Cam had agreed, and Cam was fairly and uncomfortably sure, the reason had a lot to do with the man who'd asked the question, and the idea that maybe it was time for him to face his fear of flying.

Maybe time to face a lot of things.

He grabbed his phone and dialed Sebastian's number, not completely surprised when the phone clicked to voicemail on the first ring. He pursed his lips together at the sound of his brother's voice - controlled, methodical, pre-crash Bas - telling him to leave a message.

"Hey, so… I'm going away to St. Brigitte this weekend. Last minute thing for the Fine-Tyndall Children's charity thing, and uh, I'm pretty nervous because, well, you know."

He hesitated, then plowed on. "I don't like the way we left things the other day, so I just wanted to remind you that I love you, and I want to be around for you more, okay? Maybe there are things I can do, so you don't feel like you have to grieve alone. Maybe we can go visit the cemetery when I get back, if you want." His voice had trailed off to nearly a whisper. "That's it. I love you, Bas. Be well. Talk to you soon."

He took a deep breath and slid the phone in his pocket.

He grabbed his suitcase and rolled it out the door, locked his dreary apartment behind him, and took the elevator to the first floor. The air outside was stifling hot, the humidity so oppressive his shirt was already sticking to him during the short walk from the lobby to the town car waiting at the curb. He gave his case to the driver and let himself into the backseat for the short drive to the airport.

As the car moved, his stomach began to churn. He'd been working with Dr. Meredith on the issue of his fear of flying for a couple of months. He tried to calm himself with logic and breathe consciously just the way he'd been taught. Statistically, take off was the worst time. If he got through that part, he'd be fine. *Flying is one of the safest modes of transportation. Thousands of people do it every day.*

He understood the science of flight - had made a point to study it, in fact, after the crash. But there remained a kind of elusive magic to the whole process, some kind of alchemy that transmuted drag and lift into soaring. If he couldn't fully understand it, then how could he trust it?

Heh. He rolled his eyes at himself. It seemed he had a chronic trust issue.

The airport - a private field not far from the city, came into view all too quickly, and he wondered if Cort would be waiting there. When Margaret had made their travel arrangements, she'd gotten them separate cars, and it occurred to Cam that he didn't have the first clue where Cort lived. A cute suburban house? Some crappy little place in the city? A cave covered in animal skins? He was insanely curious about the man.

Or maybe just insane.

They pulled up to a small guard house, and the driver chatted with the security guard for a few moments before the guard raised the swinging arm allowing them onto the airfield. And then suddenly they were at the plane - his parents' plane. The plane they *should* have all flown in the day of the crash, had his parents not left early. His stomach twisted with one of those stupid, unpredictable pangs of grief which came up out of nowhere. He had to work to keep his breathing steady, so the panic wouldn't take over.

He wasn't sure he could do this.

But Cam did *not* want to be humiliated in front of Cort ever again, so he forced himself to swing his legs around and get out of the car.

Staring at Kendrick Cortland kept his mind momentarily distracted from his fear. The man still looked like a Viking, albeit one who wore old, faded jeans that clung to his thighs just the right way, and a red t-shirt that stretched tight across his broad chest and shoulders. His hair was messy again today, falling in the same unintentionally perfect brown-gold waves it had the night they'd first met, and his eyes were hidden by mirrored aviator glasses which should have looked totally douchy, but on him looked fucking amazing. His jaw was set, and although Cam couldn't see his eyes behind the shades, he could tell Cort was watching him by the visible tension in his body.

The driver cleared his throat, and Cam's eyes flicked to him. "Er, if you'll step this way, sir, I'll see to your luggage?"

Oh, right. Because he was standing in the open car doorway like an idiot. Yeah.

He grabbed his carry-on bag and stepped toward the plane.

The plane looked harmless enough. Plain white, with the Seaver Tech logo on the side, just as Cam remembered it. The sun was setting, reflecting rainbow sparkles off the plane windows that were almost too bright to look at. Sebastian and several of the other executives used the plane routinely for travel and never had a problem, so the likelihood that Cam would...

"You ready for this?"

Cort's voice at his shoulder had Cam turning away from the plane momentarily. He was so close Cam could feel his body heat.

Was Cam ready? He wanted to be.

He hoped that would be enough.

"Ready," he lied.

CHAPTER THIRTEEN

Jesus Christ, it was hot out here. Cort felt a bead of sweat drip down between his shoulder blades as he stood behind Cam, who was staring at his company plane completely transfixed, as though he'd never seen the thing before. Was this one of those rich-guy eccentricities, staring in awe at a symbol of your own wealth? He rolled his eyes and felt the bad mood that had been riding him all afternoon kick up an extra notch.

Most of Cort's sourness had begun when a town car showed up to collect him from his little duplex in Dorchester. He was fairly certain Mrs. Avila, who lived on the first floor, was gonna give him shit the next time she saw him, and she didn't even know he was taking the car to a *private plane* at a *private airfield*.

One final envelope from Damon had arrived just that morning, long after Cort had woken up smiling and actually *anticipating* this weekend for reasons having nothing to do with solving a case, finding his brother, or getting justice. He'd been sitting with his phone out on his coffee table, thinking about what he should text Cam, how much overt flirtation Cam would put up with, when the intercom had announced a package for him. *Overnight shipping*. Weird.

As soon as he'd pulled the tab, the dull, black device slipped out onto the table, and realization had whacked him upside the head.

This wasn't supposed to be a romantic weekend.

He'd almost forgotten the original purpose.

Guilt had swooped in immediately, swamping any lust, any friendliness, any *anticipation* Cort had been feeling. How could he have forgotten Damon, when Damon should have been Cort's only priority?

Then a paper had fluttered out a second later, a note in familiar, blocky handwriting - "Will message this weekend," and the familiar resentment was back.

There were no messages on the phone, no numbers programmed, not a single communication from Damon asking whether Cort was okay, or making sure he'd been able to find a way to St. Brigitte, just a simple expectation he'd be there.

Not that he didn't *want* Damon to expect him, but *God*.

Bitterness churned in his gut, along with yet more guilt, a heaping helping of anxiety, and *whatever it was* he felt for Cam but hadn't quite put a name to yet. The combination set him on edge and made him sound like more of an ass than usual when he threw a hand out in the direction of the plane and said, "We gonna stand out here all day admiring the thing? It's hot as hell."

Cam startled and turned back to look at Cort. His eyes were wide and hurt.

Cort flinched.

He was being a jerk, but he wasn't sure how the hell to distance himself from Cam mentally or emotionally when every instinct told him to do the opposite.

He grabbed Cam's laptop bag from his hand, hefted his

own backpack onto his shoulder, and nudged Cam's arm to get him moving.

Slowly, reluctantly, Cam walked forward, then paused at the base of the steps, as though he was having second thoughts.

"Remember you're doing this for Sebastian," Cort warned, deliberately injecting a challenge into his voice.

As Cort had known he would, Cam sucked in a breath and straightened his spine resolutely. "Thanks so much," he said sourly. "You're not helping."

Cort shrugged. "Let's just get in before I melt."

Cam scowled over his shoulder. "You do realize we are going to a Caribbean island, right? Near the equator? Where it's likely going to be even hotter and more humid than it is in Boston?"

Cort rolled his eyes, only realizing after he'd done it that Cam wouldn't be able to see him through his sunglasses. "Well, I won't wanna stand outside down there, either, badass." He nudged Cam again, and Cam ascended the steps quickly, only to pause again when he stepped into the plane.

The door was located near the front of the aircraft, just behind the cockpit. Straight ahead was a miniscule kitchen area with a refrigerator and sink, but to the right, the cabin opened into an area that looked like a tiny living room, the kind of thing rock stars had on their tour busses.

There were two leather captain chairs, which swiveled round, along with a low wooden coffee table and matching end tables flanking a huge leather sofa. The sofa, complete with seatbelts - ran nearly the length of the cabin. At the tail of the plane, he could see an open door in front of large bed, and to one side was a closed door he could only imagine led to the bathroom.

All in all, this plane was nicer than most of the houses

he'd lived in growing up, and the price tag could probably have bought and sold *all* of those houses twice over. He wasn't sure why he kept fixating on money, except that it somehow reinforced that he and Cam, with their different backgrounds, had been doomed from the beginning.

Cam seemed to be frozen in place again, staring at a picture mounted on the wall in the kitchen area. Three guys, definitely early 90s based on the way they were dressed, huddled with their arms over each other's shoulders. There was a small shovel laid on a mound of dirt in the front of them, and they looked as giddy as toddlers who'd made a sandcastle. Cort recognized a younger Emmett Shaw, Levi Seaver, and Jonathan McMann. He had no idea why Cam was captivated by it, though.

"Cam?" Cort said impatiently. "You wanna move so I can get past you with the bags, dude?"

"What? Oh, yeah," Cam apologized. He took a small step toward the front of the plane, and Cort edged around him to the rear, plunking their carry-on bags on the coffee table before throwing himself down on the sofa. The phones - *two* phones for fuck's sake, when he'd rather not have *any* - dug into his hip as he sat, so he placed them both on the table.

"What's the deal with the picture?" Cort asked. He didn't like the way Cam stared at it - the tension in his shoulders, the way his face was pale underneath those gorgeous freckles despite the undeniable warmth in the air. As much as he tried to tell himself Cam's feelings weren't his problem, he knew it was a lie.

Cam cleared his throat. "Uh, I forgot it was here, I guess, and it's just strange to see my dad."

Cort nodded, reluctant sympathy burning off the majority of his bad mood. Grief was a bitch and it welled up at the weirdest times, Cort knew only too well.

Cam licked his lips and moved toward one of the chairs across from Cort. He sat himself down gingerly on the edge, as if he might stand up and run away at any moment, then darted an anxious glance at Cort.

Was Cam afraid of him? "What's going on with you, Cam?" Cort demanded.

Cam ignored him. "You've got two phones?" Cam remarked, as though casting around for something to talk about. "One for work and one for home?"

Cort wanted to shut down this topic immediately. "One for work, and the other for this weekend."

Cam's attention was caught. "Is this weekend not work?" His eyes sought Cort's. "I thought that was the whole point?"

Cort set his teeth. "It's a sideline investigation, and I'm waiting for contact on this phone. No more questions about that." *Ask me no questions, and I'll tell you no lies.*

Cam pressed a hand to his stomach as though sickened by the whole exchange. Cort frowned.

The captain, a stocky, olive-skinned guy about fifty years old, emerged from the cockpit.

"Mr. Seaver, we're ready to depart," he told Cam in lightly-accented English. "Looks like clear skies all the way to St. Brigitte, and we should make it there by sixteen hundred hours. Andres will bring you refreshments if you call, but otherwise he won't intrude."

The man looked back and forth from Cam to Cort, as if imagining they might need their privacy. Cam blushed, and Cort fought the urge to snicker. God, Cam was adorable.

"Great. Thank you, Stavros," Cam said, running a hand through his short, thick brown hair. Then he added, "It's, ah, nice to see you again."

"Same to you, sir," the captain said with a broad smile. "You've been missed."

Cam nodded jerkily, then sat back, found the seatbelt attached to the chair and buckled himself in.

"Must be nice," Cort said, as another uniformed attendant - Andres, probably - slid the plane door closed.

Cam sucked in a breath at the hollow *thunk*. "What's *nice?*" he snapped. His hands were tense against the chair arms, like he was really pissed. "Are you going to buckle your seatbelt?"

"Settle down, Cam, I only meant *this*." Cort gestured all around, at the furnishings, the privacy, the luxury, the *privilege*, and ignored the second half of Cam's question. "I've got to admit, I'm gonna be disappointed if there's not a hot tub in the bathroom."

"Prepare for disappointment," Cam ground out. "Maybe next time you blackmail someone into giving you a ride in their plane, you'll make inquiries first."

Whoa. So, they were back to blackmail?

"What's wrong with you?" Cort demanded again as the engine began to whine loudly and the plane rocked into motion. "I'm just saying, you're probably used to the fact that you can fly wherever, whenever, and you never have to have your knees tucked up to your chest when you do."

"No." A single, terse word, like Cam couldn't be bothered with the whole conversation.

"No? No, you're not used to it? Or no, you don't take a private plane when you travel? I'd think most people who have private planes would use them, right?"

Cam's eyes flew open, and they spat pale blue fire. "Most people? Most people haven't had their parents die in a plane crash, Cort."

Cort's jaw dropped as understanding, immediate and horrifying, washed over him in a wave. Cam wasn't angry, Cam was afraid. Absolutely, totally petrified. And he'd been so determined to keep his distance from the man that he'd completely failed to notice it. Oh, *fuck*.

Pissed off, resentful and, yeah, *guilty*, as he was, Cort hadn't considered this possibility at all, but now it seemed beyond obvious.

Without hesitation, Cort levered himself off the sofa and went to kneel in front of Cam. "You don't like to fly?"

"I don't fly at all. I hate flying."

"Not at all? Not since the accident?"

Another wordless shake of the head, and then Cam's hands were on his face, his palms scrubbing at his eyes. He sucked in air, something between a sob and a laugh. "I've tried, but I usually can't even get on the plane, and now we're already on and moving."

Cort grabbed Cam's hands with his own, forcing them down from his face. Cam's eyes were bleak, and Cort's stomach cramped painfully at the sight.

Just like that, all his doubts evaporated, any thoughts of maintaining his distance flew out the window. He could no more leave Cam like this than he could fly to the island under his own power - it was simply beyond his capability.

"Why didn't you—?" he began, but then stopped. He was pretty sure he knew why Cam wouldn't have mentioned this. Cort had forced his hand. *Jesus*.

"I'm not ashamed of it," Cam said defiantly, looking at something over Cort's shoulder. "It's my shit, and I own it, okay? It's normal."

Cort frowned. "Of course it's normal. I... I didn't think." More like he was trying so hard *not* to think about Cam, he'd missed the obvious.

"It doesn't make me weak, either," Cam continued in the same voice, and Cort realized Cam wasn't arguing with *him*, but with his own doubts. Or maybe…

"Was that something your ex said, too?" Cort demanded, and Cam's eyes met his.

Yeah, that's what he'd thought.

"Okay, come on," Cort said, quickly unbuckling Cam's seatbelt. Cam gave a terrified squeak of protest, but Cort had already picked him up and deposited him in the middle seat of the sofa, quickly locating the seatbelt, fastening it around Cam's waist, and taking the empty seat beside him.

As the plane picked up speed, taxiing down the runway, Cort fastened his own belt. Then he twisted toward Cam and pulled the man against him so Cam's face was buried in his chest while his arms wrapped around Cam's shoulders. Cam gave a shudder that might have been fear or relief, or a little of both. The man needed something to focus on, something to make him feel safe. Cort reached a hand into his pocket and grabbed his lucky quarter. He took Cam's hand and pressed the coin into his palm.

"What's this?" Cam asked.

"It's my good luck charm," Cort told him, running a hand over Cam's hair. "Saved my ass a hundred times or more."

"Really?" Cam's voice was disbelieving, as though he thought Cort was bullshitting him.

"Really," Cort confirmed. He took a deep breath. "When I was a kid, I was bitten by a dog." He hesitated before adding, "It was my stepfather's dog. A big-ass German Shepherd. I still have a little scar." He shifted his hand and moved a finger up to trace the edge of his lip. "Anyway, uh, I had this crazy fear of dogs after that. All of them, big or small, so at first they tried to place me in homes where they didn't have animals, but they can't always manage it, you know?"

Cort blew out a breath. He'd never spoken this shit aloud to anyone before in his life, and he was pretty sure he sounded like an idiot. Cam didn't move or say anything, but Cort could tell he was listening, could *feel* Cam was focused on *him*, not on the plane bouncing down the tarmac. "I was placed with the Dempseys when I was ten, and they had *three* dogs. Vicious, yappy little things. They were sweet to Craig and Rhonda, but assholes to me and Damon. They'd growl and bark and—" He cleared his throat. "Damon didn't care, because he was older - taller, bigger. But I was this tiny, scrawny, little kid."

"Not possible," Cam mumbled, making Cort laugh.

"Well, I didn't just pop out this size, badass," he joked. "But yeah, I was runty even for my age. I hadn't gotten into football or any kind of sports at that point. Craig Dempsey, he was a *man's man* kind of guy. He didn't tolerate weakness, or having a gay kid like Damon or a bisexual kid like me living in his house, either, but that's a different story coming way later. He, ah, felt like it was his duty to make me stronger by facing my fear, so he made me feed the dogs by myself every night."

Cam pulled back to look at him, his eyes wide and *angry* in a way that warmed Cort's chest. "What did you do?"

Cort shrugged. "The first time? I cried! I mean, my choices were to take my chances with the dogs or take my chances with Craig. And if Damon had tried to interfere, Craig would get pissed at *him* instead. So, Damon gave me this quarter. Told me it was magic and it would protect me."

Cam smiled, just a little. "And you believed it?"

"God, no. Even then I knew there was no such thing." He swallowed. "But, here's the thing. Damon gave it to me because he wanted me to be brave, right? Because, for whatever reason, he loved me and wanted me to be okay. And so, whenever I have it with me, I remember I'm not, you know, *alone*. That's the magic, I think."

The plane picked up speed, and Cam's hand clenched

around the quarter. He buried his face in Cort's chest again with a small moan.

"You know, air travel is really safe most of the time," Cort said, stroking his hand down Cam's back. "Way safer than cars and trains."

"I know," Cam said, the sound muffled by Cort's shirt. "And the number of aircraft accidents goes down all the time. I've looked it up."

"Just think about how much more dangerous other forms of transportation are, and how people have lived to tell the tale," Cort said, as they barreled down the runway. He felt the weightless jerk in his stomach that told him the plane was now airborne, and he began to talk faster. "Like, ah, have you ever seen how people strap those helicopter blades to their lawn chairs and stuff?"

Cam stiffened in Cort's hold. "What?"

"Seriously. I saw it on TV. One guy even took a hot air balloon mechanism and attached it to one of those plastic rain barrels people use in their gardens. You know the kind I mean?"

Cam nodded, pulling away again to look at Cort in confusion, maybe wondering what the hell Cort was rambling on about.

It was a damn good question, and one Cort didn't have an answer to. His main goal here was distraction, and he'd quickly learned nothing distracted Cam as effectively as Cort being ridiculous. Cort pulled Cam's head back against his chest, and dug his fingers into the incredibly tight muscles at the base of Cam's neck.

Cam let out a whimper - a sound so like the one he'd made last Friday, Cort felt his dick begin to swell, as though the fucking thing had a direct connection to Cam's vocal cords. *Focus, Cortland. Cam is frightened.*

"Right, so, the only problem was, he had no idea how to

steer it. The dude launches himself up - I swear to God, wearing nothing but his underwear and swim goggles. He goes so high, he gets fucking hypothermia. He passes out, and when he comes to, he's miles and *miles* away from his house, where he started the adventure. Like, in the next *state*. They had to send out people to rescue him."

"But... How did he... *Why* would he do that?" Cam demanded. He didn't attempt to pull away, and in fact he seemed to be pushing into Cort's touch, seeming to enjoy the sensation. He twisted to get more comfortable, and one of his hands came to rest on Cort's thigh.

Cort increased the pressure of his thumbs on Cam's neck.

"I don't know. Maybe because he had no idea he wasn't supposed to?"

Cort could feel Cam's frown against his chest. "That completely defies logic. How would he know how to build the mechanism but not know how to control it? Or not know it would be *dangerous* to launch himself into the air with no sure way to get down?"

Cort snickered. "Babe, have you not realized that hardly anything in life is logical? Logic and magic are both pretty scarce."

Cam shook his head, his body growing more pliant against Cort's, even though his hand was still clenched around the quarter. "You're totally wrong. Almost every-thing is logical. The sun rises in the east and sets in the west. There are three hundred sixty-five days in a year. One plus one is two."

"Those things are *facts*," Cort said, glancing out the window to see they were now surrounded by puffy white clouds. "That doesn't necessarily make them logical. *Why* are there three hundred and sixty-five days, not an even hundred? Why does the sun rise in the east instead of the north? You can't explain it, there's not a logical explanation behind it, it just *is*."

He scratched his fingers through the hair at the base of Cam's neck, felt him shudder slightly, and continued in a lower voice.

"Sometimes the truest things are the weirdest ones, the ones you think couldn't possibly work. And I think…" He hesitated. "I think a lot of the time when people do really remarkable shit, it's because they didn't know they couldn't, or they didn't listen when people told them they weren't supposed to."

Cam was quiet for a minute, digesting this. Cort watched his fingers play against Cam's neck, and felt Cam's fingers - the ones not holding his lucky quarter - contract against his thigh before the man relaxed against Cort more fully.

"Gimme an example," Cam said, one hundred percent serious, and Cort had to bite his lip to stop himself from grinning like an idiot. He couldn't remember the last time someone had listened to the bullshit he sometimes spouted and seriously considered it. He couldn't remember the last time he'd felt so *important*. It was odd, and really, really satisfying.

"Okay, think about the first dude who rubbed two sticks together and made fire. I mean, he couldn't have known for sure it was going to happen. If you didn't know anything about friction, and some guy came to you and grunted that he was gonna make a spark by rubbing two boring-ass sticks together, you'd think he was off his rocker. But he didn't *know* it was a stupid idea, so he did it, and voila. Fire."

Cam snorted. "Voila, fire?"

"Hush," Cort said, yanking a lock of hair at the crown of Cam's head. Cam inhaled sharply, but didn't pull away.

In fact, he sank further into Cort's lap. Cort lifted his knee onto the seat sideways, and shifted so Cam was leaning against him more fully.

"That actually makes a lot of sense."

Cam sounded so surprised, Cort yanked his hair again. "Thanks for the vote of confidence."

"No, no. I mean, I'd just never thought of it like that before. My dad, when he started Seaver Tech, he was the same. Everybody thought he was going to fail. His own parents wrote him off. 'Don't come crying to us when you end up bankrupt.' My mom's parents were just as bad. Nobody would invest in the business at first. I remember hearing my parents put up our house as collateral, and if he'd failed, they would've been homeless with a baby to support. That's really stupid, when you think about it."

Cort chuckled. "Massively stupid."

"But it paid off." Cam's voice was still disbelieving.

"Given that we are currently sitting on a leather sofa in the sky, winging our way to a private island, I'd have to agree."

Cam jerked his head up and looked out the window, then back at Cort in surprise. "We took off. We're already in the air."

"Yup."

Cam's eyes widened and his lips turned up in a small smile. He glanced back down at the quarter in his hand. "Uh. Thanks. I think maybe I'm good now." He held the quarter out on his open palm for Cort to take back.

Cort pushed Cam's fingers closed around the coin. All the things he could say - *My fault I made you do this in the first place.* and *Thank you for making me feel necessary.* and *Come lean on me again.* - sounded like sappy bullshit, so he stuck to a simple, "You hang onto it."

Cam swallowed and looked down at his lap. "You know,

I don't know if I could have done what my dad did. I'm, uh, *risk-averse*. I think I mostly do what I'm supposed to. One foot in front of the other, you know?"

It sounded as though Cam was reciting something he'd heard somewhere. The ex again? That asshole had better hope he and Cort didn't meet up anytime soon.

Cort frowned and ducked his head, so Cam's eyes met his. "Bullshit."

"What?"

"I said, *bullshit*, badass. You take risks all the time, and I know what I'm talking about. My friend Derrick used to say I should get 'No risk, no reward' tattooed on me someplace."

"This doesn't surprise me." Cam raised one eyebrow.

Cort chuckled. "And you still haven't seen my League of Legends skills." Cam rolled his eyes, but Cort continued, "The way you see yourself is seriously flawed, babe. You've done nothing *but* take risks since the minute we met. Sneaking up to skinny dip in the pool, making out in stairwells, flying me to St. Brigitte as your *date*. Maybe I have a good effect on you."

Cam's eyes were piercing as they focused on Cort, and then his lips tipped up into a smile.

Cort gave Cam a wink, then took his seatbelt off and stood, taking the opportunity to stretch, and adjust himself while Cam couldn't see. Whatever effect Cort had on Cam, Cam was definitely having one on him. Something about the guy's smile and the way every emotion played so openly across his face totally killed Cort's self-control. "So, do you have movies on your laptop? I brought some cards, if you want to play a game. Poker, or I dunno... Never Have I Ever?"

"Cort?" Cam said, his voice strained. Cort turned and

glanced down at him in concern, but Cam didn't look worried or upset, he seemed…

Turned on.

"I don't want to play card games," he said, taking off his own seatbelt to Cort's absolute surprise.

"You don't?"

"Maybe you're right. Maybe I want to do something a little *riskier*."

Oh. Holy. Shit. He licked his suddenly dry lips. "Riskier, as in?"

"As in, hold still." Cam reached out and unbuttoned Cort's jeans in one smooth movement. He sank to his knees beside the couch and looked up at Cort, waiting for approval, but Cort's mind was a total blank slate.

Cam wanted to…

Cort's pulse pounded, all the blood in his body traveling immediately to his cock, but still he had to ask, "Cam. Baby, are you sure?"

He didn't want to take advantage of the situation, of a moment of vulnerability Cam had shared. Cort's loyalties were all fucked up, and he didn't want to hurt Cam again.

But Cam nodded, his eyes glazed with want, and all Cort's good intentions drifted away into the cloud deck. He had no fucking clue what was happening right here, but nobody had ever accused *him* of being risk-averse. So, they'd do this. And he'd make *sure* Cam didn't get hurt, somehow.

"Do it," Cort said, low and commanding.

Cam responded instantly, pulling Cort's jeans down to his ankles. Cort toed off his shoes and stepped out of them, kicking his pants aside. Cam threaded his fingers into the waistband of Cort's boxers and looked up at him again, waiting for direction, waiting for permission.

Oh, fuck.

Cort's dick was so hard he could feel precum leaking from the tip. Cam's eyes flicked to Cort's heavy bulge and he licked his lips before looking back up at him.

"You want to take my boxers off, too, Cam?"

Cort braced his hands on the low, curved ceiling of the plane so he wouldn't be tempted to rip his *own* boxers off and take himself in hand. He was completely getting off on the way Cam was looking at him, and no way did he want this to end too soon.

"Yes," Cam whispered.

Cort hesitated for a second, wondering how far he should push, but just as before, he could read Cam perfectly. Cam needed this. "Yes, *what*?"

His eyes closed and he shivered slightly. "Yes, *please*," he begged.

And that was it. Game on. He could see the light flicker into Cam's eyes that said he was giving himself over to this, to Cort.

"Take them off," Cort instructed. His boxers were gone almost before the words passed his lips, and his cock was rock hard and pulsing in the cool air of the plane.

Cam bit his lip and sighed, and once again the sound seemed to bypass Cort's brain and travel directly to his dick. He dropped one hand from the ceiling to cradle Cam's jaw, his thumb brushing over those gorgeous, plump lips, then he cupped the back of Cam's head and gently guided him forward.

Cam didn't need any further permission or encouragement, and apparently, he didn't need a warmup. He swallowed Cort down to the root in one gulp. Cort cried out, his head swimming at the sensation.

Cam stared up at Cort and at the sight of those trusting, lust-hazed blue eyes, Cort nearly lost it. His hand clenched in Cam's hair, and he forced himself to relax, to let Cam take this at his own pace.

"So, so, good baby," he praised as Cam pulled nearly all the way off Cort's dick, ran his tongue over the tip, then sank all the way back down again, nearly choking himself in the process. "Easy," Cort said.

But Cam didn't want that. He made a small humming noise in the back of his throat, a sound of disagreement. He grabbed Cort's hand from the top of his head and moved it around to the back, pushing slightly, and his eyes pleaded with Cort as he sank down so far his eyes watered. Cort heard what Cam was trying to tell him as clearly as if Cam had spoken aloud. *Take it.*

"You want to choke on it, Cam? You want to take my cock all the way down your throat?"

The moan Cam gave, the helpless pleading in his eyes as he wrapped his hands around Cort's ass and pushed his nose into Cort's pubes, were confirmation enough. Cort wouldn't ask if Cam was sure, wouldn't discourage him from having this exactly the way he wanted it, since it was exactly the way Cort wanted it, too.

With both hands, he grabbed Cam's head, his fingers threading into the soft brown spikes of Cam's hair, and held him still. Cam's eyes burned up at him, full of love and trust Cort knew he hadn't earned. If Cam could trust him again - would trust him in *this*, at least, then Cort wouldn't let him down. He rocked back, watching Cam's cheeks hollow as he sucked, then thrust forward, into the scorching hot cavern of Cam's mouth.

Time seemed to spiral, and Cort found himself in a feedback loop of desire, the almost painfully good feeling of Cam's mouth on his dick, and the answering pleasure he could see in Cam's eyes. It was the best he'd ever had, better by far than any one-night hookup or backroom blow job, and it wasn't because Cam had any particular skill - though, fuck, could the man use his mouth. It was because of the way Cam's eyes were focused on him, wanting Cort to take him, wanting Cort to own him, wanting *Cort* himself.

And suddenly, this pleasure wasn't enough. He needed Cam to be with him. Just like last week, he needed to offer Cam something more real than he'd ever offered anyone before.

He slid himself out of Cam's mouth, a shudder wracking his body at the sight of Cam's swollen, spit-slick lips.

"Stand up, baby," he commanded.

Cam got to his feet immediately, his chest heaving, Cort's hands cradling his jaw. Cort leaned forward and kissed him, sliding his tongue along Cam's and tasting himself on Cam's tongue as though he'd embedded himself under Cam's skin. *Exactly as it should be.*

He unfastened Cam's shorts and pushed them down, along with his underwear, only breaking the kiss for a moment as he stripped off their shirts, and then he held Cam against him, skin-to-skin. His hands roamed the light muscles of Cam's abs and around to his strong back. He wasn't as obviously built as Cort, but he hid undeniable strength beneath his clothes, and that strength inflamed Cort beyond belief. He gripped Cam's hips and thrust against him, his cock sliding against Cam's stomach. Both men moaned.

His hands dipped further, skimming over Cam's ass, dipping between his cheeks. Cam broke away from their kiss and shuddered out a breath.

"Please?"

"You want more, Cam? You want me?"

Cam nodded, his eyes blazing, no trace of hesitation or shyness. "Yes," he said. "*You* are exactly what I need."

Cort swallowed, his throat tight. Cam was all welcoming

openness, giving of himself again and again with no hesitation. It was fucking *humbling.* And for the first time in a long while, Cort felt a pang of nerves, followed by a flash of resolve.

His man deserved perfection, and perfection was what Cort would give him.

His man.

His brain stuttered at the thought, but he put it aside to consider later. For now, he'd concentrate on showing Cam his faith in Cort was justified.

CHAPTER FOURTEEN

Cort smiled softly, and his hands began tracing the curves of Cam's ass again. Cam's hips jutted forward instinctively.

"I'm gonna take care of you, Cam," he murmured.

Cort leaned down, capturing Cam's mouth in a fast, searing kiss. Then his lips ghosted across Cam's jaw, and his teeth clamped down lightly on Cam's earlobe. Cam exhaled with a shudder. "I'm going to make you feel so good."

Cam was already feeling good. Downright delirious, in fact. He was still dimly aware that he was on a *plane*, but his panic had been replaced by an almost fatalistic determination. If something awful happened, if he died, then he would die this way, with his arms wrapped around Cort's shoulders with blazing trails of fire snaking up and down his spine. "More," he told Cort. More of everything. More of Cort's hands curling around his ass, more of Cort's cock rocking against his own, more of the feeling that Cort was focused entirely on him.

Cort thrust against Cam once more, and then spun him to face away. His hands swept around to Cam's stomach, and then separated, one trailing up to toy with Cam's nipple, while the other went lower... and lower.

"More of this?" Cort demanded, his open mouth sliding over the tendon at the base of Cam's neck. "Or more of this?"

Cort's hand trailed gently - way too gently - up and down Cam's cock. Cam thrust into Cort's hand and moaned as Cort chuckled.

He gripped Cam more firmly with one hand, while the other moved from Cam's chest to his back and pushed gently between Cam's shoulder blades, forcing him to bend. Cam grabbed the back of the couch, his knees coming to rest on the cushions where they'd been sitting, while Cort's mouth brushed soft, teasing kisses down Cam's spine, dipping his tongue into the grooves above his ass.

"You like this?" he asked. Cam made an inarticulate pleading noise as Cort's hand stroked him off from behind.

Then Cort sank to his knees on the floor, and both of his hands were on Cam's ass again, spreading him. He licked a path along the sensitive skin between Cam's balls and his ass. *Oh, Jesus, yes.*

"Or maybe you want me to do *this*."

Cort's thumb found Cam's opening and stroked over it once, twice. Cam whined, *honest-to-God whined*, and felt dimly perhaps he should be embarrassed by his needy noise, but he couldn't work himself around to it. Cort seemed to totally get off on it, from the way his fingers tightened on Cam's skin. Cam rocked against nothing and waited for what seemed like eternity, and then Cort's tongue found his opening, and Cam nearly lost his grip on reality.

Cort licked, swirled, and sucked, and Cam's entire consciousness became focused on that one place, on the sensations Cort was rousing in him. Then Cort's spit-slicked finger joined the mix, and Cam gasped. It had been so long.

"Fuck, you're tight, baby," Cort said, but his voice was a low growl of approval and Cam fought to relax. Cort fumbled around for his fly, and a moment later, Cam felt a cold dribble of liquid trickle between his cheeks. *Travel lube.* Cort obviously came prepared, but Cam couldn't fully process the realization because Cort added a second finger, pushing in more completely, stretching Cam further. Cam gave himself over to the burning sensation, willing himself to open. He wanted this. God, he *needed* this. He couldn't believe how far gone he was already. He bit his lip to keep from whining again.

"Talk to me, Cam," Cort demanded, pulling back to nip at the curve of Cam's ass. "I want to hear what I'm doing to you." Cort's voice, wrecked with lust, was like a siren's call, and Cam was compelled to answer.

"It's so good, Cort. Just like that." He bit his lip against another moan.

"Don't stop yourself," Cort commanded. "I want to hear those fucking sexy moans. I want to know I'm driving you crazy the way you drive me crazy. I want to know you're as gone for me as I am for you. You understand?"

Cam nodded. Cort turned his hand and curved his fingers just slightly, tagging Cam's prostate and *oh holy fuck,* Cam couldn't have helped the moan escaping from him even if he'd tried. "Cort, Cort, Cort," he chanted breathlessly, over and over again, like a mantra, like a prayer. The path to enlightenment was Cort.

"Who's taking care of you?" Cort demanded, as his fingers continued to move in and out.

"You are!"

"Who owns you?"

Oh. Oh, God. Cam knew what Cort wanted, and an

electric thrill traveled from his belly to his dick. They were only words, and he'd said them before. But this same time, he hesitated. Every time he spoke them, they meant something more, became more of an expectation. Was that the kind of relationship Cort really wanted? To own Cam that completely? Did Cort even know what he was asking?

Did it matter right now?

Risking meant offering something when there was no guarantee. And already, Cort *had* given him more than he'd ever been given by any partner. Cort saw him as strong, even when he felt weak, and somehow seeing himself through Cort's eyes *made him stronger.* Seavers never gave in, but giving Cort control didn't feel like giving in, it was more like yielding, bending.

"You do," he replied.

"Yeah, I do," he whispered, as he rose to his feet behind Cam and curled himself over Cam's back to lay a kiss at his nape. "Yes, I fucking do."

But for how long? Cam banished the thought from his mind almost as quickly as it appeared. He was standing naked, bent over a sofa, with the hottest man he'd ever laid eyes on, in an airplane for the first time in forever. If there was ever a time to live in the moment and not worry about the future, this was it.

Cort's hand trailed down Cam's spine once more, and then he reached down for the supplies he'd left on the floor. Cam heard the rip of the condom wrapper and then felt Cort's fingers again, slicking his entrance.

"Do it now, Cort. Now, *please.*"

A second later, the broad head of Cort's cock was pushing in, stretching him until Cam was utterly filled.

"Oh, fuck," Cort moaned.

Exactly what Cam was thinking. He braced his arms harder against the back of the sofa as Cort's hands found

Cam's hips and held him tightly. Cort began to move against him, harder and faster, pulling back then filling him up. It was monumental. It was earth shattering. It was unbelievably perfect.

"Cam. God, you're so tight. So perfect." The words were mindless, but the low, gravel-filled, lust-wrecked tone traveled straight to Cam's cock. He let his head hang down and gave himself over to Cort's movements, bracing them both.

Cort's hands came up to trace lazy patterns on Cam's skin as he moved, faster then slower, as though Cort was mapping his body, laying claim to every inch of his flesh. Up his back, over his shoulders, around to his chest, and then down his stomach. When Cort was bent over him completely, his warm breath in Cam's ear, his hand reached for Cam's cock and slowly began to stroke in time with his thrusts.

No more words needed to be said between them. Cam let himself become lost completely, a vessel for Cort's pleasure. Cort was utterly focused on Cam, reading every sign of his body as he showed him without words how perfect they could be together.

Cam bit his lip as the combination of physical pleasure and emotional release built inside him. It was too much, too much for him to hold onto. The steady slap of flesh against flesh filled the air, and Cam spread his knees further apart, opening himself further.

"Please don't stop," he plead. "Don't stop. Don't ever stop."

"Oh, Christ, Cam. I won't. I can't. You are the only one, the only thing. It's never been like this before. No other. Not ever."

The babbled whispers made Cam's chest swell. He wanted to be Cort's *only one*. He wanted to be the only one who could make Cort this inarticulate and uncontrolled.

Cort spread his legs and changed the angle of his thrusts, so he tagged Cam's prostate with each pass of his hard cock. Cam saw stars, and felt his body start to sway.

"Hang on, Cam. Hang on for me," Cort told him, stroking him faster, his thumb swiping the head of Cam's cock and spreading the copious amount of precum gathering there.

He wanted to obey Cort, wanted to wait, but his pleasure was climbing higher with every single movement of the man behind him.

"I'm so close. I'm so close," Cam began, then moaned as Cort's hand slapped against his ass.

"You wait for me, Cam. You hear me, baby? You don't come until I say. Wait for me."

Cam bit his lip and his eyes rolled back in his head. He'd never felt sensations like this, layer upon layer, more than he could stand. Had anyone ever known him this well? Had anyone ever understood exactly how to reach him, beyond the perfection of the hand stroking his dick and the exquisite rhythm Cort had set? Cort knew how to reach his heart, the part of him that wanted to be taken, owned, loved.

"Oh, fuck, Cam! I am so close, baby. This ass is perfection. I love the way you wait for me, the way you obey me. The way you give yourself to me so perfectly. Jesus."

Cam let out a low moan. He couldn't hang on much longer. And then Cort slid out of him completely and braced his hands on Cam's hips again.

"Turn over," he said. "And lay down on the couch."

Cam lay on his back on the leather couch while Cort hovered over him, sweat-darkened tendrils of his dark gold hair falling against his cheeks and green eyes glowing with need. He allowed Cort to arrange his pliant limbs exactly as he wanted them, so Cam's knees were drawn up to his chest and his feet were braced over Cort's broad shoulders.

"I want you like this. I want you to see me while I'm fucking you. I want you to look at me when I make you come, and I want you to scream. My. Name."

Before Cam could process the words, Cort was sliding back inside him, filling every empty inch of him. Cort braced himself over Cam with one hand on the cushions, then bent down to kiss Cam, sucking his tongue into his mouth.

Cam reached down to grab his dick, needing more friction, but Cort slapped his hand away wrapping his own around it instead.

"This is mine now, Cam. You come when I tell you, remember?"

Jesus, that should not have sounded as good as it did, but Cam was beyond caring about what he *should* want and what should turn him on. All he wanted was this man, just like this, forever.

Cort's thrusts picked up speed, faster and faster, each twist of his hips brushing his cock against Cam's prostate, making his eyes roll back in his head. He could feel his balls drawing up tight and felt his orgasm barreling towards him.

"Oh, God. Cort! Please! It's got to be now. You've got to let me!" Cam's voice was high-pitched with need and lust so acute it was anguish.

Cort's hand moved faster and faster over Cam's well-lubricated cock. "Come for me *now*, Cam, and then I'll come for you."

Once again, Cam's cock obeyed Cort's orders directly, bypassing his own brain entirely. No sooner had Cort spoken the words, given his permission, then Cam was coming, semen shooting over his stomach.

Cort paused to trail a finger through the evidence of Cam's pleasure and tasted it. "So fucking sweet, Cam."

Cam's sated dick twitched at the blatant approval in his tone, even as Cort got back to business, moving faster again inside Cam, chasing his own release. God, the feeling was exquisite - pleasure and pain combined, and Cam loved the look on Cort's face as he used Cam, his green eyes staring down into Cam's as though Cam was the most important thing in the universe to him right there and then. *This this this. Forever and ever and ever.*

Cort pulled out of him gently, his hands braced on Cam's thighs, and then he was ripping off the condom and jerking himself, his cum joining Cam's on his stomach.

He lowered himself over Cam, plastering their chests together.

They were both panting as if they'd run for miles, smiling at each other like lunatics. Cam couldn't help but laugh at the satisfied grin on his man's face.

It was silly, it was crazy. The wrong time, the wrong place, with way, way too many unanswered questions for becoming involved with Cort to be a rational decision. But maybe Cort was right. Maybe the truest things didn't run on logic, anyway.

CHAPTER FIFTEEN

The plane touched down on the small island of St. Brigitte with no fanfare. When the captain had announced over the loudspeaker that they were preparing for landing, Cam had done nothing more than shift his hips slightly, so Cort could buckle his seatbelt around him, and then leaned back against the cushions with his eyes closed once again. Cort watched Cam as he lay sprawled on the couch, his thighs draped over Cort's lap, but Cam didn't even seem to notice they were losing altitude until the plane bumped down on the runway and began to slow.

"Smooth landing," Cort remarked as the plane began to taxi.

Cam's eyes opened slowly and he gave Cort a sleepy, knowing smirk. "If you wanna call it that."

Cort rolled his eyes and Cam laughed. "I can't believe how relaxed I was during that flight."

"You need me to relax you before every flight, badass, I can make arrangements."

"Is that right? I don't know if I could afford you."

"For you? My rates are very, very reasonable. I'll take it out on your ass."

Cam snickered as if he was half-drunk. Maybe he was. God knew, the endorphins cruising through Cort's blood-stream right now were beyond anything he'd ever achieved with alcohol.

The plane taxied to a halt, and Cort tried to get his mind in order. The interlude on the plane had been incredible - so amazing it was hard for him to remember this wasn't why he was here.

Not entirely.

But he couldn't lie and say things hadn't changed either. He'd help Damon get his life back, help figure out who'd *really* caused the crash, but maybe, just maybe, there was a way he could keep Cam, too.

Cort sat up straighter. Cam frowned slightly, but seemed to take his cue, swinging his legs off the sofa and placing his feet on the floor.

Andres arrived to open the cabin door as they finally came to a stop, and Cort could see the early-evening sunlight gilding the palm trees, the small one-story white and blue hangar, and the white surface of the runway outside the door. He wondered if Damon would meet him here and now, or whether he'd call him later. Either way, he was confident Damon had a plan, and since Damon was most likely here already, Cort would be ready and waiting to follow his lead.

Cort reached over to unfasten Cam's seatbelt, then unfastened his own and stood to stretch, feeling his shirt ride up. He scratched the surface of his stomach absently, feeling the sticky remnants of the mind-blowing orgasms they'd shared only an hour ago. Though he and Cam had cleaned up as best they could in the tiny bathroom, Cam hadn't been kidding when he'd said there was no tub on board and it was impossible to get really clean. Still, Cort couldn't bring himself to care very much - he liked knowing he was wearing the evidence on himself, and he liked even better knowing Cam was, too.

Cam had started for the doorway, but turned back hesitantly to look at Cort, as though unsure whether or not he should wait for him. Cort conjured up a reassuring smile and held out his hand, which Cam grabbed eagerly. He let Cam lead him down the steps to the tarmac.

Cort felt a pang of something he couldn't quite identify as he felt Cam's smaller hand in his own. In a way, it was everything right and good - which was weird enough in a man who'd shied away from commitment as much as Cort had during his entire adult life. This thing building between him and Cam was *real*. He wasn't sure how it had happened, or why, but it was as real as anything else Cort knew, and he genuinely cared about Cam more than he'd ever cared about anyone... except Damon.

"Camden!" A smiling woman who Cort vaguely recognized from the ballroom the other night strode forward to greet them with outstretched hands. "It's so very, very good to see you, dear."

"Mrs. Tyndall," Cam said, dropping Cort's hand so he could grip her gently by the arms and lean forward to kiss her cheek. "I didn't expect you to come out to meet us."

"Well," she said in a conspiratorial tone. "I generally don't, but I asked them to alert me when *your* plane would be arriving so I could greet you myself. You've always been one of my favorites. Gerry and I are so glad you were able to make it."

Cam smiled. Mrs. Tyndall glanced around, and then back at the plane, as though expecting someone else. "Is your brother not with you?"

"Oh, uh. No. Bas still won't be coming. I'm sorry if that message was mixed up, somehow."

Mrs. Tyndall frowned. "Oh, but I was sure…" She waved a hand dismissively. "Ah, well. Never get old, boys." Her smile was rueful as she turned her attention to Cort. "And who might you be, young man?"

Cort grinned. He couldn't remember the last time he'd been called a young man.

Cam's hand went around Cort's waist. "This is Kendrick Cortland."

Cort could sense Cam's hesitation over how to introduce him - what title to give him. They weren't dating, there was no easy description, so Cort understood the dilemma, but it annoyed him anyway.

The woman was middle aged, but stylish, in an airy white dress which flowed around her despite the heat and humidity weighing down the air. Her smile was genuine and friendly - far more than Cort had expected to find in someone who had a charity named after her, but then, Cort was coming to realize that judging someone based on the size of their bank account was pretty fucking stupid, no matter which side of the income bracket you stood on.

He took the hand Mrs. Tyndall offered him. "Please, call me Cort, ma'am." After a brief handshake, he stepped back and wrapped his arm around Cam in what he knew was a proprietary way. Cam might not know what to call him, but he wanted there to be no doubt in anyone's mind that for right now, at least, Cam was *his*.

Mrs. Tyndall smiled at his display, and regarded him with a glint in her eye. "And you must call me Lydia. Camden is the only one who can't seem to break the habit of calling me by my full name, even now that he's an adult. Let me show you up to the house." She pointed up the hill, to where a large, white stone mansion was just peeking out between a heavy stand of trees. "Camden, I know you always loved the beach walk. Or maybe you'd rather see the orange trees along the way?"

Cort didn't want to head to the house immediately. If Damon was on this island - and Cort could *sense* that he was close by - he wouldn't be up at the mansion. He was far more likely to have come onto the island as a pilot, a mechanic, or even perhaps a groundskeeper. He turned around and looked back towards the plane, which was being rolled behind the hangar. If he could go and scope out the hangar for just a minute...

Lydia misunderstood his action. She put a hand on his arm to catch his attention and said, "Don't worry about a thing, dear. I'll have Tom or one of the others bring your bags to the house for you."

Cort couldn't turn back or look around after that. Mrs. Tyndall led them onward, up the path through a lush stand of citrus trees. She pointed out the varieties of oranges, lemons, and limes growing in abundance on the island, and explained how her husband's family had planted the first such trees here generations ago. She explained how the island used to be a great tourist destination, but her husband's father had bought out all the resorts and demolished them.

Cort stayed a step behind Lydia and Cam as they walked up the path, and marveled at the way Cam was able to listen to her conversation and nod seriously when she talked of the positive environmental effects which came with the clean water initiatives, and her pride in her family. The whole concept of owning an island was like the punchline to a not-very-funny joke in the world Cort came from. It was almost incomprehensible to him that the man whose ass he'd owned just an hour ago, the man who'd given himself so freely to Cort, was able to listen and comment intelligently on the potential return on investment of island ownership.

As they walked through the hazy sunshine, Cort realized they had circled around to approach the house from the rear. The path went up an incline leading to an enormous terrace with a gorgeous view of the turquoise blue Caribbean water. It was unbelievable.

"Several of the others have already arrived. Bunny and Mickey, the Taylors, the Merenskys, the Blackwells, and the Victozas. Oh, and the Shaws."

Cam paused in his walk. "Uncle Emmett and Aunt Lucy are already here?"

Lydia nodded. "Oh, yes. They arrived hours ago. Left DC after some hush-hush meetings Emmett can't help talking about. Cain made it down, as well. And Arcadia, of course." Lydia's voice had turned faintly disapproving.

"What is Arcadia doing these days?" Cam wondered.

Lydia raised an eyebrow and looked at him. "Working on her father's re-election campaign," Lydia said, rolling her eyes. "This afternoon at lunch, she regaled me with her new campaign slogan - Restore American Glory."

Cam frowned. "Sounds like something Uncle Emmett would endorse," he said with a sigh.

Cort snickered, and Cam turned to look at him. "What's so funny?"

Cort waved a hand through the air. "Nothing, nothing." At Lydia and Cam's unamused stares, he expounded, "Fine. It's just... Did nobody notice that Restore American Glory spells out RAG?"

Cam blinked and shook his head, but Lydia's warm smile turned into a genuine grin as she turned to Cam. "I approve of him, Camden," she said, then winked at Cort before she led them further on towards the house.

Several people were milling around on the patio - some admiring the view, others deep in conversation, all of them extremely overdressed, as far as Cort was concerned. The women all wore dresses, the men wore long pants and polo shirts, and Cort felt somewhat self-conscious of his own jeans and tee, until he recalled Cam himself was wearing an even scruffier outfit. Every person on the patio carried a drink in his or her hand like armor against tedious conversation. *Socialites in the wild*, he thought. *I wonder if they hunt in packs.*

"I'll let you say your hellos and grab a drink," Lydia said quietly. "But don't feel like you need to stay for too long. You've only just arrived and I know you'll want to rest yourselves. Dinner tonight will be informal, and don't be afraid to ask someone to bring some light refreshments to your room if you'd rather not join us."

Thank God. Cort couldn't imagine staying a minute longer than he had to.

Cam shook his head. "Not necessary. I'm sure everyone has plenty to do already."

"Nonsense!" she scolded. "You know Gerald and I always hire plenty of extra hands when we host these festivities."

"And it's smart thinking, too," said a gruff voice behind them. "Labor on the islands is dirt cheap."

Cort stiffened and turned to see Senator Shaw bearing down on them, drink in hand. His smiling blue eyes were fixed on Cam, his sandy hair damp with sweat. A tall, black-haired man wearing sunglasses followed in his wake. He was hot, if you went for the whole Terminator-look.

Cam smiled, and Cort wondered if the senator noticed how forced the expression was. Maybe he didn't care.

It was strange how clearly he could read Cam after such a short time… and even stranger how protective he felt.

Still, when Senator Shaw winked and stuck out his meaty paw for Cam to shake, Cam didn't hesitate.

"Uncle Emmett," he said. "It's good to see you again."

"And you, my boy, and you! It's wonderful that you've managed to peel yourself away from Seaver Tech for the weekend. You might remember my assistant, Jack Peabody?" He lifted his free hand over his shoulder, indicating the tall man, whose grim expression didn't change.

Before Cam could reply, Lydia gave Shaw a gimlet glare and interrupted. "Emmett Shaw, I'll have you know I pay the locals the same rate that I pay the catering staff I brought over from the States. *Island labor is dirt cheap.* Do you ever listen to yourself? And don't you dare launch into one of your campaign speeches. No politics this weekend."

"Oh, alright," Shaw sighed. He gave Cam an affable grin. "Lucy warned me of the same thing on the flight over. It's an occupational hazard." He took a sip of his drink and shot Cam another quick wink. Then he glanced at Cort and his smile dimmed somewhat. He held out his hand.

"I don't know if we've met. Emmett Shaw."

"Kendrick Cortland," Cort said, taking his hand. The senator's grip was damp, and a good deal firmer than necessary. The man held on for several beats, as though waiting for Cort to yield, and Jack seemed poised to intervene. Cort barely refrained from rolling his eyes. Next, they'd be whipping their dicks out to compare sizes.

"I'm sorry," Cam said, jumping into the fray. "Cort, this is Senator Emmett Shaw, my honorary uncle, I guess you could say. Uncle Shaw, Cort is my date this weekend." And to Cort's shocked delight, Cam wrapped an arm around Cort's waist as though daring the senator to comment.

Shaw's eyes turned shrewd and his lips pursed as if the

drink in his hand had suddenly turned sour. Cort bit back the urge to laugh.

"And what do you do, Mr. Cortland?" Shaw demanded.

Cort wrapped his own arm around Cam's back, settling Cam against his side. "Oh, various things," he hedged. He was fairly certain if he announced himself to be an FBI agent, the news would travel around this gathering faster than wildfire. Besides which, his status as an agent was tenuous at best just then. "Right now, I'm enjoying some time off."

Shaw's eyes turned a fraction colder. "And how do you know Cam?"

Cort hesitated, unsure of what Cam might have told the Tyndalls while making arrangements for the trip, but Cam stepped in immediately. "Cort and I met at a charity function a while back," he said smoothly.

Cort squeezed his waist in approval.

"Well, then we'll have to get to know you," Shaw said. His words were friendly enough, but his tone carried a distinct warning. "I'll ask Lucy to have you over to the house for dinner sometime once we get back." He glanced at Jack. "Make a note."

Jack nodded. "Yes, sir," he said in a faint drawl.

Cam nodded and Cort managed to smile politely.

Lydia rolled her eyes. "I don't think Camden needs your blessing on his boyfriend," she said dryly.

"What? That's nonsense. I just want to know more about the young man Cam will be spending time with," Shaw said, his cheeks turning red. "The boy is practically one of my own!"

Cort stifled a snort. *Bullshit.* Shaw was no father to Cam - he could tell Cam didn't even like the guy. Maybe if Cam's father was alive, Cam might care about his approval, but as far as Cort was concerned, he didn't care what anyone else thought. Cam was his whether or not the blustering Senator condoned their relationship. Cort fought the sudden desire to kiss Cam right then and there, and wished for a moment he'd marked him up in the plane.

"Lydia Tyndall, what are you saying to make my husband blush?" A pretty, middle-aged redhead in a sleeveless white dress strolled up to Shaw's side, along with a tall, teenage boy who looked miserably warm in a long-sleeved button-down shirt and khaki pants. The woman leaned forward to give Cam a kiss on the cheek. "Cam, sweetheart, so good to see you."

"Your husband was about to ask Camden's boyfriend his intentions," Lydia said archly.

The redhead's mouth gaped in surprise as she turned to Cort. "Boyfriend?" she repeated, looking back and forth from Cam to Cort. "Really?"

"I… well." Cam stammered, straightening slightly at Cort's side. "It's… we're…"

"Yes, boyfriend," Cort said, his hand around Cam's back tightening slightly until Cam was pressed against him again, right where he belonged. Cam glanced up at Cort in surprise, but then smiled and his own hand tightened on Cort's waist.

"Kendrick Cortland," he told the woman, holding out his hand to shake. "But call me Cort."

The lady blinked, but held out her hand mechanically. "Lucy Shaw," she said, as though surprised to hear herself speaking the words. She took her hand back quickly.

"And Cort, this is Cain Shaw. I guess he'd be my honorary… cousin?" Cam asked dubiously, as though he'd never really thought about that before.

Cort held out his hand to the younger man, who gripped it briefly, as though Cort was possibly contagious or on fire.

Lydia Tyndall rolled her eyes and shot Cort a look that said she was exasperated by the whole proceeding.

Cam cleared his throat. "Cain. Good to see you. You're looking well."

The boy blushed and nodded. He managed to squeak out, "Yeah, uh. You too."

Cort realized belatedly that if the boy was the Shaws' son, he wasn't actually a teenager but was probably twenty-three or twenty-four. And quickly on the heels of that, he recalled Cam saying he and Cain had dated briefly, once upon a time. *Honorary cousin, my eye.* Cort couldn't wait to give Cam shit for that later.

Cort's gaze on Cain turned assessing.

Cain was undeniably handsome. With deep blue eyes, a strong jaw, and a straight nose, his perfect face was the kind often featured on magazine covers, but he looked at least a decade younger than he must have been, partly because he was an inch or two shorter than Cam and a little heavier. Maybe he was still carrying a layer of puppy fat, but there was also something in his eyes. He seemed startled and uncomfortable to find someone had noticed him, and his gaze darted back and forth from Cam to his mother and father, like he wasn't sure how to behave.

"Are you still in school?" Cam asked.

"Uh, yeah. Second year law," he confirmed. "Vanderbilt."

"Oh, that's right. I remember. Good for you," Cam said. To Cort, he added, "The Shaws used to live up in Boston, but they moved south a few years ago."

"Better quality of life," Shaw informed them. "Gorgeous mountains, clean air."

"And a senator who was planning his retirement at exactly the right time," Lydia interjected.

"Lydia!" Lucy exclaimed repressively.

If not for the fact that the charged atmosphere had made his training kick in, Cort would have burst out laughing. Cam coughed and looked at the ground, while Cain became fascinated by the sight of his own shoes. Shaw merely arched a brow at Lydia, as if he expected no less from her.

"That is *not* the reason we moved," Lucy explained to Cort with a trembling voice. "We wanted better opportunities for our children! Better schools and better influences."

Though Cain's gaze was still pointed downward, Cort saw a muscle in his jaw flex, like he was clenching it hard. Cort recalled Cam saying Cain would likely never be able to come out to his parents, and wondered whose bad *influences* he'd had in Boston.

Poor kid. He made a mental note to ask Cam about it later.

"And, uh, Cady?" Cam said, once again venturing into the awkward silence that descended.

"Oh, Arcadia!" Lucy Shaw said, her eyes lighting up. "She's here, too. Probably already talking someone's ear off about her father, securing some donations!"

Cam nodded. "That's great," he said.

"It *is* great," Lucy enthused. "Oh, you and Cady used to have *so* much in common, Cam. Remember back when you two were an item?"

Cam's fingers squeezed Cort's hip. "Er…" he hedged. "It was a long, long time ago."

"Yes, but some things never change!" Lucy said. Her smile was bright and hopeful. "Maybe she can save you a dance tomorrow night and you two can reminisce!"

Cort frowned. Cain glanced up at Cort, his eyes full of sardonic humor. Cort gave a tiny shake of his head. His annoyance dissipated under a wave of sympathy for Cain.

Growing up as he had, Cort couldn't believe he'd ever

look with sympathy at someone like Cain Shaw, who'd been raised in the lap of luxury. Cort had always wanted a family of his own, wished he had parents and siblings to look out for him, but now he had to amend that wish. He couldn't imagine growing up in a family where you had to hide part of yourself to fit in with someone's career ambitions or deluded ideals. When he'd come out to Craig Dempsey - an event precipitated by Craig catching him kissing his next-door-neighbor Ethan behind the garage one sweltering summer afternoon just after he'd turned seventeen - there had been no question about whether or not Craig accepted him (he hadn't). There also hadn't been any question as to whether Cort would hide his sexuality to please the Dempseys (not a chance in hell). For the first time, Cort felt as though maybe he'd had a certain amount of freedom in growing up that way. Money seemed to bring a shit ton of posturing.

"Excuse me, please. I'm really quite thirsty," Cain gritted out, then squeezed between Cam and Lydia without saying another word and headed for the small bar set up on one side of the patio.

"I could use a drink, too." Cort squeezed Cam's shoulder. "Come with me?"

Cam nodded, but before they could turn around, an older woman on the far side of the patio squealed, "Cam! Oh, darling!" and made a bee-line for them.

Cam hesitated. "That's Mary-Alice McMann, Drew's mom," he told Cort. "I need to…"

"I'll bring you something," Cort promised, trailing his fingers over the nape of Cam's neck before he moved away, and loving the way the banked fire in Cam's eyes instantly kindled into something hotter.

Cort moved through the crowd, ignoring the curious glances from the men and women he passed. At the bar, he ordered two beers. He could have used something stronger, but he also wanted to keep his wits about him, just in case Damon made contact. His eyes circled the patio, paying careful attention to the men and women who were carrying drinks and setting up platters of fruit and snacks, but Damon wasn't among them. He tamped down his impatience.

"So, you're Cam's boyfriend." Cort turned his head to see Cain Shaw standing by the bar, his hand wrapped around a glass of brown liquid. Apparently, Cain had progressed right to the hard stuff.

"Yeah," Cort said, and Cain nodded slowly.

"He tell you about, ah…" Cain cocked his head and shrugged.

"Yeah, a little. Long time ago, wasn't it?"

"It was another life," Cain said bleakly, giving Cort a sidelong glance.

Cort dug a bill out of his wallet and left it in the tip jar, then picked up the beers that the bartender set in front of him. "Well, you can rest assured, anything Cam told me isn't something I'd share."

Cain nodded again. "I figured. Cam is a good guy." Cain's voice was low and serious. "He's never brought anyone to one of these before," he said, raising his glass to encompass the patio and the low murmur of cultured conversation. "Not sure whether to be glad for him or sad for you."

Cort chuckled. "I would've thought this stuff would be easier if you were born into it."

"Hmm. You thought wrong," Cain responded. He turned to look at the crowd and Lucy headed in their direc-tion, practically dragging a pretty girl about Cain's age. He sighed and tossed back the remainder of his drink. "I just remembered something I need to do."

"I doubt she'll ask, but I'll say I haven't seen you," Cort promised.

Cain smiled. "I owe you one."

Cort made his way through the crowd back to Cam, his shoulders tense in a way he hadn't expected. He'd blended seamlessly with the crowd last Friday night, but here, as Cam's *boyfriend*, everything was different. He hadn't been putting on a facade, and kept forgetting he wasn't here to mingle.

He wound his way through the crowd and saw Lydia was talking to the cool, elegant blonde Cam had identified as Mary-Alice McMann, while Cam stood nearby, speaking to the man Cort remembered from the other night as Drew McMann, Cam's ex-boyfriend. Jealousy rippled through Cort's chest.

Drew certainly looked the part of the young, rich guy. He was wearing chinos which didn't appear to have a single wrinkle, a tight polo shirt showing off a fairly muscular chest, and canvas boat shoes. *Too bad he's an asshole.*

Cort approached them from the side, and neither one seemed to notice him, so he hung back for a moment, watching them. Drew was speaking in a low voice, his hand slashing through the air as he made a point. Cam's arms were crossed over his chest, his cheeks flushed either with anger or embarrassment. Cort imagined himself landing a firm punch to the exact corner of Drew's jaw, and if the asshole was saying something nasty to Cam again, Cort would take great pleasure in it. He was confident he could take him down without a problem.

"But who *is* he, Cam? God, you don't know a thing about him, and you're already bringing him around to parties and introducing him to people! Don't be fooled. This isn't real. He's using you."

Cort felt a spurt of anger - both at Drew for being an

ass, and because the ass actually had a point. Cort had definitely planned to use Cam, *had* used him, in fact, but they were more than that.

"What's going on, gentlemen?" Cort asked, stepping forward and looking from one to the other.

Cam shook his head again. "Later," he murmured, his voice low.

Cort glanced down at him with one eyebrow raised, a silent code for *Can I hit him?*

Cam read him instantly, the way he had from their very first meeting, and some of the tension left his face. His lips even quirked up slightly. "Cort, you remember Drew from the other night?"

Cort took a slow sip of his beer and narrowed his eyes, implying Drew wasn't that memorable. Drew huffed.

"Oh, right. I remember that noise." Cort attempted to look innocent, but he was pretty sure the way he was glaring at Drew gave him away.

Cam's arm snaked beneath Cort's shirt to wrap around his waist, and Cort felt his temper cool just slightly.

"Is there a problem here?" Cort challenged Drew.

"You tell me," Drew said. "Does Cam even know who you are? Does he know why you're here?"

Cort's heart stuttered for a second, before he realized Drew must be - *had to be* - bluffing. Nobody knew why he was really here except Damon, not even Cam.

"I don't know what you're talking about," Cort said.

Drew sighed. "I didn't want to have to tell you this, Cam, because I don't want to see you hurt. I got all his information from Margaret as soon as I heard he was coming with you, and I ran a background check. He's—"

"Kendrick Cortland," Cam spat in a whisper to make it clear he was done with this conversation. "I know he works for the FBI. *And* I know why he's here."

Cort watched Drew's head jerk back slightly in shock which mirrored Cort's own. If Drew had done a *thorough* check, he might know of Cort's relationship to Damon, and he felt a moment of heart-stopping panic at the idea of Cam finding out this way. Cam was *his*. Cort never had anyone who was *his* besides his brother. Somehow this guy had burrowed under his skin in a very short time, and it was…

Terrifying.

"Wait," Drew said. "Do you know *everything* about him?"

Cam frowned, and his gaze flashed to Cort. *What have you been hiding?*

Lydia put a hand on Drew's arm. "I'm sorry to interrupt," she told Drew. "But Camden and Cort only just arrived, and I want to show them to their room so they can freshen up before dinner."

"I'll walk with you," Drew offered, angry eyes on Cort.

"Not necessary," Cam said. "We'll finish later."

He turned and smiled at Lydia, who led them away. The crowd of guests parted before her. Cort put a hand at the small of Cam's back as they followed, and prayed nobody else stopped them. His patience was at an end.

"Wasn't *that* a lovely introduction for your young man?" Lydia snorted as they passed through a sliding glass door and into the house. "Meeting the Shaws *and* the McManns, or at least one of them. Truly a trial by fire."

Cam made a humming noise. "They're not usually so bad."

Lydia snorted and looked over her shoulder. "Oh, yes they are. Mary-Alice was always a little high-strung, though she hasn't been quite the same since the crash, and then the divorce. Same could be said for Drew, I suppose." She sighed. "Emmett and Lucy were better when your mother was here, Camden. She was a civilizing influence on them.

But Emmett has always been a pompous prick, and Lucy lives in a fantasy world. I feel for poor Cain. There's potential there, but he needs to reach out and seize it. He's too frightened to anger his father or shatter his mother's dream world."

Cam said nothing.

"I'm not gossiping," she assured Cort with another backwards glance. "I'd say this to their faces."

Cort gave her a distracted half-smile, his thoughts still focused on Drew's almost-revelation. Every rational brain cell was screaming that he should explain things to Cam immediately or risk losing him, but something entirely *irrational* held him back. If he explained things now, would he lose Cam anyway?

Before he confessed everything to Cam, there were other, more important things he needed the man to know.

Lydia led them through a lavishly appointed living area and up the curving white staircase at the center of the house. "I put you two in the room all the way at the end of the east wing. It's the smallest room in the house," she apologized, "but it's also the one closest to the back stairs, and the—"

"Beach walk," Cam said with a soft smile. "I remember."

Lydia flashed him a grin. "Exactly." They strolled along the hallway and arrived at the room. She threw open the door, then stood back and gave the two of them a stern frown. "Now. I don't expect to see either of you again for the rest of the evening."

"You're sure?" Cam asked Lydia.

"Very, very sure. I want you to enjoy yourselves." She gave Cam a wink, and pressed a friendly hand to Cort's arm. "I expect someone's already brought your bags up. Go show your gentleman the beach and cove, Camden. Just stick to the beach path and don't go wandering the grounds unless you want to be attacked by rabid socialites."

Cam nodded and wandered into the room, while Cort turned to watch Lydia depart.

He hadn't imagined he could have so much in common with someone who owned an island, but this was turning out to be a week of revelations.

CHAPTER SIXTEEN

Cort walked into the room and shut the door behind him with no small amount of unease. Cam had heard enough from Drew to suspect Cort was still keeping secrets, and Cort expected an angry tirade the moment the door closed, complete with yelling and demands. Instead, he found Cam kneeling beside his suitcase, pulling out a pair of swim trunks and sandals.

Cort licked his lips. "Cam—"

"Let's go to the beach. Grab your suit," Cam said, dropping his shorts quickly. "And I've got some sunblock and stuff in my kit. I can already feel myself burning."

Cort frowned. "Yeah, fine. In a minute. First…"

"No. Now," Cam insisted, yanking on his trunks. "While there's still light." He wouldn't meet Cort's eyes, and Cort would be damned if he'd accept that.

He grabbed Cam around the waist and pushed him against one of the tall mahogany bedposts. He saw his own uncertainty reflected in Cam's stunning blue eyes, and it slayed him.

He needed to reassure Cam.

Hell, he needed to reassure himself.

"You calling all the shots today, badass?" he whispered, trailing his free hand over Cam's cheek and down his jaw to cup his neck.

Cam shivered and swallowed hard, but didn't reply.

"Listen to me first, for just a second. Out there, beyond the door, there are a million things happening, Cam. Things to test us. Things wanting to destroy us. Things that make the idea of us being together seem impossible," Cort said, staring into Cam's eyes. "But here, in this room? That shit is background noise. There's only you and me. Are you with me?"

Cort leaned closer, hand digging into Cam's hip, and opened his mouth over the spot on Cam's neck where his pulse beat a rapid tattoo. He sucked gently, not hard enough to leave a mark, though every instinct told him to.

"Okay," Cam said softly. "Okay."

Cort's eyes shut, and he leaned his forehead against Cam's shoulder for a second, as wild, heady relief swamped him.

"Okay," Cort repeated.

Then he lifted his head and laid claim to Cam's mouth.

Cort took full advantage of the height difference between them, towering over Cam and forcing his head back against the post. Cort's hands found Cam's hips, holding him in place, while Cort's tongue licked against the seam of his lips. Cam moaned, his lips parting slightly, and Cort accepted the invitation, delving his tongue inside to tangle alongside Cam's own with a measured thoroughness. He wanted Cam to remember this, no matter what happened between them later, wanted to ruin Cam for any other kisses.

Then Cam's arms came up to wrap around Cort's neck, pulling him them even more tightly together. The surprise of it, of knowing Cam was feeling even a fraction of what Cort felt, made Cort's heart lurch painfully.

Cam writhed against his hold, returning every bite and moan, measure for measure, until Cort knew he'd been claimed every bit as thoroughly as he had Cam.

He was Cam's.

Cam was his.

He smiled ruefully as he pulled back, pressing one more chaste kiss to Cam's forehead. The problem with acknowledging someone was *yours* was that you had to find a way to *keep* them.

"*Now* we go to the beach, badass," Cort said gently. He stepped away to find his own trunks, adjusting himself to somewhat conceal his burgeoning erection. He smiled slightly when Cam continued to lean against the bedpost in a daze.

Cort slipped the burner phone into his pocket, grabbed Cam's toiletry bag and a couple of towels, then held out his hand to Cam, who deliberately slid his palm against Cort's, twining their fingers together.

They stepped into the hall, and Cam locked the door behind them, pocketing the small key that had been left in the lock. He ushered Cort down a flight of stairs next to their room, and out through a side door. A hedgerow screened them from the view of the revelers still out on the patio as they cut across the side lawn and took a well-worn path over the rocky ledge and down a set of stone steps leading to the beach below.

The water was calm in this small cove, though they could hear the surf breaking on the rocks just beyond. The setting sun was sinking from the sky. Cort remembered reading somewhere this was the golden hour, and he truly understood it for the first time. The wet rocks and placid water seemed to burn with liquid fire, and even the air shimmered around them.

Cam still held on to his hand as they crossed the stony beach and ducked through a stone archway to a more secluded sandy stretch of seashore beyond.

"It's like an entirely separate world," Cort mused, leaning in and placing a gentle kiss on Cam's cheek. He couldn't hear any noise from the party, not a single airplane streaked across the sky. It felt as though they were completely cut off from everyone, and Cort took his first deep breath in hours.

"Mmm. I used to love it here," Cam said. He braced a hand against Cort's arm and closed his eyes, breathing in the saltwater scent that surrounded them. His brown hair was red-tinged in the sunlight, his skin was flushed and warm, and the sight of him made Cort's chest ache. "When I was a kid, I'd bring a book and come here to read, but I never ended up reading. I'd sit and watch the water and make wishes."

He could imagine that - Cam as a kid, needing to get away and find some peace. Cort had been much the same.

"What did you wish for?" he asked, his voice hoarse.

Cam shrugged. "All the usual things, I guess. To be successful - possibly as a superhero." He chuckled. "To have whatever guy I had a crush on fall madly in love with me." He grinned as he threw himself down on his butt in the sand, his eyes on the water, their towels and the case with the sunblock dropped haphazardly in a pile beside him.

Cort hesitated for a second, then threw himself down next to Cam. The sand was damp and chilly, and he fought the urge to squirm. The phone was a hard lump digging into his ass. "When I was a kid I wished for a family - a loud, boisterous family. And money. Lots of money."

Cam glanced at him and nodded. "Makes sense, I guess. We always want what we don't have."

"Cam, you know I don't give a shit about your money, right?" Cort blew out a breath. "Frankly, I think it would be easier if you didn't have any."

"What would?" Cam's eyes were wide and Cort looked away, rubbing his palms on the legs of his shorts.

"This. Us." He felt like an idiot. The words he wanted to use - *relationship, future, together* - were so incredibly silly. They'd known each other for *days*.

Cam also turned away to look at the water, but Cort could hear the change in his breathing – fast, short pants, as though he was doing something way more strenuous than sitting watching the surf. He could practically hear Cam's mind whirring, too.

"Wanna play a game?" Cort asked.

Cam huffed out a laugh. "Why not? More 'Never Have I Ever'?" He darted a quick glance at Cort. "Be careful, though. The more time I spend with you, the shorter the list of things I've never done seems to get."

Cort chuckled. "No Jameson today, anyway. Let's stick to the classic Truth or Dare."

Cam was silent for a moment, rubbing his lips together in a way that was totally distracting. Then he nodded. "Alright. I'll take the dare."

Cort laughed again. "I thought you were supposed to hear the question first, badass! But whatever. I can work with this. I dare you to go back to the party and kiss this Arcadia person I keep hearing about."

Cam gave him a look of such utter disdain, Cort laughed out loud. "So that's a no?"

"That's a *hell* no."

"So, does that mean you now have to answer the question?" Cort wondered, grinning. "How do our games get so ass-backwards?"

"Now *that* is a good question," Cam sighed, shaking his head. "Fine. What do you want to know?"

"If you could have anything right now, what would it be?"

Cam seemed startled. "Wow. You're diving right in with the tough ones, huh?"

"Well, I don't think we've really gone easy on each other this week, have we? It's been high-stakes, from the very beginning." Cort's tone was light, but he knew the words he spoke were true.

"High-stakes, maybe," Cam agreed. "But in some ways, it's still been... easy." He frowned, and Cort understood why. It was *scary* how easy this was, and part of him couldn't help wondering when the other shoe would drop.

Cam snagged a folded towel from the pile and placed it behind him as a pillow. He lay back with his hands folded on his stomach, staring up at the blue sky for a minute, giving careful consideration to Cort's question.

"Probably to be someone who wasn't me? Someone who wasn't a Seaver, I mean. I love my family, but…" He rolled on his side to face Cort and shrugged. "You probably figured money would solve all your problems. Sometimes I wish I could get rid of mine."

Cort nodded. "You know, this time a week ago, I wouldn't have believed it. Not about you, or anyone. I get it now. Sometimes money causes more problems than it solves. But Cam, I can't begin to describe to you what it's like growing up without any. How many people think you're a lower life form because you can't afford name-brand what-ever, or assume the reason you're poor is because you're lazy or weak or stupid. It's hard to fight back against that, when adults *and* their kids treat you that way. Rich kid doesn't get the question, teacher explains again. Poor kid doesn't get it, it's because he's slacking. Stupid stuff on its own, but it's like water torture, picking away at you."

"You grew up mostly in Johnsville, right?" Cam sounded hesitant, as if knowing Cort would freak if he began asking more questions.

Cort rubbed a hand over his face. He didn't want to hide from Cam anymore. "Is this my question?" he teased.

Cam flopped back down and put his forearm up to shade his eyes from the light as he looked at Cort. "Yeah."

Cort didn't hesitate. "Yep. In the not-so-nice part. It's where my last and longest foster family, the Dempseys, lived. It was a one-story house with two bedrooms, so Damon and I shared."

"Damon, your brother?" Cam ventured.

"Damon Fitzpatrick, my brother," Cort confirmed, holding his breath as he waited for Cam to recognize the name, to ask more questions.

But Cam only nodded and looked back up at the sky. "Your turn."

"Truth or Dare?" Cort asked.

Cam rolled his eyes. "I'm over the dares. Ask the question."

Cort's mind churned. He wanted to know *everything*. He wanted to know more about Cam's family, about his plans for the future, about his feelings for Cort, whatever those might be. A voice in the back of his mind reminded him he should find out more about Sebastian, for Damon's sake, but he rejected that almost immediately.

"What scares you most?" he asked, instead. "Besides flying."

Cam pursed his lips, looking thoughtful, and Cort felt his heart squeeze almost painfully. He loved this about Cam

- the way he made sure things were true before he said them, like he took Cort's thoughts seriously and wanted to give him an honest answer.

"Drew says I get scared of emotions. Since the crash. I run from things when they get real."

Cort's lingering annoyance at Drew flared to life. "That's what *Drew* thinks. What do *you* think?"

Cam shrugged. "I don't know. He's right, because I've thrown myself into work. I stopped doing things I used to want to do."

"You've been grieving," Cort pointed out. "And you've taken on a pretty huge responsibility at Seaver Tech."

"Yeah. I also ended things between Drew and me pretty easily, though, and I haven't dated anyone seriously since him."

"Well, Drew's kind of a douchebag, so I don't know if it was fear so much as good judgment," Cort drawled.

Cam laughed, and the sunlight played over the defined muscles of his abs, the freckles on the tops of his shoulders. Christ, the man was gorgeous. Cort had to look away again, pretending the water was fascinating.

"Fair point," Cam allowed. "But, should I have tried harder? Was I running away because things got real?"

"Did you love him?" Cort's chest was tight as he asked the question, but Cam's answer was immediate and unequivocal.

"No. Never. Not like that. He was a friend. Another brother, almost. But I wonder if maybe I sensed *he* loved *me*. Maybe it scared me subconsciously."

"He didn't."

Cam turned to look at him in surprise. "How do you know? I mean, you've seen him at his worst. He's not always a jerk."

"Nah." Cort shook his head firmly, completely confident. "He didn't love you. Not really. Not the all-in kind of love."

"And you know this how?" Cam's voice was amused.

"Because if he had, he wouldn't have *let* you run." He felt Cam's eyes on his face and he took a deep breath before turning to meet them. Their gazes locked and the words were pulled from his belly. "*I* wouldn't let you run."

Cam's nostrils flared, eyes wide, as parsed Cort's words. He shook his head slowly. "I don't want you to, either. I'm trying not to."

"You've been thinking about it?" Cort clenched his hands into fists because he wanted to reach for Cam, right then and there, crush him against his chest, hold him in place.

Cam swallowed and glanced down. "I have some trust issues, I guess. Comes with the name. And then the thing with Sebastian..." He glanced up at Cort. "Anyway, I'm trying. I said I'd give you a second chance, and I am, but it's a lot," he whispered. "And I know you still have secrets. What's the phone about, Cort? What's this investigation about, if it's not *work*? Does that mean it's personal? Because it seems really personal. I know it's not all classified FBI bullshit, either." His voice took on a warning edge, cautioning Cort not to play that card again. "For one thing, the FBI has plenty of ways onto this island which don't involve *me*."

Cort huffed out a breath, opened his mouth to say *something*, but Cam cut him off.

"I want to know. I do. But tell me not because I'm asking, or giving you an ultimatum. I need you to tell me because *you* want to, *when* you want to. Does that make sense?"

It made a scary amount of sense. He wanted Cort to show him the same trust Cam had been showing since their very first meeting. But the truth about Damon, what they'd learned about the plane crash - weren't entirely Cort's secrets to share.

He ran a hand over his jaw, feeling the rough stubble against his palm, and mentally cursed his brother. Where the hell was Damon? Why hadn't he made contact? The familiar anger was creeping back. Damon had disappeared from his life a *year* ago, and now Cort's loyalty to his brother was fucking things up with Cam.

Cort *himself* was fucking things up with Cam.

He exhaled. "Cam," he began. But once again, Cam stopped him from speaking.

"It can wait, is what I'm trying to tell you. I—" Cam sucked in a breath. "I'm going to *trust you* to tell me when you can. I won't wait forever, not even for very long. But a little longer, perhaps long enough. Okay?" Cam's eyes were huge as they burned up at Cort.

"Just like that?" Cort whispered.

"Ah…" Cam chuckled slightly. "No. There's no *just like that* about this. It's really, really hard for me. But I think you're worth it. *This – us,* is worth it."

Cort was suddenly overwhelmed by emotion. God, the strength in this man, *his man,* was humbling. It brought Cort to his knees.

It came to him like a burst of sunlight off the water. He needed to *show* Cam, to demonstrate in some small way how much he *did* trust him, and how Cam was worth *everything* to him, too.

Cort scrambled to his feet and held out a hand for Cam. "Come on."

Cam looked from Cort to the water and back again. "But we haven't even gone in the water yet."

"We can do it later. Come on." Cort hefted Cam to his feet, then dipped down to grab the toiletry bag and towels.

"Is everything okay?" Cam demanded, as Cort practically pulled him up the steps and along the path to the house. "Seriously, Cort, slow down and talk to me here. What's the hurry?"

Cort spun Cam around when they reached the house and pushed him up against the cool surface of the building, caging him in with his body.

"The hurry is… I want to fuck you right now, and I want to get you up to our room as quickly as possible. That okay with you?"

Cam's eyes widened and his gaze flicked to Cort's mouth.

Oh, the temptation! But Cort knew if he started kissing Cam now, in five minutes they'd be fucking against the house in front of God and everyone. And honest to God, even *that* wouldn't have deterred him if they had lube and a condom handy.

"Yeah," Cam breathed. "That's absolutely fine with me."

Cort smiled, even though he was pretty sure it was more like a grimace. His cock was pressing uncomfortably against the fabric of his shorts in a way that was quickly becoming unbearable. "Get your butt upstairs, then," he said, and when Cam turned to do just that, he couldn't resist swatting the man right on his perfect ass.

He sprinted up the stairs after Cam, following the sound of his soft laughter.

Cam unlocked their room and threw open the door, tossing the key onto a small dresser, then turned to watch Cort.

"Now what?" he demanded breathlessly.

Cort carefully closed the door, locked it behind him, then stalked towards Cam, throwing the towels and bag to the floor. He backed Cam against the tall post at the foot of the bed again and wrapped his hands around Cam's waist. "Now, I'm going to put my mouth on you."

Cam sucked in a breath and lifted his hands to reach around Cort's neck while Cort devoured his mouth. He loved the way Cam felt against him - smaller, slighter, but with a lean strength and force of will that shone through in the way he lifted himself onto his toes to kiss Cort back more fully. Cort shifted his hips, pushing his hardness against Cam's stomach, and felt him shiver with excitement.

Cort grazed his mouth lower, hitting the spot between Cam's neck and shoulder that he knew drove the man crazy. He licked and sucked right there, just over the faint mark remaining from what they'd done earlier, feeling something enormous bubbling up through his chest at the sight. Cam threw back his head and moaned, and Cort felt his dick twitching in his trunks. Like Pavlov's dog, he'd already been conditioned to respond to that sound, and he loved it.

One of Cort's hands roamed down to palm Cam through his shorts. Cam was already hard, and responded to the stroke with a needy gasp which made Cort sink to his knees and strip Cam's shorts down lightning-fast. Then Cam was in his mouth, the salty taste of him on Cort's tongue.

It was like last week but *better*, because he *knew* Cam now, and knew he'd do everything possible to make sure they had tonight, tomorrow, and all the nights after that.

Cam's hands were threading through the long strands of Cort's hair, his fingertips strong on Cort's head, and Cort loved that, too.

Tonight wasn't about asserting his dominance. He had achieved that earlier, and it had been awesome. Cort loved knowing Cam didn't submit because he was weak, but because he craved Cort's control and was strong enough to yield to that want. Now he wanted to show Cam something different.

He gave one last enthusiastic pull, then broke off, ignoring Cam's whimper.

"Shhh. I don't want you to come like this," Cort said against Cam's ear. "I want something else, baby. Now be a good boy and stay right here while I get what we need from my bag, and then you're going to give it to me."

It hadn't been a question, but Cam nodded anyway, panting. He wrapped his hands around the post behind him obediently. "If you need condoms and lube, they're in the kit by the door," he offered, as Cort went to kneel by his suitcase.

Cort glanced up at him in surprise and switched directions, grabbing the kit off the floor. "You brought condoms and lube to the beach?"

Cam shrugged. "I thought they might be necessary." He frowned. "Wait, is that why you dragged me up here?"

"Maybe." Cort gave him a smile as he threw the kit on the bed. "But that's okay. Sex on sand is one of those things that sounds better than it really is." He shuddered.

Cam huffed in frustration. "I wouldn't have cared."

Cort's smile became a full-on grin. He shucked his trunks, throwing the stupid burner phone on the nightstand, and grabbed Cam's hand pulling him around to the side of the bed. "But you won't be the one on the bottom this time." He threw himself down to lie on his back in the center of the bed.

Cam blinked, and then blinked again. "What?"

Cort unzipped the bag and found the lube and condoms right on top. *Bonus points to Cam for efficiency.* He threw the bag on the floor and pressed the supplies into Cam's hand.

"I thought maybe this time you'd want to..." He tilted his head to the side and, as always, Cam understood him without words.

His eyes flew wide. "Me? You want *me* to..."

Cort nodded. "Yeah. Oh, yeah. But only if you want to."

"No! I do! I mean, most guys assume I don't. But I didn't think you… I mean, we never really discussed it, but I got the impression you didn't like to bottom?" Cam was alternately looking down at the lube in his hand as though it held the secrets of the universe, and staring at Cort's face like he was trying to read Cort's mind and make sure he was *really* okay with this. It was adorable.

"I must admit, I haven't had the best experience with it," Cort admitted, stacking his hands beneath his head on the bed. "I'm not sure I can do it without being bossy, and honestly? I wasn't sure whether you'd actually want me this way."

"But then, why?" Cam put his knee on the mattress and leaned over Cort, running one hand up from Cort's stomach to his chest. "You don't have to."

Cort put his own hand over Cam's where it rested against his heart. "I *want* to," he said.

Cam seemed to receive the message, because his eyes turned liquid blue. He knelt beside Cort and ran his fingertips across Cort's skin. Cort shivered. He reached up a hand to touch Cam's spiky brown hair and then traced his fingertips around the shell of Cam's ear.

"Come here and kiss me," Cort said. Not a command or a demand, but an invitation, one Cam eagerly accepted. He braced his hands on either side of Cort's chest and leaned down until their lips met. The same as every time he'd kissed Cam, Cort felt his core incinerate, with hot tongues of flame running up and down his back. But unlike the crazy, hurried wildfire that had engulfed them the previous week, this burn was slower- a controlled fire, heating, melting, forging them into something different, something brand new. He couldn't stop looking at Cam, mapping the gorgeous freckles on his skin, the contours of his cheeks.

Cam lifted his knee to straddle Cort's waist and sat back so he could run his hands along Cort's skin - through the blond hair of his chest, down over his abs, and back - in increasingly long sweeps. On one pass, Cam let his hand roam up over Cort's neck to tangle into his long, golden-brown hair. He braced the other hand against Cort's chest, and their gazes collided.

"Have I ever told you I love your eyes?" Cam demanded.

Cort shook his head, unable to form words.

"I do," Cam whispered, lowering his head to bite at Cort's stubbled chin.

Cort swallowed hard. He'd been seriously trying hard to keep his hands out of this, to give Cam the unbridled access and control Cam had given to him, but he had to abandon the effort. He lifted his hands to frame Cam's face and brought him in for a fierce kiss.

Cam broke away a second later, pressing a kiss to the same spot he'd bitten on Cort's chin. "You're sure?" he whispered.

There were few things Cort had been *more* sure of in his life. "Yeah, baby. I'm positive."

Cam nodded, his eyes serious, suddenly nervous. "I *do* want this, Cam," Cort said again, more forcefully. "With you."

Cort watched the flush climb up Cam's face. *So beautiful.*

Cam pushed up on his hands and crawled backwards down Cort's body, dropping tiny kisses over his chest as he went. "I love your chest. I love the way you're so much bigger than I am."

He moved lower, and his mouth traced the Cort's hipbone. Cort exhaled in a shaky moan. "I love the sounds you make, too," Cam whispered. "Like you really want me."

"I do," Cort responded, then he arched his back as

Cam's mouth moved lower again, his warm tongue licking up Cort's shaft. "God, you make me so hard. All I have to do is see you, watch you smile."

It was too much. The heat of Cam's mouth and the needy sounds Cam made as he moved above him, drove Cort mad in a matter of moments. He dimly heard the snap of the lube container, then Cam's fingers were stroking around his opening, probing gently, pushing inside him. The sensation was so much more intense than he remembered from the few times he'd tried this half a lifetime ago, but that made sense, didn't it? After all, Cam wasn't like anyone Cort had ever known before.

Cam's fingers went away, and Cort was dimly aware of him opening a condom, adding more lube, preparing himself. Cort instinctively tensed when Cam's guided his cock to Cort's entrance, but he forced himself to relax. He welcomed the brief burn, the pressure, because he wanted Cam inside him more than he'd known he ever could. His moan mingled with Cam's as he pushed himself home, and he welcomed that, too. That signs they were together in this.

And then Cam started to move, and Cort cried out. "Oh! Christ, Cam! More. Again!"

Cam's hips moved faster, Cort gripped the bedspread in both hands, anchoring himself against Cam's thrusts and the spiral of pleasure threatening to overload his mind. He'd had sex, he knew what pleasure felt like. It had never been like this. He felt special and cherished, things he'd never known to want before.

Cam hitched out a breath and said, "Cort? Baby, I can't hold on," his voice wrecked with passion. Cort brought his hands up to Cam's cheeks, and pulled him down for a wet, thorough kiss. "Then come for me. Come for me, Cam."

Cam thrust hard one last time, then his hips froze, his

face contorted in pleasure. Cort nearly lost it right there. "You're so beautiful," Cort told him, still cradling Cam's gorgeous face in his big hands. Cam, still breathless, leaned down to kiss him once, pressing his lips into Cort's as though imprinting himself there, then he pulled back abruptly. A second later, he was swallowing Cort all the way down to the root. Cort was so primed, it was pretty much all he could take. The suction of that gorgeous mouth, the firm pressure of those lips around his dick, and Cort was coming, coming, coming down Cam's throat.

Cam dealt with the condom, then climbed back up Cort's body and stretched himself out against Cort's side.

"That was amazing," Cam offered, as though he wondered whether Cort would agree.

Cort wrapped his arms around Cam, who tucked his head under Cort's jaw, and told him the absolute truth. "It was perfect. *You* are perfect."

They lay without moving or speaking for long minutes while their breathing evened. The sun cast progressively longer orange swathes across the bed, the fan on the ceiling slowly rotated, and Cam sank more deeply against Cort, his eyelashes fluttering against Cort's chest as he blinked.

"We should really clean up," Cam said without moving. Cort chuckled.

"In a minute, baby. We've plenty of time."

Cort was aware this was the calm before the storm - the silent phone on the nightstand was a constant presence in the back of his mind. He knew he and Cam had a lot they still needed to discuss, and *soon*, but he was hopeful in a way he hadn't felt in a long time. Maybe, never.

CHAPTER SEVENTEEN

Cam was supremely comfortable, laying on the warm sand in the sunshine down in the hidden cove on St. Brigitte. His eyes were closed, but he could hear the distant crash of waves on the shore and birds calling as they dove for their supper. Everything was perfectly peaceful, and in a moment or two, when he felt like opening his eyes again, he'd grab his book and towel, and head on up the path to see whether it was time for lunch.

His stomach growled. Okay, so maybe it was closer to *dinner*. Bas, Drew, and Amy hardly ever left him alone this long, always forcing him to play some stupid game Bas was a dead cert to win. His stomach rumbled insistently again and he sucked in a deep breath. His mom and dad were probably wondering where he'd…

Reality hit him like a tidal wave - first the slow shadow falling over his mind, an awareness in his hind-brain, warning him something was off in his thinking, and then, before he could brace himself, before he could move or protect himself, the full realization crashed over his head and sucked him under.

They were gone.

His father, with his keen intellect and take-no-prisoners confidence…

Amy McMann, with her razor-sharp tongue and kind smile…

His mother, with her soft eyes and quick wit…

No one would ever again wonder where on earth Cam had got to when it was time for dinner.

No one would remind him things would get better.

No one was waiting for him anymore.

He was utterly alone.

He was sobbing before he opened his eyes. Chest heaving, stomach cramping under the weight of his grief, he sat up and wrapped his arms around his knees. It was shattering, this pain – uncontrollable desolation so vast he couldn't contain it as it welled up from his lungs and sank down into his bones. He buried his face in his hands and let the tears roll down past his fingers.

When he felt a warm hand on his naked back, he stiffened in shock and looked up to find Cort, his eyes still halfslitted and glazed with sleep, shifting to sit behind him in the bed. Cam hadn't even realized where he was, hadn't remembered Cort was also there.

He wasn't alone after all.

He *had* someone after all.

Cort didn't say a word. He shifted one leg around Cam's back, and pulled Cam to lean against him. The scruff of Cort's beard was rough on Cam's shoulder as Cort pressed small kisses to his skin and ran his hand through Cam's hair.

Without thinking, Cam twisted to bury his face in Cort's chest as the sobs came faster and harder. How could one person have so much grief inside them? Had it been there all along? Right now, it was expanding like a living entity inside him, threatening to split Cam's skin, fragmenting him into a million pieces.

Cort didn't waver. His grip around Cam tightened, holding Cam's pieces together with the strength of his embrace, and he began rocking, almost imperceptibly at first, then faster, the motion comforting and sure.

"I've got you," he whispered. "Let it go, baby. I've got you."

And Cam took him at his word, allowing Cort's soft kisses to push comfort into his skin, trusting Cort to care for him.

When his tears finally slowed, hours or minutes later, Cam noticed the room was lighter than it had been, warmer, though perhaps it had more to do with the way Cort had wrapped him up completely, arms and legs and chest, all buffering him against the world.

He swallowed, not sure how to feel once his sanity returned somewhat. Should he be embarrassed? Should he move away? Last night with Cort had been incredible, but there had been no promises between them. And still, he couldn't summon the energy to respond at all.

Cort's lips moved against his hair, his hands stroked over Cam's arm. His eyes held affection, concern - a dozen different emotions Cam could read, clear as day, because all along they'd been doing that wordless communication thing, hadn't they? And Cam hadn't even noticed.

This giant, crazy, secretive, wonderful Viking, with his green eyes and his just-fucked hair, knew exactly what Cam was thinking. He always seemed to know.

Cort frowned as Cam stared at him silently. "Can I get you anything? Water, or—"

"I love you," Cam blurted, stunning himself. Stunning Cort, too, by the way he tensed around Cam, squeezing him tight before lessening his death grip somewhat.

"You—" Cort stumbled.

Cam pulled in a deep breath and moved his head from Cort's chest so he could look directly into his face. Cort didn't look horrified or concerned, or any of the other things Cam had worried he'd find there, just completely surprised and maybe a little unsure of how to respond.

Cam shook his head. "I didn't say it for you to say it back," he told Cort. "In fact, I definitely don't *want* you to repeat it to me. Not now. I just… I was thinking about my parents. Dreaming about them actually." Cam's voice broke and he cleared his throat. "I miss them." It was so stupidly obvious, but Cam didn't think he'd ever said it aloud before. He wasn't certain whether he'd even admitted it to *himself*, because admitting it would mean contemplating *everything* he'd lost and he still wasn't sure he was ready to do that.

Cam shook his head. "Believe it or not, I've talked more about them with you this week than to anyone else in the entire past year. Maybe it was wrong or disrespectful of their memories. It's just so hard."

"Yeah," Cort agreed ruefully. "Really damn hard. But maybe it's time to talk about those hard things."

"Maybe it is," Cam said. He paused for a moment, then continued, "I never doubted they loved me. And I know they knew how much I loved them too. But I just sort of wished I had the chance to hear it from them one last time, to tell them one last time, so… I wanted… *you* to… know."

"There's no right or wrong way to grieve and process," Cort said after a short while. "They'd be so proud of you. I know I am."

His hands sifted through the hair on Cam's head, and Cam fell into a pleasant kind of exhaustion, like he'd done hard labor.

"Cam?" Cort said a moment later. "I *want* you to tell me these things. I want you to know, you *can* talk to me."

He said the words solemnly, as though he was making a promise. Cam sat up, twisting around to look into Cort's serious green eyes.

"Okay," Cam responded. Cort seemed hesitant, an unusual look for him, which made Cam need to ask, "Are *you* okay?"

Cort nodded, and his hand reached up to stroke Cam's cheek. "You have so many heavy burdens and I want… I want you to give them to me. Not because you can't handle them - you've already shown you *can,* maybe better than me. But you shouldn't have to handle things alone. I want you to trust me with this, the same way you trust me with your body."

Cam blinked, but didn't interrupt.

"You've shown me so much trust already," Cort continued. "It's time I did the same for you."

Cort reached over and grabbed the small flip phone from the nightstand, placing it on his thigh where Cam could see it. His arms tightened around Cam, as if he was afraid Cam was going to escape, to run from him once he began talking. Cam tensed, his heart beating faster. How bad would this be?

"Damon Fitzpatrick is my foster brother," Cort said, and Cam frowned. He remembered feeling the faint niggle of familiarity when Cort had said that yesterday. Cam hadn't paid attention to it then, but this morning, he focused on it. Damon Fitzpatrick… Damon…

"The pilot who caused the crash?" Cam whispered, feeling his entire body grow cold.

Cort shook his head, his arms still holding Cam tight. "He *didn't* cause the crash, Cam."

"The NTSB said differently," Cam said stiffly. His breathing was ramping up, and suddenly Cort's comforting embrace felt restrictive. "What does this have to do with anything? With the case you're working on?"

"I'm not working on a case," Cort said softly. "You accused me of it yesterday, and you were right. I'm here because Damon is alive, and I need to help him."

Cam sat up, pushing Cort's arms aside. "Alive? Cort, it's not possible. There were no survivors."

"It's possible. I have photographic proof in my bag," he said. "But you can take my word for it. Damon survived somehow."

Disbelief warred with hope in Cam's chest. "Were there other….?" He couldn't bring himself to say the word *survivors*, but Cort understood.

He shook his head quickly. "I don't… I don't think so. Nothing identifying Damon was ever recovered," he reminded Cam. Whereas Cam's parents' remains had been found at the crash site.

Cam ran a hand through his hair. "He's alive? And he wants you to help him do *what*?"

Cort winced, then his jaw hardened. "I'm not a hundred percent sure, but the things they say he did - getting drunk before a flight, failing to do the pre-checks, that's not Damon. It's not the kind of man he was… *is*." He laid a hand on Cam's thigh, holding him in place, while he explained the clues Damon had been sending him, the facial recognition picture he'd got from the security camera which had led him to St. Brigitte, the way things had gone down with his superiors, and the burner phone he'd got through the mail on the morning they left.

The words flowed into Cam's brain, but he could hardly make sense of them. His whole body was being pricked by pins and needles, like a numb limb coming back to life. Cort had lied, outright and by omission, to Cam, to his FBI teammates, to everyone.

"I still don't understand," Cam whispered when Cort finally fell silent. "He sent you pictures of Sebastian and me, things about Seaver Tech. Why?"

Cort hesitated. "I'm not sure."

"Oh, bullshit," Cam sneered, pushing up off the bed. The phone clattered to the floor, but Cam left it there and reached for his clothes, which still lay where he'd dropped them the previous night, before everything had changed. "You clearly suspect some conspiracy or you wouldn't be here."

"I don't have any proof," he hedged.

"I haven't heard proof for *any* of this," Cam retorted. "So why stop now?"

"Because I don't want to hurt you."

"Hurt me?" Cam echoed. "How could you possibly hurt me more than you already have?"

Cort swallowed. "Damon didn't cause the crash, so, who did? Who benefited most from your parents' deaths, Cam?"

Cam frowned. "Nobody."

"Is that really true?" Cort stood and grabbed Cam by the upper arms, forcing him to look at Cort, forcing him to listen. "Your brother inherited the company. You told me about it the first night we met, remember? A very wealthy, powerful company."

Cam's eyes widened as he finally understood. "And you think Bas…" His eyes hardened. "But why not *me?* I'm the president of the company, after all."

Something flickered in Cort's eyes. Cam barked out a laugh. "Oh, Jesus Christ. You actually *did* think I might have had something to do with my parents' deaths!"

Cort shook his head emphatically. "I thought so at first but after the first night we talked, I knew better. I knew you couldn't have."

"How did you know?" Cam demanded. "How do you

know I didn't just *off* them so I could have more *money,* since money is obviously the only motivation anyone has for doing anything in your world?"

"Stop!" Cort said, shaking Cam slightly. "I just know better." He lifted one hand to cup Cam's chin. "I know it or I wouldn't be here now, I wouldn't be telling you all this."

Cam shook his head and huffed out a laugh. "But you still think it was Sebastian?" He broke away from Cort, paced away from the bed. "You're crazy."

"Sometimes you think you know people," Cort ventured, but Cam whirled to face him.

"Listen to yourself. The NTSB investigation concluded *your* brother was at fault, but I'm supposed to believe he *didn't* because you *know your brother better than that.* Meanwhile, you're trying to convince me that *my* brother is a murderer, because that helps to sell the story you've been telling yourself. But you *don't* know Sebastian. You've never even met him. So, what will you do if I tell you I know *my* brother, and I know it would be absolutely, positively against his nature to do anything like this?"

Cort hesitated, and Cam could see the pain and indecision in his eyes. He wanted to believe Cam, but if he did, it would mean he didn't believe Damon.

They were at an impasse. Cam had no idea what it meant for him and Cort. Had this all been part of some larger game? Cam's head hurt from crying, his entire body felt wrung out. He wanted space and peace.

"If you really believe Sebastian is involved in this? Why isn't the FBI here officially?" Cam demanded wearily. "Why isn't there an open investigation trying to prove his innocence?"

"How would that go, Cam?" Cort took a step toward him, then stopped, running both hands through his hair. "After the crash, Sebastian ran Damon's name down in the press so badly, he became a punchline. How could Damon possibly get a fair shot? You might like to believe the FBI investigations are fair and impartial, but I know better."

Cort leaned against the end of the bed and folded his arms across his chest, totally unconcerned by his nakedness. Despite everything, Cam fought not to react to the sight of him.

"If I tell the FBI he's alive, they *will* open an investigation, but with the intent to charge him with manslaughter if nothing else. Then it will be out of my hands, and out of his hands too."

"So you're waiting for him to call you? And then what?"

"I don't know," Cort said, his eyes burning into Cam's. "I'll talk to him and then... see."

See if he had enough information to investigate Sebastian, he meant.

Cam shook his head. *Oh, Cam. You are an idiot who will never, never learn.*

"You'd do the same," Cort said, almost defiantly. "If you had to save your brother—"

"I *did* do the same," Cam agreed. "That's how you got me to come here, in case you don't remember. And now, by bringing you here, you're telling me I've essentially fucked him over instead." Cort frowned, as though he hadn't considered this. "You used me. Again."

"No," Cort said, stepping forward, reaching for Cam. "It wasn't like that, Cam. I didn't expect this. *Us.*"

"Us," Cam echoed, stepping away, holding his hands up, warding Cort off.

He'd thought he was completely cried out, that his body couldn't spare any more tears, but the damn things were welling up behind his eyes anyway, and this time he'd be damned if Cort saw him break down.

"Cort, there is no *us*. I thought..." He shook his head,

willed his voice to stay strong. "I was stupid, again. So, that's on me, *again*. There won't be a third chance."

"Cam, take a minute. Think. You *know* better," Cort pleaded. "You *said* you wouldn't run. You said you'd trust me."

Cam hesitated. Was he running? Was that what this was?

From its spot on the floor, Cort's flip phone gave a loud chirp and clatter, and Cort's head swung toward it, then back to Cam, clearly torn.

Cam would make the decision easier for him. "You'll want to get that," he said dully. He took himself off to the bathroom and locked the door behind him.

The giant bathroom featured a large soaking tub along with a huge glass-fronted shower tiled in natural stone. Exactly what he needed - to scrub himself clean and forget this entire morning, this entire trip, every second in Kendrick Cortland's company.

He turned the water to scalding hot and shucked his boxers before stepping under the spray. His stomach roiled, his eyes burned, and as the stupid tears came, Cam let himself sink to the floor.

He had to call Sebastian and warn him. He had to fly home immediately - a thought he knew would have terrified him under any other circumstances, but for now made his chest ache more intensely.

Cam lay his forearms against his bent knees and allowed the water to wash over him. He felt a scream rise up inside him, and remembered Cort's pool trick -how invincible he'd felt in that moment and nearly all the moments he and Cort had spent together. It had only taken one week for Cort to burrow under his skin this completely, to make him feel important. He had a feeling it would take a lot longer for the memories to fade.

The first clue he wasn't alone came when a chilly breeze skittered across his wet skin. He lifted his head to see Cort step inside the shower and immediately squat down in front of him, heedless of the water running over them both.

"The door was locked," was all Cam could think to mutter.

"It'll take more than a locked door to keep me out, Cam," Cort admonished. He lifted a hand to Cam's face. "I told you I wouldn't let you run."

"It can't work," Cam said almost desperately. "It's always going to be me or Damon, you or Sebastian. We'll only end up hurting each other. Or hurting ourselves."

Cort shook his head. "Trust me," he demanded, bringing his lips closer to Cam's.

Cam lifted his head, pressed his mouth desperately to Cort's, wishing and wanting, but this time he wasn't sure he had any more trust to give.

CHAPTER EIGHTEEN

"When Damon texted, he said he wanted to meet in the hangar at noon," Cort said, pulling a t-shirt over his head. The soft gray material slid down his body, clinging to his broad shoulders and the patches of skin still damp from their shower. "In about an hour."

Cam, who hadn't been able to stop himself from watching the show, turned his focus to buttoning his own shorts as Cort slid both his phones into his pockets and turned around. He looked down at the dresser, which held an assortment of things he'd removed from his own pockets yesterday - door key, wallet, cell… Cort's lucky quarter. Cam grabbed the coin and held it tightly in his palm before slipping it into his front pocket.

"You're going to meet him," Cam said neutrally. It wasn't a question. From what Cort had revealed, everything he'd had done up to this point was to help his brother, so despite Cam's hurt, this was not a surprise. It was simply the sort of person Cort was. He had a loyalty which had been embedded in him since childhood.

"*We* are," Cort said. He walked across the room and

wrapped his arms around Cam from behind, leaning down to rest his chin on Cam's shoulder. His wet hair tickled Cam's neck as their eyes met squarely in the mirror. "You and me, Cam. From here on out."

It sounded too good to be true, so it probably was, though Cam figured Cort *wanted* to believe it. He realized intention and reality often operated on two separate planes.

Still, he gave Cort's reflection a halfhearted smile. "Okay." He grabbed his wallet and put it in his back pocket.

Cort shook his head and smiled. "You don't believe it, but you'll see."

Cam nodded. They'd see alright.

A knock at the door had them both turning simultaneously.

"I thought he said at the hangar?" Cam asked.

"That's what the text said." Cort moved toward the door, taking up a defensive position to one side. With his hand, he motioned Cam to move back, out of sight of the door.

Cam rolled his eyes. What the hell did Cort think was going to happen here? He shook his head firmly. Cort had never been the boss of him, and certainly wasn't now.

Cort gestured again, his green eyes kindling with warning, sending a thrill up Cam's spine.

With a sigh, Cam walked into the bathroom. From here, he could only see Cort in profile as he took a deep breath then cracked the door open an inch. His head went back in surprise at whoever was out there. "What the hell are you doing here?" he demanded.

"I could ask you the same question," a deep voice replied, and Cam's eyes widened as he recognized it. "Bas?" he said, stepping back into the room.

Cort opened the door wider, giving Cam a clear view of

Sebastian and Drew standing in the hallway, while still blocking their entry with his arm.

"Little brother," Bas said, and Cam saw something like relief in his eyes. He was showered, dressed in impeccably clean trousers and a fitted polo, and his eyes had lost their haunted look. It was an amazing - and confusing - transformation.

"You're fine, Cammy?" Drew demanded. He looked from Cort to Cam and back again, his eyes narrowing on Cort's face.

"Yes, yeah. Of course," Cam said, just as Bas told Cort, "I've seen your face before."

Cort shook his head and his voice had a steely edge. "We haven't met. Yet."

Bas put his hand on Cort's forearm and took a step forward, a demand for Cort to move aside. Cort didn't budge.

"Cam," Drew said.

Cam rolled his eyes. "Cort, let them in."

Cort's jaw hardened as he glanced back at Cam, but he finally relented, allowing both men to step inside. Cort moved along with them, staying between Bas and Cam, almost protectively. Cam rolled his eyes again. *Like he had anything to fear from Bas or Drew.*

"What *are* you two doing here?" Cam asked Bas, hands on his hips as he repeated Cort's question. "You didn't tell me you were coming when I stopped by the other day. And my God, you look so much... better, Bas!"

Bas glanced from Cort to Cam, obviously not liking Cort's position. "I changed my plans yesterday. I arrived earlier this morning. I need to speak to you. *Alone,*" he added, when Cort made no effort to move.

"I told you he thinks he's dating this guy," Drew murmured to Bas, clearly disapproving.

"We *are* dating," Cort confirmed. He folded his arms over his chest and glared at Drew before glancing back at Cam. *Do you want me to leave?* Cam's stomach somersaulted. His choice, and Cort would let him do this alone if he wanted to.

He was tempted for a minute, but he stared into Cort's steady eyes, which seemed to be begging, *Trust me, Cam.*

Man, he was a sucker for those eyes.

Cam stepped forward and put his arm around Cort's waist. "This is Cort," Cam told his brother. He glanced pointedly at Drew. "He's staying."

Both men looked like they would balk, but Cam held firm and Sebastian finally blew out a breath and ran a hand through his short brown hair.

"Alright," he allowed, still giving Cort side-eye. "Listen, I know we have a lot to talk about, Cam, and I have a lot to explain, but first we *need* to get in touch with Uncle Shaw. We haven't been able to find him, and he's not answering my calls or texts. The service here is abysmal, so I don't know if he's even received them. Lucy hasn't seen him or Jack *or* Cain for hours." Bas gripped the back of his neck as he always did when he was frustrated.

"I don't know how we can help. We haven't seen any of them since yesterday," Cam said, shaking his head. "We haven't been downstairs at all yet today."

Sebastian raised an eyebrow at the rumpled bed, and then back at Cort and Cam. Drew made a sound of disgust.

Cam met Bas's glance with a raised eyebrow of his own, daring either of them to comment. "What's this about, Bas?"

"I need to talk to you about some… *things* pertaining to the crash," Bas said cryptically. "Things I couldn't discuss over the phone."

He glanced at Cort again, as though once again hoping

Cam would ask him to leave. Beneath Cam's hand, the muscles of Cort's spine tensed immediately as though he was worried about the same thing.

Cam shook his head. He was committed to this now, and he wanted Cort to hear everything.

Bas huffed out a breath, clearly annoyed that Cam wouldn't yield. "It wasn't an accident, Cam," he said baldly. "And I think I know how to prove it."

For one second, Cam wondered if Cort could be right - if Sebastian could have had anything to do with the crash, as ridiculous as that would have been. A quick glance at Bas's face proved otherwise. He was tense, grief-stricken, and *angry*.

"Sebastian," Cam began, wanting to be sure Bas knew Cort's identity before he revealed anything incriminating, but Cort spoke up instead.

"Cam didn't introduce me fully," he said. "I'm Agent Kendrick Cortland. I work for the FBI, for now anyway. And my brother is Damon Fitzpatrick."

Cam waited for Sebastian to explode, recalling his angry tirades about Damon Fitzgerald in the past, but Sebastian did nothing more than nod, though his face was still pinched with displeasure. "Drew told me who you are. And I would have recognized you anyway from my investigation of Damon." His eyes narrowed. "What the hell are you doing with my brother?"

Cort ignored the second half of the question. "I doubt that's how you recognize me. Not many people know there's a connection between Damon and me. We're not blood relatives, and the records of my time in foster care are sealed."

Bas waved a dismissive hand and paced toward the wall. "Likely not many people studied Damon Fitzpatrick's life as carefully as I did."

Drew snorted. "Or investigated *you* as carefully as *I* did after you came to Seaver Tech last Monday."

Cort grew even tenser, so Cam lifted his shirt slightly, sliding his thumb against Cort's skin in a soothing motion.

"You had a lot to say about Damon a year ago," Cort accused Sebastian. "Encouraging rabid reporters to dig up information on his little sister, for Christ's sake."

Bas turned to lean against the wall, folding his arms over his chest and mimicking Cort's posture. "It was an unfortunate consequence."

Anger rolled off Cort in waves, and Cam stepped forward protectively. "Could you sound a little less like a pompous prick?" he asked his brother.

Bas ran his tongue over his teeth, contemplating Cam and Cort with narrowed eyes. "No," he said finally. "I can't. Can you explain what you're doing here with Damon Fitzpatrick's brother?" He glanced pointedly at the bed again.

Drew piped up. "We, uh, don't need specifics."

Cam's cheeks heated. "None of your business. *Either* of you. Now, explain what finally got you to abandon your living room couch and your obsessive home-movie viewing."

Bas looked from Cam to Drew, then rubbed his palm over his forehead. "I think Damon Fitzpatrick might have been framed for the crash."

Cam and Cort exchanged wide-eyed looks.

"Explain," Cort said.

"As you said, I've spent a long time recently looking at old movies and TV show clips about the crash. *Wallowing in grief*, which Cam and Drew both took me to task for." He threw Drew a small smile, before turning serious again. "I actually found something rather strange. Right after the investigation, a man did a TV interview, saying he was the witness who was drinking with Damon before the crash."

"John P.," Cort said, nodding. "I remember. I tried to follow up with him."

"But he'd disappeared?" Bas guessed. "Yeah, same dead end here. I even, ah, tried to see whether the NTSB had additional information on him as part of their investigation."

"That's why you hacked them?" Cam asked, glaring at his brother.

Sebastian glanced from Cam to Cort to Drew, a small smile on his lips. "Hacked is an ugly word. I think Drew would prefer I say I *requested information through unofficial channels*."

Cort rolled his eyes, relaxing his posture slightly. "At this point, I don't give a shit if you lit the place on fire, Seaver. What did you find?"

"It's more what I *didn't* find," Bas said sourly. He looked from Drew to Cam. "All the information on the witness was redacted from the file."

"Redacted?" Cam echoed. "How? Why?"

Bas nodded. "Exactly the questions I wanted answered. So, I went back into the system and left a trail so clear, the world's most inept investigator could have followed it, but not a single person contacted me to investigate." He shook his head in disgust and looked at Cort. "I don't know what the hell they give you badges for."

Cort snorted, then chuckled, then laughed out loud, pressing a hand to his stomach.

"What's funny?" Cam asked, elbowing him. To Bas, he said, "Cort *did* investigate it. Drew was the one who squelched it." He pointed a finger in Drew's direction.

"Nope. He's right." Cort shook his head and looked at Cam. "*They* never had any real intention of pursuing it. It was quashed from above even before Seaver Tech's legal team got involved." He gave Cam an apologetic shrug and Cam rolled his eyes.

In the grand scheme of Cort's lies, this one hardly registered, but he still said in a warning tone, "I swear to God, Cort…"

Cort drew Cam closer and fitted him tightly to his side. "Never again, I promise," he vowed.

Sebastian looked back and forth between them and scowled. "Whatever touching thing you two are discussing, table it. The point is, the witness disappeared off the face of the earth, but the only reason I was looking into him in the first place, was because he reminded me of someone else, someone whose picture I saw in the footage from mom and dad's funeral."

Cam blinked. "John P. was at the funeral?"

Sebastian shook his head and reached into his pocket to pull out his phone. "Not exactly." He tapped a few keys and then stepped forward, showing Cam and Cort his screen.

On the right, was a still-shot from a TV interview showing a tall, redheaded, bearded man with a distinctive mole beside his blue eyes. On the left, was a shot of Jack Peabody, standing at Emmett Shaw's shoulder as they exited Cam's parents' funeral. His hair was black in the picture, just as it had been yesterday, but beside his eye was an identical mole.

Jesus Christ. The witness was Uncle Shaw's assistant!

Cort grabbed the phone, bringing it closer to his face. "Oh my God," he breathed. He turned to Cam excitedly. "Do you recognize this guy? This is why Damon wanted me here. He must have recognized him and figured out the same thing."

"Damon?" Drew stepped forward and grabbed Sebastian's phone back. "Fitzpatrick? The pilot?" He looked from Cam to Cort and back again. "He's dead."

Cort shook his head. He hesitated, then explained. "He's

alive, and here on the island," he told them. "He's probably trying to accomplish the same thing you are."

Sebastian's eyes widened. "Tell us what you know."

Cam felt Cort bristle at Bas's imperious tone. He folded his arms over his chest again. "It's not my information to tell."

Cam sighed and dug his finger into Cort's side. "Cort."

Cort gave him a sidelong glance. *Can I trust him?*

Cam nodded.

Cort blew out a breath letting his arms fall to his sides. "Damon contacted me for the first time about six months ago. Nothing concrete or direct - I don't know why - but he began sending me little clues. Things from our childhood only he would know. Along with information about you." He nodded at Sebastian.

Sebastian frowned. "Me?"

"And Cam," Cort confirmed. "I knew from the beginning Damon couldn't have been responsible for the crash. He would never have flown drunk, he would never have skipped his pre-check. If there was an engine problem, he would have found it."

Sebastian nodded slowly. "I checked out his record. It's spotless."

Cort shrugged. "So, if Damon didn't do it, obviously the plane must have been sabotaged." He glanced at Cam. "And the next logical step would be to ask who would have done that, and why. The obvious answer is money."

Cam rolled his eyes. It was Cort's answer to everything - money.

But Drew nodded. "He's right, Cam. It usually is. Any good investigator follows the money trail."

"Yes, but in this case Damon led Cort to investigate *us*," Cam said, leaning against Cort's arm.

Sebastian laughed.

"It's not funny," Cort grumbled. "Frankly, I still have my doubts about you." It was more of a joke than a serious statement, and for the first time Cam allowed himself to believe that maybe, somehow, this was all going to work out alright. "It was a very real possibility. Until I met Cam." The look he gave Cam was affectionate and exasperated all at once.

Bas shook his head. "Cam's sparkling personality aside, the only way you'd think that was if you never bothered to read the terms of our parents' wills."

Cort frowned. "Wills? Everyone knows you and Cam inherited everything."

He gave Cam a blank look, and Cam bit his lip. "Yeah, I hadn't fully explained that part."

"The company assets don't belong to Cam and me," Sebastian told him. "We have trust funds, and we draw salaries from the company - very decent salaries - but the company itself is in trust, and the beneficiary is the Seaver Charitable Trust. All the money we were ever likely to inherit from our parents was already ours long before they died."

"And you didn't tell me this, why?" Cort demanded, turning to Cam.

"Oh, please. Like you didn't keep secrets. I wanted you to believe me about Bas because you believed *me*, Cort."

Cort gave him a look as if to say they would be discussing this later. Cam felt a tingle in his stomach, and cleared his throat. "The better question is why you didn't share all these suspicions with *me!*" Cam challenged Bas.

Bas pushed his lips together. "Lots of reasons. For one thing, it's been the only thing keeping me sane for the past few months. And for another... You've taken on enough this year, Cam. I know I've mostly checked out. I didn't want this to fall on you too. I wanted to protect you if I could."

"Keeping secrets isn't the way to do that," Cam said, glaring at Sebastian and Cort in turn. "*Jesus*. I am a capable adult."

"I know," Cort murmured, turning to rest a hand on Cam's cheek. "I've never doubted it."

Drew grimaced angrily. "Don't feel too bad. Bas didn't trust me either, Cammy."

Bas rounded on Drew. "And I told you *why*!"

Drew glanced away and didn't respond.

Cam sighed. "So now what the hell do we do?"

"We find Uncle Shaw and show him these photos," Bas said. "I don't know what Jack's endgame is, but if he had something to do with the crash, it's possible Uncle Shaw may be in danger."

"Have you done any digging into Jack Peabody's financials?" Cort demanded. "Any idea where the money might have come from?"

Bas shook his head. "Not yet. Locked up tighter than a drum."

"You can't get into his system?" Cort snorted. "And here I thought you were some computer genius."

Drew smirked. "He didn't say he *couldn't*, Kendrick, he said *not yet*."

Cam winced internally. Trust Drew to have somehow figured out Cort detested his first name, and made sure to use it.

Cort ignored Drew. "Cam and I have a meeting with Damon in…" He checked the time on his phone, then showed it to Cam. "Fifteen minutes."

Cam nodded as Cort put the phone away. "We've gotta go. Meet us at the hangar after you find Uncle Shaw," he told his brother. "And we can make a plan for dealing with Jack."

Bas frowned. "You should call in backup," he told Cort. "See if you can get an FBI team out here."

For a second, Cort hesitated, but Cam placed a hand on Cort's back and shook his head.

"It's not going to happen," Cam said. "If Cort contacts them without proof, they'll likely end up investigating Damon. After all, he was the official cause of the crash. And don't you dare give me that face," he said when Bas scowled. "Keeping secrets to protect a brother is something you should understand."

CHAPTER NINETEEN

Cam and Cort arrived at the hangar to find it mostly deserted. Unlike the day before, there were no planes arriving or departing, and the crew mostly seemed to have the day off.

Two men in blue coveralls stood chatting to one another, eating their lunch. Cort didn't recognize either of them, but they spotted Cort and Cam right away. One of them, an elderly man with dark eyes and a gap-toothed smile approached them.

"Can I help you gentlemen?" he asked, wiping his hands on a rag.

Cort hesitated for half a second. He didn't want to call attention to Damon for any reason, he simply needed to have a look around and allow Damon to approach him.

Cam wrapped both hands around Cort's forearm and leaned against him heavily, giving the mechanic a wide smile. "Oh, perhaps you *can* help us. We just want to have a quick look around. See, Kenny promised me a plane for my birthday - I'm going to be twenty-seven in October," he confided in a stage whisper. "And I really think it's time to *upgrade*, you know? But I need to see which kind is the prettiest so that Kenny knows what to buy!" He added a bright laugh at the end which was so completely unlike Cam, Cort fought the urge to turn and stare.

The mechanic blinked. He looked at Cort with wide eyes, and Cort shrugged. "If it's what he wants," Cort agreed with a shake of his head. "Gotta keep my boy happy."

"Uh." The mechanic's eyes widened as he looked from Cort to Cam. "Well, I guess it'd be alright then," he agreed grudgingly. "Long as you don't touch anything or try going inside."

"Wouldn't *dream* of it!" Cam said, making an exaggerated cross over his heart with his index finger.

The mechanic nodded, then turned away shaking his head. "All these crazy rich folks wanna hide out in their planes, ain't my business," he muttered to himself.

Cam smiled brilliantly at Cort, who rolled his eyes. "Pick out your plane, darling. Did you want something diamond-encrusted?"

Cam laughed. "Oh, *Kenny*, that's sooo last season," he drawled, laughing even harder when Cort reached over to smack him on the ass.

"Don't call me *Kenny*, brat."

"Don't call me a brat, *Kenny*," Cam retorted, smiling as he maneuvered away from Cort's reach.

God, the way Cam smiled, all blue eyes and warmth, the way he'd claimed Cort in front of his brother and his friend, the way he gave Cort chance after freakin' chance…

Cort loved him. How could he not? And he felt like the world's biggest chicken-shit for not telling him so this morning, for taking the out Cam had given him. He'd known since yesterday afternoon this was more than a passing thing. It was *everything*. Or it could be, if Cort let it.

He held out his hand for Cam, who grabbed it, letting Cort reel him in closer. "Cam," he said.

"Cort."

Behind one of the planes off to the side, someone else spoke up. *"Cort."*

Cort blinked, then glanced around.

Holy shit.

"Damon?" he demanded, walking towards his brother's voice. Cam's hand squeezed his tightly, whether with nerves or as an offer of support, he wasn't certain.

Then Damon stepped out from behind the plane and Cort froze.

If not for his hair - long and distinctively gray - and the familiar lines of his face, Cort would not have recognized his brother. He was tall and broad-shouldered, as always, but he walked with a distinct limp now, his right leg dragging somewhat behind him, his forearms crisscrossed by shiny pink scars. His hair was bedraggled and greasy, and his normally clean-shaven jaw sported a scraggly salt-and-pepper beard which aged him far more than his hair ever had. But it was his eyes which truly halted Cort in his tracks. The expressive hazel was now hard and cold, devoid of all the humor and warmth Cort used to see there.

"Cort," Damon said, making no move to step closer. His shocked gaze moved to Cam, who had halted just behind Cort's right shoulder, and then back to Cort. "What the fuck is he doing here?"

"He brought me here," Cort said simply, still drinking in the sight of his brother. "Damon, where have you been? What happened?"

Damon eyed Cort's right hand, which was still wrapped around Cam's. He balanced his weight on his left leg and folded his arms across his chest. "I'll explain later. We don't have much time. Get rid of him," he said, nodding at Cam.

Cam tensed, and Cort gripped his fingers more tightly. He shook his head at his brother. "No. Listen, Damon, I have so much to tell you."

"Jesus, Cort. This isn't a game!" Damon scowled, glaring at Cam, and then towards the other side of the hangar, where the mechanics were laughing while they sipped their coffee. "Did you not understand all the messages I sent you? You used to be a lot smarter than that."

Cort blinked in surprise. This wasn't the happy reunion Cort had imagined. Damon had never spoken like this to him before. What the hell had happened to his brother? There was a hard edge to his own voice when he replied, "I understood, Damon. That's why I'm here. But you were wrong about some things, too."

Damon gave a quick shake of his head. "I'm not discussing anything with him around."

"I'll go," Cam offered, but Cort shook his head.

"That's too bad," Cort told his brother, when Cam tried to extricate his hand from Cort's grasp. "He's with me. We're together."

Damon's lip curled up in a sneer. "With a Seaver? When the fuck did that happen?"

"Sometime between the time you disappeared without a trace and the time I flew here to help you," Cort retorted. "If I'd had your *number*, I could've called."

"God, Cort. I thought you, of all people, would know better than to get involved with the likes of him." He huffed out a breath and his voice became even harder. "Here's the deal. I don't trust him. Can I trust *you*, or was this whole thing for naught?" He threw his hands in the air, encompassing the hangar, the island, and the entirety of whatever plan he'd worked out in his statement.

Cort hesitated, torn. His brother was behaving crazy -

one hundred percent ridiculous. He'd expected Damon to listen to him, to give him the benefit of the doubt. To *trust* him for God's sake. Combined with all the questions he still had for Damon - like where the hell he'd been, and why he hadn't contacted Cort directly even *once* in the last year - he was working his way from merely pissed to truly *angry* with each passing second.

But was he really willing to walk away without helping Damon? Without finding answers to the questions he had?

Cam cleared his throat and slipped his hand from Cort's. "I'm going to stand over there," Cam whispered in his ear, pointing towards the front of the hangar, far away from the mechanics. "And I'm going to pretend to pick out a plane for my birthday. You let me know if you need me."

"Cam," Cort said, turning to look at his man. "I don't want…"

"He's your brother," Cam said. He flashed a smile that didn't quite reach his eyes. "I get it. No contest. You can come find me when you're done, or whatever." He gave Cort an awkward pat on the shoulder as he moved away.

Shit.

Cort grabbed his hand once again. "Five minutes," he told Cam firmly, willing him to believe it.

Cam nodded. "Sure."

Cort could tell that he was anything *but* sure. Damn Damon, and damn *himself* for every secret he'd ever kept from Cam. How could he convince Cam he was all-in when he kept acting like he wasn't? But then Cort glanced back at Damon, at the livid scars on his arms. Whatever had happened to his brother, he couldn't let him walk away, either.

Cam pulled at his wrist, but Cort didn't want to let go. "Trust me?" he asked, looking into Cam's shining blue eyes.

Cam smiled softly, then leaned up and brushed a kiss on

Cort's cheek. "Good luck," he said, then he walked away without looking back. Cort watched him go. When he'd ducked behind a plane and out of sight, Cort turned back to his brother.

Damon's sneer was still firmly in place and he was shaking his head at Cort. "He's playing you and you don't even realize it."

"Enough!" Cort said, allowing frustration to color his voice. "I'm here, Damon, because you asked me to be. I blew up my career. I tricked the guy I love. I have done everything you asked me to do. Now *you* answer *my* questions. Where the hell have you been?" He took a step closer to his brother. "Why the hell didn't you call me?"

"Love!" Damon's eyes goggled and he sneered. "Oh, my God, that's rich! Does he know? Is that—"

"Answer. My. Questions!" Cort hissed impatiently.

Damon clenched his jaw. "Fine. Where have I been? Well, you might have heard I was a little busy crashing a plane into a mountain. Believe it or not, I didn't walk away unscathed." He nodded down at his leg, his arms. "I was in a medically induced coma for a few months."

Cort rocked back on his heels. "Damon," he murmured.

Damon shuffled to the side and leaned back against a tall tool chest, grimacing in relief as he took the weight off his injured leg. "After I woke up, I still wasn't in very good shape. Guy who found me brought me to the hospital, said I was in a car wreck up in the mountains. Guess they never suspected I was the guy on the news. This probably helped," he said, stroking a hand over his beard. "At first, I had no idea what had happened. I started to piece shit together, a little at a time."

"Did you think of calling me at any point?" Cort demanded. "Maybe letting me know you were alive?"

Damon shook his head. "I felt guilty, Cort," he whispered, his eyes to the floor. "I had no idea what had actually happened, but I was the sole survivor of the crash. Those people, the Seavers, were nice. They were decent to me. I figured somehow I'd missed something during the safety check, or maybe I'd been too sleepy to fly. I felt so guilty, I didn't want to live anymore." He looked up and caught Cort's stare. "Until I saw a news interview with John." His face darkened.

"Jack Peabody, you mean?" Cort asked, and Damon looked surprised. "Yeah, I just heard about him, from Sebastian Seaver."

"*Sebastian*? On a first-name basis, are you? You're, what? A part of their family now?" Damon spat. "Just how deep in their pockets are you?"

"Fuck you," Cort said, congratulating himself for mostly keeping his temper. "Damon, he wants to find out the truth as badly as you do. I checked up on them, I followed the hints you sent me. I thought at first Cam might have been involved, but he's not. You have to take my word on that."

"Here's what I know, Cort. I wasn't drinking with Jack, I did the safety check and everything about the plane looked normal. Jack had to have…"

"Sabotaged the plane," Cort finished. "I know. I believe you. Sebastian believes that too."

"Sebastian. That asshole would have raised me from the dead and shot me himself if he could have," Damon said.

Cort leveled a look at his brother. "Can you blame him?" he demanded, taking Sebastian Seaver's side for possibly the first and only time ever. "What would you have done if an official investigation showed some guy was at fault for killing your parents and your fiancée?"

Damon swallowed and looked away. "Looked like a sign of guilt to me," Damon declared. "Someone had to have paid Jack. The asshole didn't work for free." His voice was bitter.

"*Someone* paid Jack, but it wasn't the Seavers. I really believe that," he told his brother. "Levi Seaver's will left the company to charity, so Sebastian had no motive, Damon." Cort frowned. "And how did you know Jack, or John, or whatever the fuck his real name is, in the first place?"

Damon's cheeks flushed beneath his beard. "We were sleeping together. Had been off and on for a few months before the crash. He works for Senator Shaw, and happened to fly the Senator into my airport when Shaw was visiting family in Boston. He made a joke about the irony of Shaw trusting a gay pilot. Seems so stupid now," he said bitterly.

"Anyway, we'd been together for maybe two nights right before the crash. Taking time off, he said. We had some wine." He looked at Cort. "One glass, I swear."

Cort nodded.

"I fell asleep *hard*. I don't know whether I was drugged or what." Damon sighed. "When I woke up the next day, I was really groggy. Jack offered to help me with the pre-flight check since he's a pilot himself, and I agreed. But I checked everything myself, anyway. Or I thought I had." He shook his head angrily. "If Seaver didn't pay Jack, who did?"

"I don't know," Cort said. "But why not at least listen to..."

"Hey, Cortland!"

Damon straightened and Cort craned his neck around to watch Sebastian and Drew jogging toward them. Drew wore his perpetual scowl, while Sebastian looked worried.

"What's up?" Cort asked Bas. "Did you find Senator Shaw?"

Bas shook his head. "But one of the gardeners saw him

headed this way a little while ago, along with his assistant. He's not here?"

Cort glanced at Damon, who shook his head. "Shaw? Fuck, no. I haven't seen him, but I've been avoiding this place more or less since his plane landed. Jack's been promoted from pilot to personal assistant, and I don't want to take any chances he might recognize me."

"So, you're Damon Fitzpatrick?" Drew accused. "Back from the dead?"

"Shockingly brilliant *and* handsome," Damon sneered. "The girls must love you."

Drew snorted and glanced around. "Where's Cam?" he demanded.

"He stepped away to give us some privacy," Cort said, glaring at his brother. "He's waiting over there." He waved a hand toward the front of the hangar, the same direction Sebastian and Drew had come from. "Didn't you see him?"

Bas shook his head slowly, darting a glance at Drew that made Cort's pulse skip a beat. "We definitely didn't see him, and we were looking out for you both."

Cort glanced toward the other side of the hangar, where the mechanics had been talking, but there was nobody around anymore. *Shit.*

And then an ominous clanging came from a plane nearby, the unmistakable sound of metal-on-metal.

The four men exchanged glances and, as one, hurried toward the noise.

"Come on, boys!" a voice drawled. "Don't be shy. The mechanics are having a long, sleepy lunch break on me, and if you're not over here in one minute, I promise you Cam won't be either!"

Heart racing, Cort dove around the nearest plane to find Cam caught in a chokehold by Jack Peabody. Jack's left elbow encircled Cam's neck, just below his chin, and he was holding Cam up so his toes barely touched the floor. In Jack's right hand, pressed against the sweaty hair just above Cam's ear, was a .45 caliber pistol.

"Aw, see that? I knew they'd come for ya, Cam," Jack sneered, bringing his mouth to Cam's ear.

Rage, hot and fluid, bubbled up inside Cort as Cam looked at him with wide eyes. "Let him go, Jack," Cort demanded, just as Sebastian asked, "What do you want? Name your price."

Jack smiled at Sebastian. "I have all the money I need, friend. What I need now is a way off this island. I saw all the texts you were sending Shaw. Imagine my surprise when I saw you'd pieced together my identity." He turned to look at Damon. "And imagine my *shock* when I found *you* were still alive." He smiled, a cold and menacing expression. "How are you, lover? You're looking pretty good for a dead man. I've missed you so much."

Damon's hands were braced on his hips and his eyes bored into Jack's. "Fuck you. You set me up back then, and if you think I'm gonna let you get away…"

Cort reached over and hit Damon in the stomach, hard. "Shut the fuck up, Damon." He turned to Jack. "If you leave now, I'm not going to come after you," he vowed, deadly serious. "I won't let anyone come after you."

"You're a pilot, from what I understand," Drew said, almost sounding bored. "You can pick any plane you want from this hangar and leave." He didn't even glance in Cam's direction. His posture was relaxed and almost friendly, and Cort suddenly understood how the sullen man could be such a good attorney. "You can take my mother's plane and disappear. I promise you, we won't even report it missing."

Jack's eyes crinkled as he chuckled, and Cort thought once again this guy *could* have been good-looking, if he wasn't a total psychopath of course. "God, you guys are funny. *Take my money, take my plane.* Hilarious. Naive and trusting, just like your parents." He moved his arm, jiggling Cam slightly. "They were saps, too."

Cam didn't answer, and Cort realized it was because he couldn't. His face was turning red as Jack slowly cut off his air supply, and his feet scrambled for purchase against the hard, concrete floor.

"Let him go," Cort said, stepping forward, "and I'll go with you."

Jack turned the gun on Cort. "You back the fuck up right now," he said. "But that's sweet, friend. Real sweet. I'm sure your man here really appreciates those heroics."

Cort took a step back, and Jack returned the gun to Cam's temple. "Here's how this is gonna work, boys. I'm gonna take Cam along with me when I leave." Cort's heart sank as he stared at Cam, who was clawing at the back of Jack's forearm.

Cam's blue eyes were firmly fixed on Cort's face, as though he was trying to send him a message. *I love you*, he could hear Cam saying. *I love you.*

"And now I'm thinking I'll also take Damon along for the ride."

Cort's jaw fell, and he saw Damon's had, too. "Me?" Damon demanded.

"Yep. If I'm going to keep an eye on my hostage, I'd better have someone else at the controls, and I remember you being an excellent pilot before you had that whole plane crash debacle." He smiled broadly and nodded at the plane, banging the side of it with the edge of his gun, as though to get their attention. The plane's clamshell door was open, forming a small set of steps, and Jack began to back towards them. "I already prepped the plane an hour ago. All fueled up. Of course, you'll have to trust I did the proper checks." He laughed. "Better than last time, anyway."

He put his heel to the bottom step, keeping Cam in front of him as a shield. "Cam and I are gonna go up first and you can follow after," he told Damon. "And you," he said, exchanging glances with Cort, Drew, and Sebastian. "You won't alert a single soul, you hear me? Or I'll kill Cam and tell the authorities it was all *his* fault for kidnapping us." He nodded at Damon. "I work for a well-connected Senator, if you recall. And he'll be none too happy when he finds his plane is gone." His drawl was smug, but carried a thin thread of wildness to it, like he had been driven to the edge.

That hint of madness caused sweat to dot over Cort's brow. He'd been in worse situations than this thousands of times, but he'd never been more afraid. He'd honestly never had so much to lose. His eyes were locked on Cam's as Jack dragged him up the stairs, and he willed Cam to read his mind, to understand all the things he hadn't said but should have.

"I will *not* let this happen," Sebastian said, running at Jack. He hadn't gone two steps before Jack sent a bullet flying toward Sebastian's feet that hit the floor inches away. Sebastian stopped in his tracks.

"Stay back," Jack warned, his eyes glinting.

"I'm not going with you!" Damon called. He folded his arms over his chest and stared at Cam, his jaw working. "This is ridiculous. You'll kill us both the second we land."

Jack smiled, a leer which was not even a little sane. "So suspicious, lover. Alright, have it your way. I'll kill your brother's boyfriend right now and fly myself out of here."

He placed the gun more firmly against Cam's head, and Cort realized the safety was off. Cam's tear-filled eyes burned into Cort's, one final *I love you*, as he struggled against Jack's choking hold but couldn't break it. Then Cam squeezed his eyes tightly shut, preparing for the worst.

"No!" Cort cried, taking a step forward. "Cam!"

Damon pushed Cort out of the way, sending him sprawling to the floor. "Fine," Damon told Jack, rushing toward the steps. "Fine, I'll fly."

Jack smiled. "Always so predictable."

"Jesus! Damon!" Cort cried, pushing himself up on his hands.

Cam opened his eyes as Jack heaved him backwards, and Cort saw Cam try to shake his head, telling Damon to stay back. Damon either didn't understand or purposely ignored him. He mounted the steps after them and drew up the door.

Belatedly, Cort saw the blocks had already been removed and the plane had been prepped for flight - Jack had obviously been planning for this.

Sebastian ran toward the plane, banging on the door before Cort had even pushed himself to his feet. "No! Cam! Open the goddamn door, Jack! Cam!"

Still, he wasn't prepared for the way the plane flared to life, the engines firing up while the plane was still in the hangar. He coughed as a storm of dirt and debris whirled around him, tiny shards of stone and sand from the floor pinging against his skin and eyes. He covered his eyes with his forearm.

"He's insane!" Sebastian yelled. "What the hell is he thinking, starting up inside like this?"

"He's thinking I would have climbed up the side of the damn plane if he'd waited thirty more seconds," Cort said, coming to his feet to stand beside Sebastian. Damon quickly guided the plane out the open door of the hangar, barely pausing before picking up speed and taxiing over to the runway.

"Now what?" Drew demanded of no one in particular, throwing his hands in the air. "We can't call the authorities."

"The local authorities would know nothing anyway," Sebastian said, running a hand through his hair. "We need American authorities involved. I'm asking Uncle Shaw to call in a favor." He panicked for a second. "Unless Jack hurt Shaw, too. Let's find Lucy, and…"

"No! No, I've got this." Cort licked his lips and pulled his phone from his pocket - not the burner phone Damon had given him, but his space aged, FBI phone, the one with the important phone numbers. "I have someone I can call instead."

"Hey," he said into the phone a minute later. "It's Cort. I need your help."

CHAPTER TWENTY

Cam sat in the leather chair of Emmett Shaw's plane, staring down the barrel of Jack Peabody's gun just as he had been for the last hour or longer. In that time, he'd invented a dozen potential ways of getting out of this situation, and dismissed them one after the other due to his lack of weapon, muscles, and ability to fly.

The layout of this plane was the same as his family's. The furnishings were more upscale, but far less comfortable. Cam surveyed the clouds passing by the window, surprised at how un-freaked he was about being in a plane. Then again, being held captive by a guy who'd likely shoot you as soon as the plane landed really put the risks of air travel into perspective.

Jack sat in a chair opposite him, swiveled sideways, so he could keep one eye on Damon in the cockpit, while keeping track of Cam in the living area. Cam hadn't heard from Damon since they'd first taken off. Jack had shoved him into a seat near Damon in the cockpit and then forced Damon to input coordinates and take off in some crazy-ass way that had made Damon flush red and mutter things about recklessness and suicide. Then Jack had yanked Cam up again, as soon as they'd reached cruising altitude, and brought him back here, no doubt the better to keep him away from Damon, who vibrated with crazy anger at approximately the same intensity as Jack.

Cam needed to talk to Damon if they were ever going to find a way out of this alive, and Cam needed at least *Damon* to survive, for Cort's sake. Bas and Drew would have each other, plus Bas had his work, and Drew had his mom. But Cort... Cam couldn't imagine what he must be feeling now, having his brother ripped away from him again, after all that Cort had gone through, all he'd sacrificed. Cam rubbed his thumb over the pocket of his shorts, feeling the outline of Cort's lucky quarter against his finger. A lump lodged in his throat.

He needed to get Damon back to Cort.

He watched the madman sitting across from him, gun in one hand and cell phone in the other. Jack was hunched forward in his seat, elbows on his knees, breathing erratically. He kept running the cell phone across his forehead in a nervous way, like he was waiting for it to ring with a call from wherever the hell they were headed. Would Jack deliver him and Damon to his real bosses, the people who'd paid Jack to kill Cam's parents?

"Jack," Cam began, and Jack's head flew up, eyes wild. Cam shrank back, making himself as non-threatening as possible. "I just... I was wondering. Who paid you?"

"What?"

"A year ago, the crash," Cam whispered. "We already figured out someone must have paid you to kill my parents."

Jack's head went back, a smile forming on his lips. "Why the hell would I tell you?"

"Why wouldn't you?" Cam swallowed. "I mean, you're going to kill me anyway when we land, aren't you?"

"Maybe," Jack shrugged, his eyes cagey. "I haven't decided yet. Might be better to keep a hostage for a little while, and you're a better bet than Fitzpatrick."

"Right, okay. Well, I'm assuming you will at some point," Cam said sadly, letting real fear thread through his voice, real tears spring to his eyes. "I think I'd kind of like to know the truth before it happens. Wouldn't you? Call it my last request."

Jack laughed, a single quick bark, then a longer stream of chuckles. "Aw. You're scared aren't you, Cam?"

Cam nodded seriously. "Of course. You're the guy with the fucking gun."

"Hmmm. Yes, I am," Jack agreed. His smile turned smug. "Crazy thing about your parents. Had to set it up to look like an accident. I had to be above reproach." He rolled his eyes. "Harder than you'd think."

Cam nodded and glanced away, and as he did, he saw something move from the corner of his eye, a sliver of reflected light from further down the hall, from the bathroom and bedroom area. He kept his gaze trained there, hoping Jack would think he was trying to compose himself, and he saw it again - a definite flash of light, reflected off the surface of a picture in the gangway.

Was there someone else on this plane? Cam's pulse kicked up and he sat straighter. Had Cort or one of the others somehow managed to sneak aboard? How could he twist this to his advantage?

"Who engineered it?" Cam demanded, wanting Jack's attention focused on him.

Jack snickered and leaned back in his chair. "You wouldn't believe me if I told you."

"Can't be any crazier than some of the thoughts I've entertained this week," Cam argued. "Cort thought for a second Bas was involved."

"Bas? You mean your brother Sebastian?" Jack laughed out loud. "Oh, God! I wish I'd thought of that. Did you believe it?"

"Not really," Cam said, watching the light creep closer along the gangway. "But I wondered who else it could have been. Maybe one of his competitors?"

Jack shook his head, enjoying the game. "Nope. Much, much closer."

Cam ground his teeth together at Jack's taunting tone and looked to the side again. The light had gone, but now Cam could see a shadow. Someone was standing right in the bedroom doorway, listening to them. "What would you say if I told you it was one of your father's most trusted friends?"

"One of Dad's friends?" Cam repeated. His attention was caught now, between the shadow in the bedroom and the story that Jack was telling. "Who?"

"Guess."

Cam rubbed at the back of his neck impatiently. "I-I don't know. I can't imagine why anyone would want to hurt my dad. Was it someone from the board? Mitch, maybe? Or maybe the guy below him in the department, David?"

"Closer than that." Jack's voice was sober now, all his humor gone. "One of his best friends ever. Someone he trusted implicitly."

Jack's eyes darted unconsciously to the cell phone in his hand, and Cam saw what he'd been missing all along.

They were in Emmett Shaw's plane, with Emmett Shaw's assistant. "Uncle Shaw," he breathed. "Not possible. He loved my dad."

Jack nodded. "He did. Killed him to do it, but your dad had made his bed." Jack shrugged.

"What the hell is that supposed to mean? What did Dad ever do to Uncle Shaw that could possibly have led to this?" Cam fought to keep his temper in check, but how dare this man talk so casually about ending his parents' lives?

"The usual." Jack shrugged. "Screwed him over. Left him hanging in the wind. Your dad made it clear he couldn't be trusted."

"You're wrong," Cam argued. "Dad was totally trustworthy."

Jack shook his head with mock regret, then smiled. "You still think your dad was a saint. It's so *cute*. Probably better you die thinking that way, huh?"

The shadow was still standing in the doorway, and Cam wondered for a second if it could be Uncle... *no*. Emmett Shaw was *not* his uncle, and it couldn't be Emmett out there, or he doubted Jack would have spoken so frankly. If it was someone who could help Cam and Damon, he had to get them in the proper position and somehow neutralize Jack's gun. Whether Cam made it off the plane or not, he needed to make certain Emmett Shaw would pay.

He forced himself to shrug and look unconcerned. "Maybe we won't die today anyway."

Jack smiled and turned the gun so it pointed directly at Cam. "I think it's up to me though, isn't it?"

"Well, Damon's flying the plane," Cam said. "Who knows where we'll end up?"

"Nah," Jack said, but his eyelid flickered. "He inputted the coordinates for a small airport outside of Miami, just as I told him to."

"He can't change them in flight?" Cam asked innocently. He was pretty sure Damon could, and probably *would*. "You'd know better than me."

Jack's eyes narrowed as he realized the flaw in his plan. He glanced back at the cockpit and his breathing hitched.

"You're just trying to get me to leave you here while I go see to Damon," he accused.

Cam's eyes widened. "Of course not. What could *I* do? I don't have a weapon."

Just as he'd hoped, Jack looked more suspicious than ever. "Get up," he commanded. "We can both go sit in the cockpit."

Cam stood slowly and pretended reluctance. "I could just stay here…"

"Get your ass over here," Jack said, rising to his feet and backing up, leaving plenty of room for Cam to precede him. Cam stepped forward, until he was blocking Jack's view of the cockpit. He turned his head to glare at Jack *and* get a direct line of sight into the tiny bedroom in the rear of the plane. He caught the faintest glimpse of a man - average height, short dark hair - before Jack barked at him to get moving.

Cam's stomach plummeted. Was that Cain Shaw? Had he been involved in this plot the whole time? Was he working with his father and Jack? Suddenly, being trapped in a cockpit with Damon and this madman didn't seem like any sort of a decent plan.

"I was just messing with you," Cam said nervously. "Damon wouldn't play games like that, not with me on board."

"Too late for second guessing," Jack sneered. "Move your ass."

Cam didn't have to feign his reluctance as he walked the short distance into the cockpit.

"Sit," Jack said, gesturing towards the copilot's seat. Cam glanced out the window, but there was nothing to see except unrelenting blue - clear blue sky over a darker blue ocean, no land anywhere in sight. He swallowed hard, felt his stomach lurch, but he didn't have time for a panic attack right then. Death was a lot more certain than a plane crash.

Damon glanced over as Cam sat down and stared at him, but unlike his brother, Damon couldn't relay messages to Cam with just his eyes. Cam had no idea what Damon was trying to tell him.

"I'm sorry," Cam said instead. If it hadn't been for Cam, Damon wouldn't have been on the plane after all.

Damon lifted his chin, an acknowledgment. But he said, "I didn't do it for you, Seaver. I did it for Cort. He loves you."

"Shut up," Jack said, motioning with his gun. He glanced at the instrumentation and must have somehow determined that they were still on the correct course, because his posture relaxed. "Not a word from either of you."

But Cam was done following orders. If he was going to die, there were things he needed to say first.

"It's not like that for him," he explained to Damon. "Cort... we... I don't know what we could have had, but he wasn't there yet. It's okay, though. I know he cared, and he knows how I felt." He dug into his pocket and retrieved Cort's quarter.

"Hey! Keep your hands where I can see them," Jack said, but he relaxed when Cam displayed the simple coin in his hand.

Cam held it up, turning sideways in his seat to show it to Damon, and he saw that Jack's attention was riveted on it, too. From the cabin beyond, he saw movement and prayed whoever was out there wasn't working with Jack.

"Cort let me borrow this," he told Damon. "He told me *you* gave it to him a while back."

Damon looked at Cam like he was crazy. Maybe he was. From the corner of his eye, he watched the shadow outside the cockpit door creep closer. Whoever was out there was trying to conceal their presence. Cam knew he needed to distract Jack and give them the element of surprise.

"I figured you'd want it back," Cam told Damon, trying to convey with his eyes that Damon should play along. And then he flipped the quarter in a perfect arc.

Jack's attention was focused on the coin as it sailed through the air, heading for Damon's outstretched palm, and he never noticed the arm reaching around to grab him from behind. Cam jumped from his seat, both of his hands reaching for the wrist of Jack's gun hand and forcing it up to the ceiling, even as the fourth person yanked Jack backwards, trying to wrestle him to the floor. Cam lost his grip for a split second, falling forward as Jack was wrenched back, and in that second, Jack fired.

Damon cried out as sparks shot from the control panel. The plane dipped precariously.

Cam's stomach rolled, but he levered himself up anyway, grabbing Jack's wrist again, his knee digging hard into Jack's thigh as they wrestled on the tiny floor. The other man – *Cain*! It *was* Cain! - was trapped underneath Jack, his arm still around Jack's neck, but he was losing the struggle as Jack elbowed him relentlessly with his free arm.

Cam made it up onto his knees, gaining leverage over Jack and pushing his wrist in the opposite direction, so Cain could have more room to maneuver himself free. Cam pinned Jack's wrist to the floor, moved his knee onto Jack's forearm, then grabbed the gun from his hand. The men on the floor continued to wrestle, Cain's thin form no match for Jack's extra bulk and muscle.

"Stop!" Cam shouted, holding the gun in both hands. He was balanced on his knees, his back braced against Damon's seat as Damon struggled frantically to bring the plane under control. "Jack, I *will* shoot you if you don't leave Cain alone," he promised.

Jack froze, belly to the floor, and Cain scrambled away from him. The younger man's nose was bleeding copiously and he kept a protective arm coiled around his ribs.

"Cain?" Jack asked dumbly, as though he'd only just processed who he'd been fighting with for the past minute.

"Are you okay?" Cam demanded as Cain backed himself over to the cabin wall. He managed to get his feet underneath him, and slid himself up the wall using the wall for support. He looked as though he might vomit.

"No," Cain whispered, staring at Jack with disgust and betrayal stamped onto his features. "I am not okay. You *killed* them?" he demanded.

"Cain, baby, I can explain!" Jack pleaded.

Baby? Now the utterly wrecked look in Cain's eyes made so much sense.

And also, *holy shit.*

"You were working with *him* the whole time, and I thought... I thought we..." Devastation was evident in every word Cain spoke.

The plane dipped again. "*Fuck.* The electronics are damaged," Damon said, his voice thick with tension. "We need to make an emergency landing. The communications system isn't working, Cam. I need a cell phone."

"Cain, get Jack's cell and give it to Damon," Cam demanded. "Now!"

Cain dropped to his knees, still clutching his ribs, and wrestled the cell phone from Jack's back pocket, handing it to Damon.

"I have my phone, too," Cain said, bracing himself against Cam's shoulder as he heaved himself to his feet.

"Cain, call your dad," Jack said. "Explain what's happened. He'll help you."

"*Fuck you.* Don't even talk to me," Cain said. He stepped to one side and kicked Jack in the ribs, flinching and clutching his own stomach tighter. "I heard what you said about him. I heard everything."

"Cort? Cort listen to me," Damon said into the phone. "No, don't put me on speaker. Are you listening? Cort! He's fine. He's *fine,* I swear. Yeah, I'm fine, too. The Senator's kid is here, and he's fine as well. Cam got Jack's gun. There was some damage to the plane and I'm setting it down early. I need you to… You did what? *Oh my God.*"

Cam fought the urge to swivel his head as Damon groaned.

"No, no, it's fine," Damon sighed. "Yeah, I know. I get it." His tone was wry. "It'll be alright. It was going to happen anyway. Listen, are you alone? I need you to be alone, Cort," Damon commanded. He paused for a minute, then said, "Listen, we know who paid Jack. It was Emmett Shaw."

From the corner of his eye, Cam saw Cain bury his head in his hands. Meanwhile, Jack punched the floor and screamed, "Fuck!" He tried to stand, as though trying some misguided, last-ditch means of escape, so Cam instinctively reached out, bringing the butt of the gun down hard on the back of his head.

Jack collapsed back to the floor and didn't move.

"Uh… That was nothing," Damon said, obviously trying to soothe Cort. "Just a little trouble with Jack, but your boyfriend took care of it."

Cam sat back, his hands trembling as he continued holding the gun tight. *Holy crap, what did I just do?* He couldn't tell if Jack was still breathing, and he was too afraid to check.

Damon paused. "Yeah, I guess he is. Jury's still out." Damon coughed slightly. "Anyway, I'm turning back, heading for St. Michel. They have a tiny airport, you need to radio ahead and make sure... Right, yes. Exactly. Okay, and whatever you do, don't tell... Alright, okay, you know how to do your job. Yeah, I've got this under control." Damon's voice was confident. "You can tell him yourself. We're landing in about fifteen minutes." Another pause. "Yeah, brother. I promise."

"What now?" Cam asked. His head was spinning and his voice was thin. He was barely hanging on.

"Now I land," Damon said. "I've got this, Cam. Just pull down the jump seat and strap yourself in."

"What about him?" Cam said, indicating the body on the floor.

Cain swiveled his head and caught Cam's eye. "Leave him. I hope his balls are whacked all the way up to his tonsils when we touch down."

Cam nodded. He unfolded the seat Damon had indicated and strapped himself in, closing his eyes as he felt the plane begin to descend. He thought about Cort and Sebastian, then about his parents, and he sent a prayer out to nobody in particular.

If we make it, if we land safely, I will never hesitate again, he promised. *I will celebrate every single day. I will hug Sebastian, and maybe even Drew. I'll volunteer again. I will make sure Emmett Shaw gets what's coming to him. I will not be a martyr anymore. I will make Cort tell me he loves me, even if he tries to be a stubborn idiot, because no matter how it started, loving him is the truest thing I know.*

"Brace yourselves," Damon said as the plane slipped slowly down from the sky.

CHAPTER TWENTY-ONE

"Where is he?" Cort demanded.

Sebastian, jogging into the airport from the blazing-hot tarmac alongside him, shook his head. "I don't see any of them."

The airport on this small island was a tiny building, hardly more than a rain shelter, and today, the place was packed with law enforcement personnel - local police, international investigators, and even a few people wearing FBI jackets who were here in an 'unofficial' capacity.

"If it hadn't taken so long to get here..." Cort fumed, running a hand through his hair.

Sebastian glanced at him with a raised eyebrow. "Hardly my fault, Kendrick, that almost every plane in the hangar was damaged by the wash from Shaw's engine."

"What good are your billions if you can't get us a plane in less than five hours?" Cort scoffed. "People from the *States* are here already."

As it was, they'd had to co-opt another pilot staying on the island to fly them over in his tiny prop-plane, only big enough for two passengers. Cort had never been particularly frightened of air travel, and even *he'd* had to fight the urge to puke.

"You could've stuck with Senator Shaw and Lucy," Sebastian said, a hard edge to his voice.

Cort noticed he'd immediately dropped the *Uncle*, and winced. As hard as this day had been for him, it had to have been even harder for Sebastian, knowing someone he'd trusted had betrayed him so acutely.

"Yeah, no thank you," Cort said. "Fortunately, the *yacht* will take another few hours to get here."

Once Bas had relayed the message that Jack had taken off with Cain, Cam, and Damon as hostages, Shaw had been beside himself. As soon as Drew informed him his plane had touched down on St. Michel, Shaw had insisted on taking one of the yachts docked on St. Brigitte and traveling to St. Michel by boat, rather than waiting for a plane as Cort and Bas had. It turned out not to have been a wise decision.

Cort turned in a wide circle, searching for Cam, when a hand reached out to clasp him on the shoulder.

"Cort," Sean Cook said, and Cort caught him up in a hug.

"Thank you so much for getting here," he told his former boss.

Sean pounded him on the back, obviously taken aback. "Kid, I'm just glad you called me," he said. "Derrick and Nat are so pissed I didn't let them come, but there was no time."

"You kept things on the QT?" Cort asked, already knowing the answer but wanting it confirmed.

"Yeah. I haven't said anything about the senator possibly being involved." Sean blew out a breath. "Good luck to you with proving that." He glanced at Bas, and Cort belatedly introduced them.

"Well, we apprehended the guy who arranged the incident," Cort reminded him, as Sean and Bas shook hands. "But Senator Shaw's not much of a flight risk. I don't think you need to take him into custody until we get our guy to turn him in."

"Jack Peabody?" Sean's head tilted to the side and he looked at Cort appraisingly. "I dunno if it's gonna be as straightforward as you think. He's clammed up. Not a word since we got here. Locals were already on the ground waiting for them when they landed, brought him out on a stretcher because he was knocked out cold, apparently by your boyfriend." Sean didn't even try to hide his amusement. "I like him, by the way."

Bas rolled his eyes, but Cort didn't give a shit what Sebastian thought. As long as Cam would have him, that's where he'd be. Speaking of which… "Where is Cam?" he asked Sean.

"Outside. Come on, I'll show you." He walked them to the front of the small building, pointing to a closed door as they passed. "That's the manager's office, where we're keeping Peabody for now. He woke up pretty quick after they got him inside. No lasting damage. But now he's looking for an attorney. Not a big surprise, but don't start thinking you've got an easy case," Sean warned.

"Yeah, but from what Damon said when he called from the plane…"

Sean stopped still. "Who?" he demanded. "Sorry, I don't know anyone by that name. Certainly no one who was on the plane. Both Cain Shaw and Camden Seaver have stated for the record it was only the pair of them, along with Jack. And… *anyone else*… was already gone by the time I got here." He smiled at Cort. "Apparently he said to tell you he'd call. Soon."

Sebastian's head went back, a small smile lifting his lips. "Well done," he said.

"Incredible," Cort corrected, shaking his head in gratitude.

"Incredible? I'll take it as a compliment from the guy who carried a thumb drive of hardcore porn in his pocket, just when he knew Porter was gonna go looking for it." He rolled his eyes, and Cort felt a flush spread across his cheeks.

In retrospect, perhaps not his wisest choice. "You, ah… figured it out?"

"Told you before, Cortland. You don't *have* any tricks I don't know about. Cam Seaver and Cain Shaw plan to say Jack flew the plane in, and they clocked him after they'd landed, when he attempted to kill them." Sean gave them a quick wink. "Just FYI. And between their testimony and the interview footage from after the accident, I think they're going to have a solid case against the guy without involving your brother at all unless he wants to come forward."

"Thank you," Cort told him, clapping a hand on his shoulder. "I'm really glad I called you."

"Don't thank me, kiddo," Sean said, shaking his head. "I'm fucking glad you realized you *should* call. Like something I said finally penetrated that hard head of yours."

Cort smiled. Some*one* had gotten through to him, alright, but it had nothing to do with Sean's words.

They resumed walking until they got to the front entrance of the airport. Outside, the setting sun reflected off the windows of a few cars, and tall palm trees swayed in the hot breeze. Off to one side, there was a small seating area and a picnic table with benches on either side. Cain Shaw was curled up awkwardly on one of the wooden chairs, his weight on one side. When he saw the men appear in the doorway, he stood up slowly and began walking towards them, clearly hurt.

Cam sat on the far side of the picnic table, facing away from them. He was hunched over, elbows-on-knees, staring into the distance. He was so real and so *alive*, Cort had to stop himself from jogging over and wrapping him up in a hug.

You're gonna have to do some convincing, he reminded himself. But it would be worth it.

He put a restraining hand on Sebastian's arm. "Hey, can I?" he said, nodding at Cam.

Bas looked at Cort grimly. Cort bristled as he prepared for some sort of threat or warning which, frankly, the guy didn't deserve to be handing out. But Bas surprised him. "Hold him tight," was all he said. He looked over at his brother sadly, then clapped Cort on the shoulder. "And don't fuck up."

He turned and walked back into the airport.

Cort took a deep breath, walked toward Cam, his feet moving faster and faster, until he was full-out running. Cam turned as soon as he heard someone approaching, and stood with a bright smile on his face as Cort crashed into him, throwing his arms around his man and picking him up off the ground.

"Hey," Cam said.

"I was so fucking scared." Cort spoke the words into Cam's thick hair. It wasn't what he'd intended to say, but then nothing seemed to go according to plan when he was with Cam. He'd learn to just enjoy the ride. "And I love you," he blurted out. "Not... not because I was scared, okay? Just... I should have said it before. I knew it yesterday... hell, I probably knew it last week, and I was just too afraid to tell you."

He set Cam back on his feet and pulled away slightly so

he could see his face - the liquid blue eyes, the constellation of freckles, the blush Cort loved to put on his cheeks. "I know this has all been my fault Cam. It was my fault you weren't standing beside me in the hangar. Hell, my fault you were on the fucking island in the first place. I lied to you, and took the easy way out."

Cam shook his head and Cort panicked. *Be more convincing, Cortland.*

He ran a hand through his hair. "Listen, I know this is deja vu, me convincing you to give me another chance. What am I on now, my fourth? My fifth?" He winced. "And it's not like I can say this is gonna be the last chance I need, either. I mean, I'm probably gonna need six more before we get back to Boston. But I learn from my mistakes, Cam." He swallowed. "I just need you to trust me."

"You called the FBI," Cam said, when Cort finally gave him a chance to speak.

Cort frowned. *Oookay.* Not quite the return declaration he'd been hoping for. He let his hands drop from Cam's waist.

"Yeah, of course. I called Sean Cook," he said, hooking a thumb towards the building. "The second you guys took off. I was scared to death. I had no idea what else to do."

"No, Cort," Cam said, his own arms still wrapped around Cort's neck. "*You called the FBI.* You called your team to come and save us, even though you knew it might get Damon in trouble." He grinned. "I'd already figured out you loved me. I promised myself if we landed safely, I would tie you up and force you to tell me."

Cort's chin went back. "Is that so?"

"Yup. Maybe I still will." His gaze was teasing, and Cort became lost in it. "But when we landed and the authorities were here, that's when I *knew*. There was no way you'd risk

Damon unless... unless you already realized you loved me, too."

Cort shook his head. "I couldn't let anything happen to you. I love Damon, but you... you've become everything somehow. It's crazy, huh?"

Cam's smile was bright as the sun. "Yeah. Totally illogical. But this really smart guy once told me, the most illogical things are sometimes the truest."

Cort leaned forward and gently took Cam's mouth with his, nibbling at the gorgeous lower lip that had fascinated him from the very beginning. "We'll see who ties up who, badass," he warned Cam. And then he leaned forward and claimed the laughing mouth with his own - slow and easy and forever.

EPILOGUE

"Marcus, how about you fill us in on the modifications for the…" Sebastian's voice carried across the table as he spoke to the manager of a Seaver Tech research division in Spokane whose face was plastered on a giant wall-mounted flat-screen, but Cam could barely force himself to listen. Despite the bright sunlight flooding the conference room through the floor-to-ceiling windows behind him, and the extra-large coffee on the table in front of him, Cam was *tired*. On the other side of the thick, glass-block privacy walls which cocooned the conference room from the rest of the office, no doubt the employees of Seaver Tech were moving around, hurrying to finish their work before they could leave for the weekend. Cam was just a tiny bit jealous. He wondered for the twenty-seventh time why Bas always scheduled these meetings on Friday mornings.

Not that having Sebastian at the helm again was in any way a bad thing. In fact, it was one major silver lining to all the shit that had had gone down on St. Brigitte and the even bigger mess they'd found when they returned. Emmett Shaw's betrayal and the ramifications of it were things Cam and Sebastian would struggle with for a long time, but it helped to know Sebastian was back among the living, no longer swamped under the weight of his own grief, and he and Drew were closer than ever.

Cam's cell phone buzzed almost imperceptibly, and he withdrew it from his pocket.

[Cort:] *I feel like we need a vacation.*

Cam rolled his eyes as he read the message, but couldn't stop the smile from tugging at his lips. He glanced across the table to find his boyfriend, the newly appointed head of Seaver Tech's new Internal Security Division, waggling his eyebrows meaningfully.

Kendrick Cortland was completely incorrigible, and unconditionally *his*. He typed his reply quickly, knowing exactly how to provoke his man.

[Cam:] *You do realize we're in the middle of a board meeting?*

[Cort:] *Think you mean a bored meeting. Ha!*

Cam stifled a smirk – the dad humor was terrible - just as another text buzzed through.

[Cort:] *FYI, Margaret agrees. We need a vacation.*

[Cam:] *Margaret? My assistant? You chatted with her about this?*

[Cort:] *Yup. We talked. Last night while I was waiting for you. She's very concerned about your stress levels. You're not getting any younger you know.*

No surprise there. Of course Margaret had agreed with whatever scheme Cort concocted; she'd been Cort's BFF since pretty much day one. She told Cam she loved the way Cort had lightened his heart… which was such a sweet and *accurate* way of putting it, Cam couldn't be mad even when she conspired with Cort behind his back. His heart *was* lighter these days. And fuller, too.

[Cam:] *I am twenty-six, Kenny.*

[Cort:] *And apparently too senile to remember my name, brat.*

Cam pushed his lips together, fighting the pulse of heat rising from his belly. With Cort, arousal was a steady current always running just beneath his skin.

[Cam:] *Shhh. I need to pay attention to the meeting.*

[Cort:] *Bullshit. You're not paying attention. You're probably thinking about last night.*

The annoying man was not wrong, but Cam would be damned if he'd admit it. He put his phone facedown on the table and pretended to watch Marcus talk about... *something*... from the flat-screen on the wall, but in reality, Cam was definitely thinking about last night.

It had started out with a stupid bet, the kind that had become a daily occurrence in their relationship. Cam hadn't known quite how competitive he was until Cort started turning every thrown wad of paper into a game of basketball, and every glass of wine into a round of Never Have I Ever. He also hadn't known it was possible to laugh as much as he did with his rule-skirting boyfriend.

Sadly for Cort, who was arguably even more competitive than Cam, his League of Legends game had never quite picked up, probably because he insisted on playing with Cam sitting beside him, leaning against his arm, massaging his shoulders and... other things. Cort's matches invariably involved him being killed early on, while people on chat swore ripely and suggested anatomically-impossible moves in angry Russian. Six months after his first game, he was still unranked... but it didn't seem to dull his enthusiasm for "practicing."

Last night, however, Cort had suggested Cam demonstrate his own skills, while Cort took careful notes. Cam hadn't been particularly enthusiastic. Only a month ago, he and Cort had bought a townhouse of their own, and they were still in the process of moving in. Between painting the rooms - and the laughter-filled competitions required to determine the colors each room would be painted - moving furniture around until Cort lost his temper then decided leaving the whole lot in the middle of the room would be a great way to start conversations, and the emotional rollercoaster ride of unboxing and hanging the family pictures Cam had taken from his parents' house, he'd already been tired, but Cort had insisted. If Cam could finish a match before Cort got him off, he'd win the forfeit of his choice. Otherwise, Cort would have to settle for an IOU.

It had been too tempting to resist.

Besides which, Cam knew that he'd been able to complete matches in less than twenty minutes - sometimes less than fifteen. Tired as he was, distracted as he was, he was confident he could hold out. Cam had already decided he would hold onto that IOU because there was something special in the works for their first Valentine's Day together.

"Fine," he'd told Cort. "Let's do this."

But of course, Cort hadn't been able to resist stacking the tables against him. Within the first minute of the game, Cort had been naked and hard, and he'd stripped off Cam's clothes, too, in record time.

Cort had started off with a slow, sensual massage that had completely killed every one of Cam's defenses, then he'd crawled beneath Cam's desk, like a fantasy come to life, and used that extremely-skilled mouth of his to make Cam scream before five minutes had even passed.

It had been the hardest, most satisfying orgasm Cam had enjoyed in weeks of very satisfying orgasms.

He'd also been utterly crushed in his match.

He shifted his legs beneath the table now, just remembering the sensation of Cort's mouth on him. His phone buzzed again, and Cam turned it over, desperate for distraction.

[Cort:] *Imagine if I were kneeling in front of you right now, in the boardroom. I'd be under the table looking up at you…*

[Cort:] *My hands would be on your thighs, rubbing them. Can you feel it?*

Oh, fuck. This was exactly the kind of distraction Cam didn't need.

He glanced down the table at Sebastian, who was listening intently to Marcus, and along the other side, toward Drew, who was watching Sebastian. Neither seemed to notice the flush creeping across Cam's cheeks, but David Pearce had. He cocked a concerned eyebrow at Cam.

[Cam:] *David is looking at me right now. Do you want me to be rock hard while he's watching me?*

Cam already knew the answer to this question. Cort was uncompromisingly protective of Cam, including Cam's privacy. There was no way Cort would want David to suspect anything. And while Cort wasn't overbearingly jealous, he was definitely territorial. Sure enough, Cort sent a dark glare down the table at David.

Cam stifled a laugh and realized he didn't give a shit about the meeting anymore. He bit his lip as he typed.

[Cam:] *That's probably the hottest thing I've seen today.*

Cort's brow puckered in confusion.

[Cort:] *What? The Marcus guy from Seattle?*

[Cam:] *Spokane. And no.*

[Cort:] *You don't mean David.*

Cam snickered. Poor David.

[Cam:] *Not David.*

[Cort:] *Then what?*

[Cam:] *There's this guy across from me.*

Cort raised an eyebrow, then bit his lip.

[Cort:] *Do tell.*

[Cam:] *He's totally built, and just a tad jealous. Broad shoulders, green eyes, makes me hard instantly, has these hands…*

[Cort:] *Hands?*

[Cam:] *Yup. Big, beefy hands. Can't text for shit, but they're amazing on my skin…*

[Cort:] *Yeah? I'm calling in my IOU.*

Cam frowned at Cort across the table.

[Cam:] *For what?*

[Cort:] *Tell you in a minute.*

[Cort:] *Now about that vacation.*

Cam looked at his boyfriend suspiciously, wondering what the hell he had in mind. It wouldn't be office sex, or at least he didn't think so. They'd done that already, christening both Cam's office, Cort's brand new office, as well as the elevator and several other key places Cam couldn't remember without blushing.

When Cort had chosen to leave the FBI, rather than wait to hear the outcome of their internal investigation into his conduct, Cam had been a little worried Cort would regret his decision. He'd come to realize just how much that badge meant to someone who'd struggled to find his place in the world the way Cort had. He'd wondered if Cort would ever find a job he enjoyed half as much. And then Sebastian had announced the need for more internal security and decided to set up the new division - people who could prevent individuals such as Emmett Shaw from taking advantage of them. When he'd mentioned to Cort that part of the job description would be protecting Cam, Cort had rolled his eyes and leaped at the chance.

Then Cam had been concerned that working closely together might be slightly too much stress on their new relationship… but the exact opposite had been true. As with moving in together - a choice several people, including Sebastian, had felt they'd made too soon - they found things were simply better when they were together. The more time Cam spent with Cort, the more confident and grounded he felt in himself. Cort was a strong guy with a powerful personality, but when it came to Cam he was nothing but protective and supportive.

[Cam:] *We only took a trip to a luxurious private island six months ago.*

[Cort:] *Funnily enough, the kidnapping kinda kills my buzz when it comes to thinking about that trip.*

[Cam:] *Don't say that, Cort. I remember with fondness several parts of our trip.*

[Cam:] *My favorite part was the Friday night…*

Friday night on the island was the first time Cort had let Cam top him. It wasn't the only time it happened over the past few months, but it was definitely less common - both of them usually preferred when Cort was in charge. Still, nothing set his man on fire like the memory of that night.

Cort's eyes met his across the table and then narrowed. Tension crackled between them as if a live wire had fallen across the table, and Cam knew Cort was replaying every second of that night.

He shivered. He wasn't quite sure how tonight was going to play out, but he knew it would be fun.

He glanced at the clock to see how much longer this meeting could possibly last, when his phone buzzed again.

[Cort:] *You cannot distract me badass.*

[Cort:] *Let's play a game.*

[Cort:] *Never have I ever gone to a place with a private pool.*

Cam rolled his eyes across the table. His boyfriend had an inexhaustible supply of games. Fortunately, almost all of them ended in a win for Cam.

[Cam:] *This game doesn't work over text. We've established this. Besides, you and I have been in a pool alone. Our first night together, remember? Which makes it sort of private.*

[Cort:] *Oh, I remember. I'm feeling the need to blow off some steam.*

[Cam:] *Want to scream underwater and see if I hear you?*

[Cort:] *Want to make you scream under water.*

Cam shivered and put the phone facedown, glaring at his man across the table. Cort's face seemed all innocent, despite the long hair and scruff which Cam loved to rub with his fingers.

[Cam:] *David is getting ideas.*

Across the table, Cort hid a chuckle behind his hand.

[Cort:] *You getting excited, Cam?*

[Cort:] *Maybe I don't care whether David knows something's up, as long as he sees those glassy, blue eyes are watching ME, your cheeks are all red because of ME, and you are MINE, down to the very last freckle.*

Cam pressed his lips together and fought not to shiver.

[Cam:] *Such a Neanderthal.*

[Cort:] *And you get off on it.*

Truth. Undeniable truth.

[Cort:] *Never have I ever had sex on a beach.*

[Cam:] *Seriously? Still doesn't work over text, babe. But you know very well I hadn't the last time we were at the beach, and I'm not likely to have accomplished it since then without you.*

The closest he'd come had been on St. Brigitte, and as much as he enjoyed that memory, he was in no hurry to fly back and repeat it.

[Cort:] *God, you know I love it.*

[Cam:] *I know. You love having my firsts.*

A few weeks before, Cort had taken great delight in showing him just how *much* he loved being Cam's *first* at so many things - first man he'd fallen in love with, first man he'd lived with, first man he'd ditched condoms with.

Cort frowned down at his phone as he read Cam's message, and his expression had Cam frowning, too.

[Cam:] *What's with the face? You rethinking your stance on firsts?*

[Cort:] *Hmmm. Maybe I am a little.*

What the hell? Since when? Cam scowled as he typed.

[Cam:] *Well, you're a bit late!*

[Cort:] *Your firsts aren't good enough.*

Cam stared at his boyfriend, but Cort was looking out of the window behind Cam's head, a small smile playing on his lips. Was he trying to be funny? If so, he was failing miserably.

[Cam:] *Fine, then. Maybe I'll see if Drew or David is interested in giving me some more experience.*

Fighting words, and Cam knew it, but he was more than a little pissed at the curve this conversation had taken. He jabbed at the Send key with more force than necessary, then placed his phone facedown on the table and pointedly turned his attention to Marcus.

"Thanks, Marcus. Send me that proposal and I'll have Drew's team jump on it," Sebastian said easily. "Sounds like a great fit, and thanks for bringing it to our attention."

From down the table, Cam saw Drew lean back with his hands folded across his chest, and nod once.

"Janine, can you switch to Dr. Grayson, please?" Sebastian asked one of the techs. Janine cut Marcus's feed and switched to another image, this one was a young brunette with long curly hair and dark eyes. Cam recognized her right away.

"Pam," he said, momentarily forgetting he was pissed at Cort. "How's it going?"

Pam smiled and proceeded to fill them all in on the great progress they'd made in implementing and testing the new virtual reality surgical techniques Cam had greenlit on behalf of Seaver's biomedical division.

"We've already helped save lives thanks to this technique," she told the board.

Sebastian glanced down the table at Cam and met his eyes for a moment. From the minute he'd taken up his CEO position again, he'd been filled with nothing but praise for Cam's performance in holding down the fort during his absence. At first, Cam had rolled his eyes - he'd felt as though he was barely getting the job done from day to day, and anything he'd managed to accomplish was based on nothing but sheer good luck. Slowly, though, he'd started seeing things with new eyes, seeing *himself* with new eyes. And yeah, maybe some of this had to do with the annoying jerk sitting on the other side of the table who Cam was pointedly *not* looking at.

A few minutes later, Sebastian drew the meeting to a close and everyone slowly began gathering their things, pushing away from the table, and breaking off into smaller conversations. Cam sat where he was, doodling with his pen on the edge of a piece of notepaper. He didn't want to give Cort the opportunity to explain quite yet. He wanted to stew for a minute or two first.

But the door to the conference room suddenly locked with a quiet *snick*, and Cam looked up.

Everyone was gone. The room was completely empty except for Cam... and the bane of his existence, who was looking at him with smoldering green eyes.

"What are you doing?" Cam demanded.

Cort stalked toward him, all long limbs and bunching muscles beneath his casual Friday polo and the jeans he had insisted on wearing. For just a second, some primal part of Cam's brain lit up in warning. *Prey, we have spotted a predator!* But this prey had finally learned better than to run away.

He remembered Cort walking into the ballroom exactly

the same way the night of the gala, the first night they'd met.

"Once upon a time, I thought you looked like a Viking," he said coolly when Cort was just a few steps away from him.

"A Viking?" Cort repeated, amused. He spun Cam's chair around by the arm and scooped him up bodily, depositing him on the cool, black tabletop.

Cam's pulse picked up, but he bit his tongue against the squeak that threatened to burst from his throat... and the moan that always followed when Cort demonstrated just how much bigger and stronger he was. Cam loved that about him - loved the way Cort made him feel safe and protected *always*. But he also *lived* to remind Cort that while *he* might be in charge in the bedroom, he was *not* dominant all the time. They had a constantly evolving set of rules, made ever more exciting by the fact that Cort tried to change them whenever it suited him, but Cam thrived on it. From the time he and Cort had embraced again at the airport on St. Michel, he'd never for a second doubted he had one hundred percent of Cort's focus, attention, and most importantly, his heart.

Still, the man needed to learn, his texts weren't always as amusing as he thought they were.

"A Viking," Cam agreed coolly, as though he hadn't just been plunked bodily onto a new piece of furniture, and his man wasn't pushing Cam's knees wide apart so he could step inside them. "Like Fabio."

Cort grabbed Cam's neck and yanked it to the side, biting down firmly on the exposed tendon between Cam's neck and shoulder. It was his favorite spot to mark Cam, who felt his dick becoming hard immediately. Conditioned response. When Cort claimed that spot, Cam wanted nothing more than to submit.

But not today.

He bit his lip and fought the instinctive sway toward his boyfriend.

"You're saying I look like the 'I Can't Believe It's Not Butter' dude?" Cort snickered. "That's okay. I'll take that. Dude had thighs for days."

Cam rolled his eyes. Trust Cort to focus on the man's legs. He opened his mouth to make some snarky retort - likely something that would amp up his boyfriend even more, but then Cort did a thing with his tongue, curling his lips around the spot he'd bitten and sucking hard, and Cam couldn't keep up his pissy attitude anymore.

Within seconds, his eyes were closed, his lips moving under Cort's, his hips sliding forward, as Cort pushed his back down on the table. Cort braced himself on one hand and lifted Cam's shirt, running a hand over Cam's abs in a way that made Cam shudder *hard*.

"We haven't christened this conference room yet," Cort whispered.

Cam groaned, and his eyes flew open to meet Cort's heated gaze. "True," he whispered back. His boyfriend had a thing for semi-public sex, and Cam was totally on board with it. *So* on board.

Cort grabbed Cam's chin and held it firmly. "Yeah. So, what do you *say?*" he demanded.

Oh, the bastard. This was a game for *home*, not the conference room.

But the light in Cort's eyes wouldn't be denied, and today, just this once, Cam didn't want to.

"*Please*," he whispered in Cort's ear, feeling the lightness that always came from admitting what he wanted to the one man he could trust would always give it to him.

Then Cam was on his stomach bent over the table, his

pants down around his ankles while Cort worked him open from behind.

Cam's boyfriend was all about making the most of the travel-size lube.

Cort pushed inside him the next instant, and everything froze. Tingles of sensation floated up and down Cam's legs the way they always did, and his heart nearly hammered through his ribcage. Having Cort like this, being taken by Cort like this... it was everything to Cam.

Cort shifted, tagging Cam's prostate like a professional, which Cam had to admit by this point he kind of was. He moaned as pinwheels of color exploded behind his eyes.

"More," Cam whispered, and Cort gave it to him over and over and over again. The conference room with its beige walls and beige carpet floated away, the whole building, all of its inhabitants, ceased to exist for him, and Cam forgot his own damn name. He was Cort's, and that was enough.

Later, when he was laying on his side on the cold, hard table catching his breath, Cort's arms wrapped loosely around him, his thighs wet with Cort's come, Cam remembered their earlier argument and began to chuckle.

"What's funny, badass?" Cort asked in the gravelly voice Cam loved.

"Here I thought firsts weren't good enough for you anymore," Cam teased. He grabbed Cort's hand and brought it to his mouth, biting it firmly between his front teeth.

Cort hissed. "You didn't see my reply?"

Cam rolled his eyes. "You know I didn't."

"Hmmm... Well, let me explain it to you, then." He pulled his hand away from Cam's mouth and rolled until he was poised over Cam - a position Cam couldn't help but feel would be more comfortable in their bed at home. But when

Cort opened his mouth again, Cam forgot any complaint he'd been about to make, because the words Cort spoke were devastating and true.

"Firsts aren't good enough," he said, as serious as Cam had ever seen him. "Because I don't *just* want your firsts. I want your onlys, Cam. Your lasts, your in-betweens. I want your always."

Cam's heart, already filled to bursting with everything that was Cort, somehow managed to double in size.

This man, *his* man, was the most complicated, provoking, agitating, vexatious, aggravating man on the planet, but falling in love with him had never been anything but, plain, simple, and easy.

Thank you so much for reading *The Easy Way!* If you enjoyed this book, or even if you didn't, please consider leaving a review!

Want more Cam and Cort? Check out the FUN bonus epilogue just for newsletter subscribers here → https://dl.bookfunnel.com/145mkbcq5c

Thanks!
~May

ALSO BY MAY ARCHER

<u>Love in O'Leary Series</u>

<u>Whispering Key Series</u>

The Sunday Brothers Series

<u>The Way Home Series</u>

Licking Thicket Series

(cowritten with Lucy Lennox)

<u>Champion Security Series</u>

(cowritten with Lucy Lennox)

<u>Honeybridge Series</u>

(cowritten with Lucy Lennox)